W9-BLP-610

SUMMER HAWK

SUMMER HAWK

Deborah Savage

HOUGHTON MIFFLIN COMPANY
BOSTON 1999

More thanks than I can say to my friend Robbie, whose love, patience, and insight helped me in my journey through this story.

With grateful appreciation to Tom Ricardi of the Massachusetts Bird of Prey Rehabilitation Facility, who generously shared his expertise with me during my research for this book.

The quote on page 207 is from
"The Heaven of Animals" by James Dickey
Poems 1957–1967; Collier Books 1972

The text of this book is set in 12 point Palatino.

Library of Congress Cataloging-in-Publication Data
Savage, Deborah.
Summer hawk / Deborah Savage.
p.   cm.
Summary: When her rescue of a baby hawk takes fifteen-year-old Taylor to a raptor rehabilitation center in rural Pennsylvania, their offer of a summer public relations job seems a step toward her dream of becoming a journalist.
ISBN 0-395-91163-X
[1. Birds of prey — Fiction.   2. Wildlife rescue — Fiction. 3. Journalism — Fiction.   4. Country life — Pennsylvania — Fiction. 5. Pennsylvania — Fiction.]   I. Title.
PZ7.S2588Su   1999
[Fic] — dc21   98-29651
                                                                              CIP
                                                                              AC

Manufactured in the United States of America
HAD 10 9 8 7 6 5 4 3 2 1

For Eleni,
who danced in a red skirt

1

I HAD HEARD of the hawk lady, of course. Anyone in Hunter's Gap could tell you how she prowled around with a high-powered rifle, shooting at any person who dared to set a toe on her property — and if she missed, she'd take you to court for trespassing. But even though my father's land bordered hers on one side and the Hunter's Gap school lay along her southern boundary, I'd never seen her. Betsy Warren insisted that she had spoken to her once, naturally. Anything that wasn't nailed down tight, Betsy claimed for herself. Kevin What's-his-name said he'd seen the hawk lady, too, last fall when he'd gone hunting with his dad on the first day of doe season and they'd blundered onto her property in the fog. He swore she was way over six feet tall. Since I never paid attention to anyone in Hunter's Gap, I figured they were both lying and forgot about it.

But on the morning of my last day in ninth grade, the blessedly last day I'd ever have to spend at the school in Hunter's Gap, I saw the hawk lady for myself in Bitsi's store. My father drove me to school, stopping at Bitsi's Gas and Lunch so I could get something to eat. When my mother was away in Philadelphia, neither my father nor I bothered to plan for meals. But Bitsi's was a last resort, even for us. My father always said the "Gas" part of the sign should come after the "Lunch," since that was the order in which they happened. A smaller sign beneath it, with "Worms and Crawlers" crudely lettered, didn't exactly add to the appeal, either.

"Did you at least have breakfast, Missy?" my father asked as he rattled his old Chevy truck over the broken pavement in front of the store.

"The milk was bad," I shrugged. "And it's *Taylor*."

My father gave me a quizzical grin as he swung down from the truck. "Taylor — my name," I persisted. "You promised you wouldn't call me Missy anymore, remember? When I go away to school next year, everyone will call me Taylor. You may as well get used to it."

Giving my door the requisite special tug, my father let me out of the 1955 Chevy my mother called "the death-trap." She periodically tried to forbid me to ride in it, but since she wasn't around much I ignored this, keeping the fact from her as naturally as I did all the other secrets I shared with my father. "Taylor," he pronounced with a courtly bow, taking my hand to kiss it as I jumped down.

He'd already been at work in his studio for hours and was still wearing his leather apron. Even at eight-thirty the air was muggy and hot, and he had no shirt on under the apron. Marble chips stuck in his long hair, and the white stone dust accentuated the heavy muscles in his shoulders and arms. After a day of work, my father would look like the sculptures he carved from marble.

I loved the way my father moved, the way he walked around things or held them in his hands, as if the hard elements of earth revealed their fluid, internal shapes to him. He seemed to speak to the world with movement and touch. But today, his rough hand holding mine, I was embarrassed. "Quit it," I muttered, glancing toward the store. Bitsi was sure to be peering out from her rocker next to the door. "Bitsi'll think you're weird."

"So I am," laughed my father, dropping my hand. "And so, I might add, are *you*. We're partners in crime."

His words bothered me on this particular morning, although ordinarily I would have been proud to be his partner in anything. Certainly, if being *weird* meant being different from the people in Hunter's Gap, I was only too happy for the distinction. When

I'd walked into Mr. Beecham's classroom for the first time last September, eleven pairs of eyes stared at me as if I'd just landed from outer space. As far as they were concerned, I suppose I had. Even to me now, after ten months' exile in Hunter's Gap, Philadelphia seemed a universe away. And I didn't think any of *them* had been farther away from Hunter's Gap than Alton. Practically everyone in the whole class was related — no new blood, my father said — and they'd all been at school together since first grade, without a single new person joining them. Until I came along.

When I'd come home after that first day of school and told my father what had happened, he'd rolled his eyes and laughed. "So," he'd said, putting down his chisel to give me a hug, "that school really hasn't changed since I went there — astonishing. But why should I be surprised?" He'd waved his hand toward the open door of his studio, shadowed in early afternoon by the mountains rising to an endless sweep of ridges on the far side of the creek. "Look at this place. Beautiful as hell. But nothing gets in and still less gets out. I guess you'll just have to look at this year as a valuable life experience, Missy. Don't worry about school too much — you know I think it's a waste of time for creative people anyway."

That was fine for him to say. My father was an artist, and artists are different. My mother told me he'd never cared about what kind of grades he got.

But if I was going to compete someday for a place in a journalism program at one of the best universities in the country, not to mention competing later in a high-powered career as a television reporter, I *had* to worry about school. And I was worried. I paused, glancing down the road from Bitsi's toward the school. I wasn't looking forward to my final report card. Not for the first time, I wished I could believe my father about grades and school. I wished I could be the creative person he thought I was. "Grades don't matter," my father always told me. "What matters is that you make a difference in the world. That you shine your light, even if it's only a single candle. Illuminate the darkness." Up until this year, I'd shone at school like a hundred candles. But in Hunter's Gap, all my candles had gone out.

I slammed through the door into Bitsi's store ahead of my father to prevent him from performing any further antics. As I did, Bitsi smacked at a fly from her chair, rocking forward so violently the Chihuahua dog she always had clutched under her huge arm was dislodged and skittered across the floor. I sidestepped warily. "Good Tiny. Good dog," I said. Tiny would bite without warning, scooting out at passing ankles from behind the counter. Under his colorless, chewed-up fur, Tiny's skin was as dirty as the rag Old Mr. Bitsi had hanging from his back pocket.

Bitsi settled her enormous haunches back in the rocker. That was what my father called her rear end:

her haunches. "Ain't you supposed to be in school by now?" she asked suspiciously. "'Stead of slammin' in here like you was on your way to a fire?"

"It's the last day of school," I said with joyful triumph. "We don't have to be there until nine."

"Mrs. Bitsi," said my father, greeting her with his inevitable bow. "I hope you're managing to keep cool on this torrid day."

Bitsi didn't understand half of what my father said, but she never let on, hiding her bewilderment behind a glower. Besides, she couldn't help but be charmed by him, even when he was poking fun at her. Everyone was charmed by my father. My mother grumbled about his baiting Bitsi. "She may not be the brightest soul on earth, but you might show her some respect," she'd say. My father would wave his hand in airy dismissal. "Oh, Bitsi and I have a perfect understanding. Goes back years," he'd tell her. "She knows I think she's the very salt of the earth."

This morning, as I poked around in the soursmelling bin by the soda fridge, I kept my ears focused on their conversation out of habit. It was part of my ongoing training as a reporter. Finally, finding nothing but a few worn-out turkey sandwiches, I called out, "Haven't you got any just cheese?"

"What's wrong with them ones?" snorted Bitsi.

"I don't eat meat," I said.

"Ain't natural, not eatin' meat," Bitsi stated, slapping the fly swatter on the arm of her chair for emphasis. "Only them tree-hugger perverts don't eat meat. And religious freaks."

"But you're religious, Bitsi," I pointed out.

She humped herself back in the rocker. "I'm a Christian," she said haughtily. "An' you know that ain't what I'm talkin' about." She swung her massive, disapproving head around to my father. "It wouldn't kill youse to get this girl to church sometimes, Bobbie Armstrong. Just because you been livin' in a big city all these years don't mean you can forget how your Aunt Grace did a good job of bringing you up an' gettin' you to church when you was a kid."

"Yup, she sure did a good job on me," muttered my father under his breath. He hardly ever liked to talk about his childhood in Hunter's Gap, and now that I lived here, I could see why. For a moment he stared darkly at the cans of motor oil he was examining. Then he winked at me. I was twisted practically into a pretzel, trying to read the headlines on *The Alton Register* that Bitsi kept out of reach behind the counter. She couldn't bear to have people get anything for free, including a look at the day's news. When I straightened up, the hawk lady was in the store.

I don't know how I knew she was the hawk lady. I certainly didn't recognize her from Kevin's idiotic description. She was tall, but she wasn't way over six feet. And she didn't look mean enough to shoot anyone. Strong enough, maybe. Not mean. I stared at her. I couldn't help it. She was beautiful. Not beautiful in a movie star kind of way, but like something my father might carve out of a magnificent piece of marble. She appeared so tall because of the way she held herself, majestic and watchful. Her movements seemed calm, but her eyes had a life of their own, alert, with a distance in them that was like a promise you aren't sure will be kept. She made me think of the way my father's sculptures looked when they were incomplete, before he had released the whole of a strong figure from the stone.

She seemed to move naturally toward my father, as if she'd come especially to meet him, and they stood talking. I could see my father's eyes get deep and full. They almost changed color when he talked from inside himself, instead of in that chatty, silly way he did with people like Bitsi. I moved back unobtrusively until I was hidden in the aisle, and listened. Even Bitsi was so curious to hear what the hawk lady was saying, she forgot to keep one of her beady eyes trained on me. If she'd been smarter, Bitsi would have been a crack reporter.

"I haven't seen Tim around for . . . I don't know. Three or four weeks, come to think of it," my father was saying. "He seemed all right then . . . have you called him?"

"Of course," said the hawk lady, with slight impatience. "Twice. He promised he'd come over, but he's never showed up. I'm worried. I can't always tell if he's all right —"

"Ain't never no way of tellin', with Tim," said Bitsi, shaking her head and elbowing her way into the conversation. She didn't usually speak in such a soft voice, and I had to strain to hear. She fixed the hawk lady with a stern eye and admonished, "But don't you give up on him. He's a good man, and Lord knows he needs the work."

My father grinned and touched the hawk lady lightly on her arm. "Thus spake the Lord's spokeswoman," he said. "I wouldn't ignore her command."

The hawk lady turned to go past him down the aisle, but my father moved at the same moment, so it seemed as if they were dancing together. They stopped, and in the sudden moment of stillness my stomach jumped. Then the hawk lady laughed. The sound glittered through the store as if she'd tossed up a handful of golden coins that hung suspended in the low light. She said something in too soft a voice for me to hear, her eyes flashing up to join her laughter, and my father moved to let her pass. "Missy! Melissa!" he called.

I ducked farther behind the shelves and pretended not to hear. I felt a strange loss, as if a spell had been broken before it had worked all its magic. I did not want to meet the hawk lady. I was afraid to come any closer to her. She was like the Grand Canyon or the idea of stars or the faint aftertaste of a dream, impossibly and wonderfully far away. There are some things so beautiful you know they can stay perfect forever only if you don't get too close. My throat grew tight with that strange, longing sorrow. I hid behind the shelves and knew I would never come close to really touching the hawk lady.

I waited until Bitsi rang up her purchases and the hawk lady left the store, then strolled toward my father, studying two boxes of crackers as if choosing between them. "Who was that?" I asked casually, hefting the boxes.

He smiled at me from eyes still deep inside himself. "She was beautiful, wasn't she?" he answered softly. I should have known. We didn't just share secrets, my father and I; we shared a heart. Sheepishly, I tried to shrug, but he laughed away my nonchalance and put his arm around my shoulder. "She's our neighbor. Haven't you ever met her? Rhiannon of the birds . . ."

"Who?"

He gazed out the screen door, momentarily pensive. "Oh, her name. Rhiannon. It's from the Mabinogion . . . an ancient Celtic legend. Rhiannon's Penance. Very sad story, really —" He paused, then chuckled, glancing at Bitsi who was, as usual, all ears. "She was called Rhiannon of the birds because she spoke their language and they helped her. Appropriate, huh? Our neighbor — Dr. Rhiannon Jeffries, Professor of Wildlife Biology, licensed raptor rehabilitator and master falconer, and Director of the Hunter's Gap Raptor Rehabilitation Center. I have only the vaguest notion of what all that means. I'm just repeating what she told me."

"She must be some kind of vet," I said. Bitsi snorted. Tiny stood on her lap and growled. "I bet Bitsi can tell you all about her, can't you, Bitsi?" I prompted.

"I can tell you it ain't natural," Bitsi said, her voice sounding about the same as Tiny's.

"What isn't natural?" I asked, plunking a box of crackers and a container of yogurt by the register.

"What that woman's doin', livin' way out there all alone, without no one but them college boys around —" Bitsi gave my father a look of profound significance. "She ain't that young, either. She's gotta be more'n forty, if she's a day. *And* single, too. Now, what business does a single woman have livin' way out there all by herself? Ain't no wonder she's so unfriendly — it's enough to make anybody a pervert —"

Bitsi had a limited stock of labels, and so far she had evaded all my attempts to get her to define them. But I tried again. "Specifically what kind of pervert is she?" I asked, ignoring my father's quick frown. Bitsi looked at me with disdain.

"I know what I mean, an' that's good enough for me," she announced, moving like an almost-extinct dinosaur to the cash register. "All's I got to say is, there's something ain't natural in a single lady livin' on her own, messing around with nasty birds an' them college boys . . ."

"Hawks aren't nasty. They're important predators in the food chain," I pointed out. "And there must be college girls, too. Alton University isn't all boys."

"That's even worse," snapped Bitsi. "And don't you tell me about them kind of birds, Miss Know-it-all. *I* know all about them. An' I know plenty about *her*, too — she's runnin' some blasted state program that's eatin' up all my tax dollars. Her an' them blasted college kids —"

"What do you think they *do* over there all alone?" I asked in my most persuasive interviewer manner. It was too much for Bitsi. Her glower settled danger-ously down into her many chins. My father deftly in-tercepted further dialogue by opening his wallet and taking out a twenty dollar bill. For a moment, as she punched each item into the register, Bitsi was silent. But I knew she hadn't said all she intended, because she neglected to ring up the total, thus preventing us from leaving. She was clever, Bitsi was. She knew how to hold her audience.

"I ain't the only one around here who thinks there's something wrong," she said portentously. "Junior Fenstemacher asked me just the other day, what did I think possessed Duane MacGaw to sell his daddy's farm to that danged university in the first place. Now we got them college kids drivin' around over here gettin' in trouble, 'stead of staying in Alton where they belong. Just look what happened last week —"

I looked a question at my father, but he shrugged. Bitsi leaned heavily across the counter and poked a finger at him. "Oh, I know what you're thinkin'," she said. "You was just as bad, when you was their age. But that university's always been full of radicals and Commies . . ."

"Oh, you and your Commies!" laughed my father. "You were blaming everything on them when I was a boy. Don't you think, with the demise of the Soviet Union, the world is safe at last from Communism?"

Bitsi looked blank a moment, then continued. "You go ahead and laugh. But look what them Commies did to poor Tim Bogart, half blowin' him to bits like that . . . that university's been on the side of the Commies since before you was a boy. Nobody in Hunter's Gap wants anything to do with that place. You mark my words — that woman's trouble."

"Your words, as usual, are marked indelibly in my memory," said my father solemnly, giving his arm to Bitsi to help her make her ponderous way back to the rocking chair. "And now, Missy — I believe you have one more day of your sentence to serve . . ." He handed me the paper bag with my lunch and we left.

Bitsi was still muttering. The last thing I heard over the creak of her chair were the words, ". . .all my tax dollars wasted on them killer birds. She don't let decent hunters on her land, but she lets them blasted birds loose to kill everything in sight. Figure that out. When Mr. Bitsi and me raised chickens, we shot every hawk we found and hung 'em by their feet all around the coops . . ."

A good news reporter has to observe everything without getting involved. Always alert, always listening and watching for the chance information that could lead deeper in — because even the most important stories start small. You never knew when something hidden might reveal a tiny corner of itself. So an investigative reporter has to pay attention to the facts and can't get distracted by personal feelings. A reporter has to keep digging away at that corner, because that's how the truth is exposed.

But as I left the store with Bitsi's attack on the hawk lady still in my ears, I wasn't thinking about the facts. I didn't know the facts. I only knew what I felt. And what I felt was the echo of Rhiannon Jeffries' golden laughter, the unsettled longing, the indefinable something that tingled through my blood. The hawk lady was an outsider in Hunter's Gap, just as I was. I wondered if she minded feeling alone.

The spell she'd cast still seemed to resonate around me when I walked into Mr. Beecham's classroom for my final day at Hunter's Gap school.

2

I WAS FATED to sit next to Rail Bogart alphabetically, no matter which of my names was used. Armstrong or Brown, I would have to sit on one side of him or the other. And even knowing it was the last day of school, the day I'd been waiting for ever since we'd moved so unexpectedly to Hunter's Gap last September, I resented the seating arrangement as much now as I had from the start. No one was comfortable around Rail Bogart. He was obviously the class pariah.

He was a year older than all of us because he'd had to repeat fourth grade. And even though half the people in the class were his cousins, second cousins, or step-cousins, the girls all complained that he looked at them "funny" and the boys scorned him because he refused to fight "normal." The standards of Hunter's Gap school aside, I hadn't noticed Rail look at anyone in a way I would call *funny*. His gray eyes were unsettling because they were so light, set wide apart and rimmed with dark lashes. He reminded me of the rangy, solitary cheetah I'd once seen loping back and forth in a cage at the Philadelphia zoo. But Rail rarely looked *at* anyone. And I'd never seen him fight. He was taller than anyone in ninth grade and always wore old army camouflage pants tucked into the tops of his hunting boots, even today with the temperature already above eighty degrees. He looked as if he was prepared in case a rattlesnake struck, and even though he wasn't a fighter, it often seemed like he expected something to jump out of the shadows at him.

The other boys sometimes ganged up and tried to goad him. But they could never get Rail Bogart riled in a way that gave them an excuse to attack him. Art Schumman tried hardest. He was a cousin of some kind, but Art's side of the family apparently declined to acknowledge their relation to the Bogarts. Once, early in the spring, Art found a couple of frogs in the creek and showed them to Rail. "You ever seen your mother doing this?" Art had sneered. The frogs were mating, clasped together one behind the other, and they didn't break apart even when Art thrust them in Rail's face.

Rail took the frogs away from Art and held them gently, shielding them from us with his hands. For a few moments, no one moved. Then Rail took a step closer to Art, his eyes intent, as if he meant to inspect the mole on Art's chin. Without seeming to move much at all, Rail finally stood so close to Art they must have been breathing in each other's breath. At least, Rail was — I don't think Art was breathing at all. As still as we all were around them, Rail Bogart was even stiller. His stillness made him appear larger, and all he had to do was wait while Art sweated and Art's imagination did the damage for him. Rail never even touched him.

But that wasn't the real reason Rail Bogart was different. He was different because, along with me, he was the best student in the class. And he shouldn't have been. Not only had he failed a year, but he was one of the vast Bogart clan, and the Bogarts weren't known for their brains. Even at Hunter's Gap school, where no one was academically inclined, the Bogarts had a *reputation*. But Rail studied and worked with a silent, ferocious intensity and all year, to my surprised humiliation, I'd had to struggle to keep up.

Today I glanced at him from the corner of my eye. I would never have to sit next to Rail Bogart again. I would never have to watch him attack his school work, his pencil plunging across the paper, thumping down each punctuation mark as if some invisible monster was waiting to pounce if he stopped for an instant. He created such an overwhelming intensity around him I could hardly concentrate. He would frown, leaning over his desk as if he had to protect his work from an enemy, and burn every mark into his paper so it would last an eternity. Once he ran out of notebook paper halfway through an essay, and I truly thought he might explode. He never made a sound, but there was something awful in the frantic way he pummeled through his desk searching for more paper. He glanced at me once, as if to see how far I was getting ahead of him, until I couldn't stand it. I tore out a handful of paper from my own notebook and shoved it across to him. He'd grabbed the paper without a word and gone back to his race with the monster, pressing down so hard with his pencil he made indentations in the desk top.

He'd gotten a better grade on that essay than I had. And as for our final essays at the end of the year, we weren't even in the same league. I still couldn't believe it. I'd written a neat, succinct piece on the problem of homelessness in the cities. Rail had written a paper about deer hunting that had rambled on for pages. Apparently Mr. Beecham considered deer hunting the superior social issue. This was Hunter's Gap, after all. You could cut the ignorance and bigotry here with a knife, my mother had complained to my father more than once. *Hunting.*

Last fall, when I'd first seen all those slaughtered deer tied onto the roofs of cars or slung up in trees with gaping cavities where their insides had been, I thought I'd be permanently ill. As if there wasn't enough killing in the world.

But no one at Hunter's Gap school seemed to care about homelessness or violence in the cities, or about acid rain or the destruction of the rain forest or nuclear waste. Hunter's Gap didn't inspire anyone to bother about the real world; as long as they could hunt and race their pickup trucks along the Flats and hang out at Stovic's Cafe or the firehouse, they were happy. As far as I could see, Rail Bogart was no different from the rest of them, even if he did manage to get good grades.

And that was what drove me crazy. Because of those grades, right from the first day practically, everyone had lumped Rail and me together. In *everything*. In class. In the stupid school play where we were forced to sing a duet together. In gym, where we were always left until last while the team captains argued over which one of us they'd have to take. We were the only two people in the school who never had to take tests over. We were *geeks*. Nerds. We may have been different from the others — but no one seemed to understand that we were completely different from each other. The teachers were the worst offenders. "Rail and Melissa, you two can study together — you're so far ahead," Mr. Beecham would say. Or, "Rail and Melissa manage to do their homework," he would remonstrate the apathetic class, holding our work up for everyone to see. There were days I became so enraged, my face would burn for hours and Miss Lovett would ask me if I had a fever. I was different because I *wanted* to be different. Rail was different because there was something *wrong* with him.

"Melissa."

I couldn't quite put my finger on the wrongness, but there was something about Rail that unsettled everyone. Maybe it was the way he worked so relentlessly, fueled by his invisible fire. Or maybe it was the way he stared off into the sky, as if he saw something he knew you could never see. Maybe it was just his father, Tim, who Bitsi said got "blowed up by the Commies" in Vietnam and who everyone else said was nuts. But what I found most disconcerting about Rail was the perverse way everyone just couldn't leave him alone, even if it was to torment him. And because of that, I was never left alone either. From the very first day I'd walked into Hunter's Gap school. . . .

"Melissa Armstrong-Brown!"

I jumped. "What?" When I looked up, Mr. Beecham was standing in front of an empty classroom holding out my report card. I took it and shoved it into my pocket. Mr. Beecham smiled at me. "Good job, Melissa," he said. "I know it was a difficult year. Now, go on out to the field — everyone's there already. Miss Lovett has a game planned."

"Couldn't I just read in here? I have a headache," I begged, knowing it was hopeless.

"Your headaches are imaginary, Melissa. You know your mother explained it to me," said Mr. Beecham. "Wait. Here — I meant to give this to you a few days ago. You might be interested — for next year . . . since you want to be a reporter —" He was shuffling through the papers on his desk, speaking in little puffs.

"Thanks, but I'm not going to be here next —" I began lamely, but he thrust a manila envelope at me and I didn't have the heart to finish. With remorse, I realized Mr. Beecham had always *tried*.

"No, don't read it now — go on out, Melissa. It's your last day at Hunter's Gap school. Try to have a nice time." Mr. Beecham sounded almost pleading as I left, plodding down the hallway. I ran my hand along the dented lockers, trying to ignore the yelling and pounding of feet outside. I traced each locker number slowly. Number 14. Number 15. Number 16 — there. My father's locker, from more than thirty years before. I leaned down to trace the initials R.A. elaborately gouged into the metal through the red paint. Robert Armstrong, already carving in eighth grade.

"Go *on*, Melissa," called Mr. Beecham.

"Taylor," I muttered. "Why can't anyone call me

Taylor." But I knew he couldn't hear me. I ran out into the hot sun.

I kept as far from Miss Lovett as I dared, hoping she would not notice me. Betsy Warren and Kevin were bouncing up and down in front of her, the way they always did when they were feeling important. They had no dignity. But Miss Lovett wasn't leaving it up to Betsy and Kevin to pick teams this time. I shifted warily away from her range of vision, noticing too late that it brought me closer to Rail, who was also standing apart, hands in his pockets, staring off into the sky.

There was no time to change tactics. Miss Lovett reached behind her and grabbed me with one red-nailed hand and Rail with the other. "Melissa. Rail. Everybody." In the heat her perfume was almost unbearable, shimmering around her like gas fumes on a highway. Unexpectedly, Rail caught my eye; his nose crinkled. Otherwise, his face remained expressionless.

"I really don't want to play, Miss Lovett," I pleaded.

"Oh for goodness sakes, Melissa. It'll be fun. Round-up . . . just for old times' sake. You've all played it every year since —"

"Melissa never played it," Kevin pointed out. "She's only been here one year. She doesn't know how."

"See?" I said. But Miss Lovett was firm. "Traditions are important," she said. "And it's important to welcome newcomers into your traditions. Anyway, next year you'll all be gone."

"It's just to high school in *Alton*," said Kevin in disgust.

"It doesn't matter. Next year won't be the same. You'll see. You have all been together since first grade, and now you'll be in different classes with different people . . ."

"Melissa wasn't with us since first grade."

Miss Lovett blew her whistle and shoved Kevin away. "Come on, divide up. If you don't care about this, *I* do. I remember you all playing Round-up when you were this tall." She held out her hand halfway down her thigh. The girls began to mill around in a suspiciously horsey way. Miss Lovett turned to me. "The girls are the wild horses and the boys are the cowboys," she explained as the class began to trot out into the field. I scuffed out a few steps reluctantly.

It was midday and there was no shadow. Not even the row of hickory trees that divided the school from the hills on the hawk lady's land left more than a faint smudge in the undergrowth. I wondered for the hundredth time why everyone was convinced the hickory nuts were poisonous. My father said all folk superstition had some basis in fact, but I was certain this was just plain ignorance. When I'd first started school in Hunter's Gap the nuts were beginning to fall. Betsy Warren had offered me a handful, cracked open with a rock. I took them, noting how carefully everyone was watching me.

"Go ahead," Betsy had said. "They're really good."

"Sure," I'd answered, sarcastic, wondering why on earth she would imagine I *wanted* to eat hickory nuts all smashed up with bits of shell.

"No, they aren't," said Rail Bogart, the first I'd ever heard him speak more than the bare minimum. "They're poison. Don't you eat them."

I'd dropped the nuts and walked away, nonchalant, but when no one was looking I'd scrubbed my hand hard on my jeans. I'd felt foolish, but Rail's words had an authority that matched the expression in his eyes, and Betsy's hadn't.

Now, slowly following the others, I looked beyond the trees to the scrub-covered hills. Kevin accused the hawk lady of being a mad scientist who had put something in the ground to make the hickory trees yield poisonous nuts — to keep kids off her land, he said. It was an idiotic theory, but I didn't blame the hawk lady for wanting to keep everyone from Hunter's Gap away. I'd spent the entire school year doing the same. Not that I'd ever had friends, but at least in Dressler Academy in Philadelphia, I hadn't had to contend with people who knew nothing and cared nothing about the world. At Hunter's Gap school, when I'd mentioned Bosnia in history class, someone thought it was a city in Massachusetts. When I'd suggested the school start recycling bottles and cans, Mr. Beecham was sure it would be too confusing to remember all the different categories. And as for trying to start a school newspaper —

"Hurry *up*, Melissa!" screeched Betsy, waiting for me with her hand on her hip. "You have to *gallop*. You're supposed to be a horse. And stay together — that's the rule," she announced. She and Cindy Hubbel, her best friend, did some kind of ridiculous prance, giggling and tossing their heads like demented ponies. I wondered what it was like to have such a good friend you didn't care how silly you looked to the rest of the world. Cindy and Betsy were always clinging to each other, practically attached at the heads like Siamese twins with all the whispering they did. They sent each other notes all day along the secret pathways in the classroom as if they were making a million important plans.

By now the group of six girls were jostling together, running seriously, and I was caught among them. I had to gallop, had to pound across the field with the dust gritting in my teeth. When the herd swerved I had to go with them, our bodies bunched so close I could hardly breathe. The girls played at first, squealing and bucking and rolling their eyes to tease the cowboys who prowled back and forth in a ragged line. Gradually the boys loped closer, forming a circle around us, watching intently for an opening.

The herd of girls packed even closer together, each high squeal escalating their excitement as we raced over the hard ground. I couldn't see anymore. A foot slammed into my shin. I tripped as a girl lurched into me. We swerved again. There was a violent flurry of movement, a shriek, and silly Jean Hocker was caught. Through the dust I saw her thin white legs kicking as a boy yanked her by the arm back to the edge of the field.

The herd was silent now, tense with apprehension, running faster, heads down. My heart was pounding and there was a gritty, salty taste of sweat in my mouth. I had to run. In the heat of the others pressed around me, I sensed the cowboys circling closer and closer. I was trapped in the herd's fear. I don't know what made me look up.

I don't know how the dust cleared for that one moment, so I could see the hot blue sky. A hawk was gliding toward me down a mountain ridge. In that moment, I broke stride and fell behind the herd of girls. The hawk swooped low over the hill beyond the field, rose again, circled over me. I watched as it cut across the sun; I blinked, squeezed the spots from my eyes, and looked again. The herd was gone. In sudden panic, I tried to catch up. But when I swung around the cowboys had cut between me and the girls. I turned sharply again, stumbled, and paused.

The hawk dropped out of the sun. Straight from the fire-white center, the dark bird sliced through the sky toward me. My heart swept up to meet it. In the high, wild cry of the hawk I heard, clear as the flash of sun on wings: *You don't have to run with them! You can run alone!*

And then I was running free. The field opened before me and I ran, the hawk chasing its shadow ahead of me. My strides found the rhythm of flight, my lungs filled with the sweet endless sky, my heart beat along invisible currents — and I followed the hawk. I had no weight, no fear; nothing pursued me. I was the hawk's dive, the sun's light; I was air and space and flight. There was no end to the field and no end to me.

I ran until I lifted free of the earth, like the shadow of the hawk rising off the mountain's blue flank. My blood raced through me and my heart pounded with the beat of the hawk's wings. And then a sharp pain shot up my leg through the sole of my foot. When I lifted my foot, the pain was gone. I'd only stepped on a pebble. But I had plummeted to earth. I was only me again, running across the dusty field, alone. I couldn't seem to stop. My breath tore gasps from my throat and sweat stung my eyes. I ran farther and farther out, abandoned by the empty sky.

I caught a movement at the edge of my vision, and the movement became a figure obscured by dust, running after me. Instinctively I turned away, and the figure swerved to follow. I became something seeking escape, but the field was huge and I didn't know which way to turn. Now the figure pounded behind me, now beside me, running alongside.

But he did not reach out to lasso my arm with his hand. He glanced at me as he ran, his stride matching mine, his pants tucked into his heavy boots. I thought for a moment he'd smiled, but it was only his gray eyes seeming to dart out, the way a wild animal might dart from the cover of the woods. Our feet hit the ground together and I could not tell my stride from his.

I turned, and Rail Bogart turned with me; I turned again, and he matched my movement, and now he *was* smiling and so was I. Suddenly I felt that I could run with him forever, in our perfect, tireless stride. The earth seemed to hold us as if we occupied the same space and time. I was no longer a shadow dissolving into a limitless sky.

Only when I heard the whistle, a thread of sound dropping around us like a rope, did I see how far we were from the others, who watched us from the school side of the field. Rail was loping easily beside me. I knew he would have to catch me now, drag me back by the arm in front of everyone. I veered away, but the other boys moved to intercept. Rail said, "We have to go in now, Taylor. Just pretend I caught you."

He dropped back so he was a step behind me, and we jogged unevenly toward the school. The other boys grinned and cheered. I hoped desperately everyone would think my face was red from running and I held my head up and looked straight at them. Betsy smirked. "You didn't play it right, Melissa," she said. "You aren't supposed to run way out there like that. What'd you do that for?"

"She wanted Rail to catch her," Kevin said, grinning, but keeping a wary eye on Rail. "See, Miss Lovett? I told you she didn't know how to play."

Miss Lovett gave me a conspiratorial grimace. Her makeup seemed to be melting, taking her face with it. "Well, I don't know . . . she looked like the fastest horse in the bunch," she remarked to Kevin. "And Rail had to work pretty hard to catch up to her."

"But you're *supposed* to get caught. That's the *rule*," complained Betsy.

"Oh for goodness sakes, get on the bus, Bets," Miss Lovett sighed. "Have a good summer. Tell your mom I'll be at the church Saturday night to help set up . . . Melissa, wait. Your mother's come for you."

I expected Rail to look back at me. I expected, at

least, a little flicker of triumph in his eyes. I would rather anyone else had caught me instead of Rail Bogart, even Kevin. But Rail had climbed on the bus and was staring as usual through the window up at the sky. So intent was his gaze I looked involuntarily in the same direction. But the sky was an empty blue, hard as the glass in the bus window that reflected my face. There was no hawk. Perhaps I had imagined her. Without warning my eyes blurred, and I ran to the car where my mother was waiting.

3

AT DRESSLER ACADEMY everyone knew my mother
was a psychoanalyst. Tom Keegan's mother was
some kind of surgeon, and Caitlin's mother was a
lawyer, and another girl had a mother who ran for
Senate. So no one thought there was anything unusual about my mother.

But at Hunter's Gap school, my mother was a psycho*path*. They never tired of this hilarious joke. Early
in the year, before I knew better, I'd made the mistake of telling the class about my parents. Mr.
Beecham had asked, and I never forgave him for
leading me into the trap. The class managed to handle the fact that my father was a sculptor — Mr.
Beecham explained it was something like being a
carpenter — but when I began telling about my

mother's job, all they heard was "psycho." For the rest of the year, Melissa T. Armstrong-Brown's mother was a psychopath. The joke gave them hours of comic relief from their strenuous academic studies.

Only Rail Bogart had never laughed at me. But he didn't laugh at much of anything. They called *his* mother a tramp — she'd run off when he was twelve, leaving her family for the UPS man who delivered packages at Bitsi's store every week. She had an absurd name: Queenie. Queenie MacGaw Bogart. She was his dad's third cousin, but that wasn't unusual in Hunter's Gap. Bitsi told me all about it. Bitsi could tell you about anyone in Hunter's Gap, but she seemed especially fond of the story of Queenie MacGaw. "It happened right here," she'd always say, waving her hand around the store in indignation. "She just walked right out that door with him, got in that big brown truck, and she ain't never been back." She told the story so many times I suggested she should put up a plaque, the kind they have at historical landmarks, which would read: "Queenie Bogart betrayed her husband in this store, April 1992." But Bitsi had silenced me with a scowl. As long as she was alive, she wanted the pleasure of telling the story herself so she could embellish it with choice tidbits of her opinion. "Poor Tim got even worse from that day on," she'd told my father. "And that boy of his. Rail. He had to stay back that year in school, it shook him up so much. Now what kind of mother would up and leave her kids like that?"

My mother was waiting for me in air-conditioned comfort, motor running, the opera on her CD player wailing. I was grateful she'd kept her windows shut so no one could hear, and I pulled the door closed quickly. "Hi, Mom," I said, and she leaned over to give me her usual awkward hug. I hadn't come up with a diplomatic way to tell her I didn't need a hug, but if I could, I know she'd be relieved. She was dressed in a neat linen suit which, after the hug, she smoothed with a furtive gesture. She'd gotten her short hair styled and with her tailored, colorless clothes it made her seem even smaller than ever. Small and plain. Like her name: Anna Brown.

I settled back in the seat and tried to relax. "Is your conference over already?" I asked brightly. But she was maneuvering the car up to the pump in front of Bitsi's without hitting the pothole I was sure Old Bitsi had dug there on purpose, and she used that as an excuse not to answer. I could feel her waiting, though, like a tiny brown adder hidden in the leaves. I took a deep breath. Better to grab the snake before it bit. I pulled the report card out, gave it to her, and gazed out the window.

Usually, I was fascinated by watching Old Bitsi shuffle around the car while he filled the tank with gas. He would circle each car that came in at least eight or nine times, as if performing some kind of ritual dance. Sometimes — if the spirit moved him, my father said — he'd take a swipe at the windshield with his filthy rag. He never said a word. Never.

Old Bitsi was on his sixth pass around the car, and my mother was still reading my report card. Out of the corner of my eye I watched her fingers drumming silently on the steering wheel. I didn't have to see her face to know her expression. Lips pressed into a thin line. Eyes narrow. Old Bitsi flicked the rag right in front of her open window, but she didn't seem to notice.

"Jesus, Melissa," said my mother.

I wondered if Old Bitsi might shrivel up and burn to a blackened crisp at hearing his good Lord's name taken in vain. Old Bitsi and Mrs. Bitsi were seriously religious, like everyone else in Hunter's Gap. At the very least, he might take his rag and wipe out her mouth. . . .

"Melissa, what is going on here?" my mother asked. She didn't look at me, just stared down at the report card. "What is this B in History? And a C in *English*? A C?"

"It's a C-plus," I said weakly.

Now she did look at me. "This is the way you plan to start your year at the Porter Phelps School? One of the best private schools in the country? With a C in English? Do you expect them to admit you into their Advanced Writing program *now*?"

"Couldn't we talk about this tomorrow?" I muttered, glancing anxiously down the road. Everyone who walked home from school stopped at Bitsi's to stock up on junk food. "I mean, couldn't we wait until Dad sees it, and then talk about it? As a family?"

It was a deliberate low blow, and my mother knew it. She didn't answer. You could hardly call us a family. Not since we'd moved to Hunter's Gap. Probably even before, although it hadn't been so noticeable in Philadelphia. But now, since my father's Aunt Grace died and left him the old farm, my mother had been staying most of the time in the city to maintain her practice. And to teach seminars at the university. And to write her book. And to speak at important conferences all over the country. She said she couldn't concentrate way out in the middle of nowhere — but the truth was, she just hated Hunter's Gap. But she didn't have as much reason to as I did.

"I was doing great at Dressler!" I burst out. "Why did you make me go to this stupid school?"

My mother's face went flat and still. "You know there was no time to enroll you in a decent school by the time we decided to move here," she said, scanning the report card again. "Class Rank — you're number two? Who was number one?"

"I told you you should have let me stay in the city with you!" I cried. "I could have finished ninth grade at Dressler . . . you could have —"

"You know that wouldn't have worked. We've

discussed this before, Melissa. I'm gone most of the time," my mother answered, in the cold, professional voice that made me feel helpless. She tapped the report card. "Who was number one?"

I muttered, "Some guy . . . I don't know —"

"The Porter Phelps School is my alma mater, Melissa," my mother continued, as if I'd hadn't said a word. "You aren't just any old student coming in there. They value the children of alumnae, but they also have very high expectations of them . . ."

"Well, they may as well lower them, because I'm just not a genius, the way you are!" I cried.

My mother gave me an irritated frown. "Don't be silly, Melissa. You're a far better writer than I am, you've read more widely than I had at your age, you've got real insights into world events —"

It wasn't me. I don't know how she did it, but when my mother talked about me, it wasn't *me*. Everything she said was true, of course; she had the facts right. But there was something missing, something so big a huge hole always opened inside me as she spoke. Yet it was impossible to fight, because everything she said about me was true.

Old Bitsi had been standing silently by the window for several minutes, waiting for my mother to pay for the gas. He wouldn't think of *telling* us what we owed. You had to crane your neck around to read the figures on the pump. "We'll pay inside," my mother said curtly, opening the door so abruptly Old Bitsi had to scamper back. I gave him a guilty grimace and followed my mother into the store.

After inspecting every package of hot dogs Bitsi kept in the fridge, my mother seemed to relax a bit. Now she gave me one of her melancholy smiles, which was much worse than her anger. "I know you've had a difficult year, Melissa," she said, reading the ingredients on the packages as she spoke. I could have told her hot dogs contained nothing but poison, not to mention meat, but I knew she was trying to avoid looking at me. "I want you to go to school at Porter Phelps as much as you do. But it's so important that you give yourself the best possible chance there — otherwise it's a waste of time. It's a highly competitive school. After a good three years there, you'll have your pick of universities . . ."

I'd heard it all before, of course. How important it was to make good contacts. How important the right college was. How important it was to be better than the best . . . and I'd *been* better than the best. Always. Top grades. Right up until I'd landed in Hunter's Gap, at the far edge of the civilized world.

". . . and I want you to make friends. Real friends. People who want to contribute in important ways to the world the way you do," my mother was saying as she carried everything to the counter. By now we were within hearing distance of Bitsi, who was, as always, tuning her internal wavebands in our direction. "I'm not the kind of person who makes friends," I said haughtily.

At that moment, Betsy Warren and Cindy Hubbel came in the store, giggling, their heads practically stuck together as they whispered. A fierce pang shot through me, and I said unpleasantly, "I'm not eating any of that stuff." My mother put the hot dogs on the counter with a liter of Coke and a bag of chips. She shrugged, trying hard to manage a cheerful smile. "Well, your father'll love it. Nothing healthy for *him*, right? May as well make someone happy."

I tried to make amends. "I'll eat potato salad," I said, anxiously remembering the fridge of uneaten, spoiled food my mother was going to find when we got home. She always left us stocked up, but when she was away, my father and I existed on pizzas and hoagies from the take-out place in Alton. So far, we'd always had time before she returned to "give the food back to nature," as my father called it. But every time I threw a load out in the woods, I thought of famines in North Korea or Bosnia and resolved to make a schedule of meals and stick to it. But I never did. It was too much fun keeping the secret with my father.

Bitsi began to ring up the food. Betsy Warren paused behind me, Cindy looking sick on her feet as usual and clinging to her arm. "Kevin said you liked

Rail Bogart," Betsy observed casually. "What'd youse guys *do* out in the field all that time?"

I swung around so fast I think Cindy thought I was going to hit her, because she flinched and shut her eyes. Betsy stood in front of her. "Just you shut your mouth," I warned her. Bitsi watched, eyes as bright as laser beams. Cindy tugged at Betsy's arm and they sauntered off to the candy section.

My mother gave me a sad smile and shook her head. "Small minds," she said to comfort me. "The world is full of them. You'll always have to contend with small minds. Just try to remember how unhappy they are."

I didn't care one bit how unhappy Betsy and her tiny mind was. What I cared about was how Bitsi would report the information she had just received to the entire Hunter's Gap community. Rail Bogart and Melissa T. Armstrong-Brown. I could practically see the heart drawn around those names already. It would provide hours of entertainment.

But Bitsi surprised me. "That girl's growin' up silly as her mom," she snorted. "There ain't nothing wrong with Rail Bogart, to tease somebody about. He's worth a hundred Betsy Warrens put together. Ain't natural for a boy his age to have so many worries as that one does, but I ain't never heard him complain. He just about raised up them two little sisters of his, 'cause his own poor dad ain't much good." She put down the bag of chips she'd been about to ring up and leaned her huge elbows on the counter. "You know, Tim Bogart was a real decent boy, before he went off to Vietnam," Bitsi continued, passion making her jowls quiver. "You wouldn't be right in the head, neither, if'n you saw a bunch of kids killed right in front of you." She paused, almost pensive. "It weren't his fault — any more'n it was his fault his wife Queenie was a tramp. But he's the one gotta live with it. Well, he sure tries to make it up to his kids. Can't fault a man who loves his kids, can you? Still, it's awful hard on that boy."

I was staring at Bitsi in fascination. "Wow. You mean the other kids weren't lying, for once?" I said. "Rail's dad really is —"

"Melissa, we need to go," interrupted my mother, giving Bitsi a pointed look.

But Bitsi ignored her and went on, "Oh, that Tim, he just gets a little confused . . . he don't always know where he is. It ain't all the time. Just sometimes, when something reminds him of them little blowed up children . . ."

My mother practically shoved the chips into Bitsi's chest. "I'm very uncomfortable with this conversation," she said firmly. "Tim Bogart and his family have a right to their privacy. There's no need to discuss their affairs."

I hoped Bitsi would ignore her again and at least finish her last sentence. All my reporter's curiosity was aroused. But she rang the chips up huffily, and I could tell she'd decided to deprive us of any further information. Outside, my mother snapped, "There wasn't any need to encourage her, Melissa."

"Reporters have to ask questions," I protested. "That's how they find things out."

"You were baiting her," said my mother abruptly, dumping the bag in the back seat. "Just like your father does." For the first time, I noticed the dark circles under her eyes and the thin, pinched look of her mouth. She'd lectured at a conference all week and then driven five hours up from Philadelphia today. Now she tried to smile in apology. "I'm sorry, Missy," she said softly. "I've had a long day. Let's go home. I wanted to have a picnic to celebrate your last day in ninth grade. I've got to drive back tonight."

I got in the car. "You mean you're still at the conference? You came all the way up here just because it was my last day of school?"

My mother gave me another brief smile. "Of course I did, Melissa. It's the least I could do. I know I'm gone too much —" She stepped on the accelerator. Even if you weren't from Hunter's Gap, it was too much to resist speeding down the Flats along the creek. But unlike my father, who yahooed out the open window of his Chevy like a banshee, my mother didn't look as though she was enjoying herself. She looked as if something was driving *her*. We didn't speak. There wasn't anything to say. I knew I should appreciate that she'd come home to give me a picnic, but all I felt was guilt.

The Flats ended when the road curved away from the creek toward the foot of the mountains. Broad cornfields gave way to woods, deep green and still in the early afternoon, shadowing the slopes. Rail Bogart and his sisters and his father lived back in those woods somewhere — at least, the bus dropped them off at the end of a dirt road that I always pictured led to a rundown, tarpaper shack next to a swamp. My father said we were neighbors, since Aunt Grace's land bordered the Bogarts' somewhere up in those woods. But I had no idea how far away it was. I wasn't much for exploring the wilds. I was a city girl — you wouldn't catch me out there with the bears and poisonous snakes.

About two miles from home, we passed the drive leading up to the Hunter's Gap Raptor Rehabilitation Center. I'd passed the sign every day this year in the school bus, but now I looked at it with more interest. As I did, a blue van with the words ALTON STATE UNIVERSITY DEPARTMENT OF WILDLIFE BIOLOGY stenciled in white on the sides came down the drive and stopped as we went by. A bird swooped low across the road in front of us and my mother had to brake, and in that one instant I glanced through the window of the van and caught her eye — Rhainnon of the Birds. The hawk lady. It was only for a moment. But it was enough time for her eyes to pierce straight into mine, as if she was searching for something.

It happened so fast I didn't think my mother noticed, but I forgot she was trained to catch the smallest signals. And to poke around until she figured out what they meant. "Do you know that person?" she asked.

I shrugged, keeping my face turned away, even though I knew it would put my mother on the alert. "No," I grunted. I had to lie. I don't know why. It wasn't far from the truth; I didn't really know the hawk lady. But I suddenly knew I had to keep her a secret from my mother.

"I'm sorry about the report card," I said, changing the subject abruptly. "I don't know what happened . . ."

My mother skidded to a stop by the mailbox at the bottom of our drive. "Oh, I know it's not all your fault, Melissa," she said, tired. She jerked open the box and yanked the mail out. "It's this *place!*" she cried. "I don't know what your father was thinking of, dragging us all to live up here. *He* hated it when he was growing up. He couldn't *wait* to leave."

Only in the last year had I begun to see my mother get as agitated as this. It was happening more and more, almost always when she talked about my father. "Maybe he thought things had changed . . ." I began tentatively.

"Oh, for God's sake!" she snapped, flipping through the letters. "It's because your father's an artist. Artists, especially male artists, seem to need to set themselves apart from the system. They aren't happy if everyone accepts them — that was his problem with the city. It wasn't just lack of studio space — He just wasn't *different* enough there. Cities are full of artists. In Hunter's Gap, he can really stand out —"

"But you're different."

"I *had* to be different," she said defensively, giving me a look I could not read. "I had to be better than everyone. How far do you think I would have gotten in a field that's predominantly male? I had to be the *best*. And so do you, Melissa. Do you think it's easy for a woman reporter on the front line, the way you want to be?"

I couldn't stand it when she talked like this. I couldn't bear her attacks on my father. She was so tense the muscles in her neck stood out. But for a moment, I felt her hand on the back of my head, smoothing my hair. When I looked up, she pulled her hand away and gave me a tight smile. "There's no point in being different just for the sake of being different," she said. "It's a waste of energy."

She turned the car up the drive.

4

I EXPECTED WE'D HAVE TO DRAG my father from his studio for our picnic. But he was in the kitchen when we got in, and he barely greeted my mother before he began an excited account of his latest commission. "Didn't I tell you last week that this would happen, Anna?" he said in disgust, following her out to the car while she brought her bags in. "It's the town — they're dragging their conservative little feet over funding the sculpture. It doesn't matter to them that the university's already allotted their share of the money, and I've done the preliminary sketches —" The screen door slammed behind him and he straddled a chair backwards while my mother got the food ready. "Fred Drumheller told me, off the record, that *I'm* the one the town council had reservations about! Can you believe it! Something about my personal history being in conflict with the subject . . ."

"Well," my mother remarked dryly, without turning around, "you *are* a strange choice to create a Vietnam war memorial for this town. Did you think no one would remember?"

I tried not to look at him. I'd probably helped that memory. I'd made the major mistake of announcing, during history class, that my father had gone to jail during the 1960s for being a conscientious objector to the Vietnam War. In the shocked silence that had followed, I'd added proudly: "And if you don't know what that means, it's that my father refused to kill people in an unjust war." Only Rail Bogart had glanced at me with interest. The others had recoiled as if I'd told them I ate snails.

"I'm not a strange choice," protested my father now. "I gave up a number of years of my life protesting my peers being sent off to the slaughter. As did *you*," he pointed out to my mother. "And anyway, do you know of some other Alton native who could create a real work of art for a memorial — not just a cement slab with names on it?"

"You aren't a native. You came here when you were seven, after your parents died," my mother said shortly, and I felt the chill rush up between them.

My parents weren't the kind of people who screamed and yelled at each other. People who didn't know them would not realize they were fighting. My mother would stick to the facts, nipping each word off as if she was breaking her sentences into little shards, and my father would answer her with jokes. Then he would just wander away as if nothing had happened. But they were deeply unhappy. I knew it, and I knew why, too.

They should never have had *me*. That's the truth of it. Some people are meant to have families and some are meant to just be a couple. My mother and father had been together since college, more than ten years before I was born. I had a photograph of them from those days, taken at an antiwar demonstration. Except for the longer hair and beard, my father looked the same. But my mother wore a brightly flowered skirt and her smile was sweet and warm like the bloom on a tropical plant. I'd never seen that smile, except in the photograph.

Having me was my father's idea. He wanted a baby. He told me once that my mother had been so worried about whether she could take care of a baby that he'd brought her a ten-day old kitten to practice on. She'd had to feed it every few hours with an eyedropper.

"Did it live?" I'd asked.

My father laughed. "Did it *live*! My God, it tore the

house to shreds. Strong as an ox. It was a girl, but we named it Hercules."

"What happened to her?"

"Oh, we had to give her away . . . we didn't really have time for a pet —" My father had waved his hand vaguely and gone back to tap-tapping his chisel on the stone.

Since we'd moved to Hunter's Gap, I would sometimes hear my mother crying late at night after she'd driven up from the city. I could never get to sleep on the nights I knew she was driving home, and I'd become convinced that I *had* to stay awake, to prevent something terrible happening to her. On the nights she'd cry, I'd hear my father talking softly to her down in the kitchen, and above his soothing voice I'd hear her repeat over and over, "I'm not good at this, Bobby. I don't think I can do it anymore. I don't think I can do it. I'm no good for either of you —"

I grabbed my pack now and escaped to the back porch. There was a warm breeze under the shade of oaks, but I still felt cold. I stayed there for a long time, gazing beyond the overgrown orchard toward the wooded hills, until my mother called me to dinner.

We ate sitting on a blanket in the yard my father never had time to mow. Both my mother and father were taking a special interest in the food on their plates, and I kept making inane remarks so I wouldn't have to listen to their silence. Several times, my mother looked as if she wanted to say something, and once she actually caught my eye and opened her mouth, but my father stopped her with a loud, jovial "So, Missy!" He slapped my back and I almost choked on a mouthful of salad. "You made it through your year in Purgatory. How did you manage not to get yourself tarred and feathered and run out of town for the sin of intelligence?"

"Quit it," I mumbled, trying to swallow. "You said ignorance wasn't anything to joke about."

"What a serious little person you are!" he laughed. "If anyone can save the world, it'll be you." He sounded almost wistful, as if he was thinking about someone else. He glanced briefly at my mother, but she had half-turned away from us both.

"Stop making fun of me," I grumbled.

"It isn't a joke, Bob." My mother spoke now, quietly, with a quick frown sideways at me. "Intelligence doesn't mean much without hard work, and Melissa's got a lot of work to do if she wants to go into Porter Phelps with a good record."

"What work?" I asked.

My mother speared a potato on her plate. "I spoke to the Headmaster, Mr. Hawkins, and he —"

"You called the school already?" I cried, flushing.

"I'm going to be busy all week, Melissa," she

snapped. "I needed to take care of this now. There isn't any chance for you to get into the Advanced Writing program with your grades the way they are. You need —"

"What about all my perfect grades at Dressler!" I said bitterly. "I suppose they don't mean anything."

"What it *means,*" my mother interrupted, "is that you *can* do the work, and didn't. Porter Phelps doesn't have room for students who aren't motivated. They reject two-thirds of their applicants, Melissa. Believe me. The competition is *real.*"

My father had stopped eating. He was staring at my mother as if he didn't recognize her. I said hurriedly, "Okay, okay. What work? I'll do it. Just tell me."

My mother was gathering up the plates with jerky movements. She even took mine with the remains of my salad still on it. Some picnic. I tried not to look at my father. "The Headmaster would be willing to overlook the grades if you demonstrate 'exceptional motivation and skill' in your work over the summer vacation. That's what he told me," my mother said. "You need to come up with a research project. Mr. Hawkins was quite specific — you have to be personally involved in the subject, you need to do extensive background research, and then you need to write an essay of at least fifteen pages and submit it to him by mid-August."

"For God's sake, Anna!" exclaimed my father. "It's her summer *vacation*. She's not going for her doctorate — she's fifteen. Summers are for *fun*."

"When I was fifteen I was taking an advanced summer course and working full-time as an aide at the city hospital," said my mother fiercely. They stared at each other. Then my mother went into the kitchen. My father scrambled up to follow her.

I sat by myself under the tree. The air had become oppressively still, as if the tension between my parents permeated the whole atmosphere. The grass smelled hot and pricked my legs. From beyond the mountains, black in early evening, thunder rolled in along the ridges. The oak leaves quivered suddenly.

I went into the kitchen. They barely noticed me. "Annie. Stay tonight," my father said quietly. He and my mother did not take their eyes from each other. I wanted to go up to my room and shut the door. I couldn't understand them at all. If they were so unhappy, why were my parents looking at each other the way they were now? As if the rest of the world didn't exist. Including me. I stood pressed against the door. A hot gust of air came through the screen with a low moaning sound, and the thunder felt as if it came from the pit of my stomach.

"A storm's coming..." I said, but my voice cracked into a whisper.

"I have to go back," my mother said, her eyes

never leaving my father. "You know I do. Bobby. Don't make it harder for me."

It always happened this way. After weeks of acting as if they came from two warring planets, my parents could inexplicably and suddenly shift into the same orbit. And each time, I would think: They *do* love each other. They *do.* I would think it over and over, like a chant, trying to drown out how awful I felt. But the awfulness always beat me. When my parents came together like this, I began to feel myself disappear. No, worse: I felt as if I'd never really existed at all. As if they'd never even *imagined* my existence.

Lightning slashed across the mountains. The kitchen had grown very dark. When I was younger, I would run to hide in my parents' bed during thunderstorms. But I couldn't do that now.

"You can't start out in a bad storm, Annie," my father murmured, moving closer to her. My mother didn't pull away. When the rain came, lashing across the fields and whipping the trees against the house, neither of them went to shut the windows. I could not move, either. I was trapped between their tension and the storm. Then my mother turned and walked from the kitchen, waited silently for my father in the hallway. She brushed her hand against him. She would stay. At least for the night.

I sat on the back porch during the storm. Maybe I

needed to be afraid of something I could see. Each crack of lightning made me flinch, but it made me feel *real*, like the rain that stung my face. I couldn't hear myself cry over the thunder. I couldn't even feel my tears for the rain. But no matter how hard I pressed my fists against my ears, I could hear my own thoughts.

My mother was right, of course. I had blown off the whole year and I was blaming it on Hunter's Gap. But it was no one's fault except my own. I just didn't have what it took. Not the way my mother did. This year had been hard for her, too. She hadn't stopped working, though. She was still the best.

I clapped my arms around my head as lightning and thunder crashed simultaneously. But I couldn't block out my thoughts. I knew the real reason why my mother was pushing me into the best school, into the top classes . . . because once I went away to school, she wouldn't have to come back to Hunter's Gap. She could stay in the apartment in the city, she could leave my father, and she could tell herself it was all right because at least her daughter was getting the best education money could buy. She'd be able to focus entirely on her own work then, she wouldn't have to support my father or make those five-hour trips between Philadelphia and Hunter's Gap. The dark circles under her eyes would disappear, the lines would soften around her mouth.

Maybe she'd even get that smile from the photograph back —

My father was finally becoming known for his sculptures and my mother had built a thriving practice — what did they need each other for now, after all? But they thought *I* needed them. So they were staying together. The only way out of the trap was for me to leave and for them to believe I was happy. For my mother, being happy meant being the best. So I had to be the best. It was the only way.

It *had* been my suggestion to go to my mother's old school. Of course I wanted to go to Porter Phelps. And what was I so miserable about my parents for? More than half the students at Dressler Academy came from divorced families. It was obvious my mother would be better off on her own. She was a loner, like me. And my father —

My father would be alone in Hunter's Gap. He'd work in his studio all the time. I wouldn't be there to remind him to eat, and I wouldn't be around to pester him about wearing his respirator so he wouldn't breathe in the marble dust, and he'd have no one to watch his stupid Star Trek videos with. I couldn't stand thinking of him here on this rundown old farm, all alone. And I couldn't imagine my own life, without him to talk to. My father was my best friend. My only friend.

But there was no sense in thinking about that. I

certainly wasn't going to start tenth grade at Alton High School, riding the bus every day with Betsy Warren and wimpy Cindy and that idiot Kevin. And Rail Bogart. No. I was committed. I would go to Porter Phelps, and I would get into that Advanced Writing program. Whatever it took, I would do it.

I jumped up, knocking my pack off the table. Books and papers spilled across the wet floor. I grabbed everything up and saw the envelope Mr. Beecham had handed me as I left the classroom. Slowly, I opened it. Across the top of the flyer inside, I read: ALTON REGISTER YOUNG INTERNSHIP PROGRAM. I skimmed the guidelines, interested in spite of myself. The internship was open to applicants from the local high schools. The chosen student would work for the school year at *The Register*, the biggest newspaper in the county. The winner's feature story would be published.

I crumpled the application impatiently. My reporting career was not going to develop by getting published in a little backwater paper like *The Alton Register*. If I was going to write a story, I was going to make sure it had a real chance to make a difference in the world. At the very least, my story was going to make up for that C in English and get me into the Advanced Writing program. I was going to Porter Phelps the way my mother had: by being the best. As far as Hunter's Gap went, *The Alton Register* was welcome to publish any story I might write. Maybe it would make the people here sit up and take notice of the rest of the world. But I didn't need their internship.

The storm gave a terrific crack of thunder as a streak of blinding light ripped across the sky. A gust of wind almost tore the papers from my hand. There was an explosion so loud it zinged up through the soles of my feet and a flash illuminated the top of a distant hill. In a few moments, I caught a sharp whiff of fire drifting in on the cool air.

With that last crescendo, the storm seemed to die down. Cautiously, I pushed open the screen door and peered through the twilight rain. The hill was barely visible. I stood for a long time in the doorway, clutching the papers and watching as darkness lowered over the dripping trees and fields. I imagined a glow on the far-off hill, but when I tried to focus, I saw only the light from the house reflected on the mist sifting up from the ground. The rain slowed to a whisper on the roof. The crickets came with the darkness, trilling first singly, then in a chorus.

I was shivering with the wet. I took a final deep breath of the clean air before going inside. I slipped upstairs quietly, past my parents' closed door, and shut the door of my own room. I threw the internship application in the wastebasket and went to bed.

5

I woke early and lay gazing out the window. The leaves shimmered watery shadows over the walls of my room. The house was silent. I jumped up to look down in the yard. My mother's car was still there. The door to my parents' room was shut, and in the kitchen, I found the table still piled with dirty plates and leftovers from our picnic. I shoved them aside to make a space and plunked down a bowl of cereal. Some picnic. If it was meant to be a celebration of my last day at school, why did we have hot dogs? There hadn't been anything I could eat but potato salad and a bun.

I listened for sounds that would indicate my parents were getting up, knowing that my mother wouldn't have time for more than a few words before she rushed out the door. Then I'd have to watch her driving off down the road. I pushed my spoon dejectedly around in the soggy cornflakes. My father would disappear into his studio, and I knew I might not see him for days. He'd work late into the night, sleep half the days, and leave me to deal with my first summer in Hunter's Gap alone.

How was I going to find something in this place to get involved in? What went on in Hunter's Gap, anyway? The Lutheran camp run by the church ladies? The organizing committee for the annual Firemen's Community Picnic? Right. I could really light up the world writing about something like that.

I slammed the door loudly and went outside. The sun was steaming off the grass and the air was heavy with humidity. I wandered lethargically across the lawn, glancing now and then up at my parents' window. Paint was peeling in patches all over the house. Ever since we'd moved here, my father had been promising to clean the place up, but here it was mid-June and he hadn't done a thing. Mid-June. Two and a half months of summer vacation stretched before me like a dismal swamp.

If I could just stay in Philadelphia with my mother, there would be plenty of worthwhile things to do that I could write about. I could volunteer at the soup kitchen or help out at the Greenpeace office downtown. I could get to places myself on city transit. Research? Not a problem — Philadelphia had wonderful libraries and I had cards for several of them. I loved everything about the city — the noise and bustle on the streets, the little Russian man who stocked the newsstand on the corner with newspapers from all over the world, the librarian in the hushed Public Reading Room who spoke only in an impressive array of facial expressions. . . . Last summer I had pretended to be a reporter on assignment in a foreign country. I would sit at sidewalk cafes drinking cappuccinos, observing every detail of the street around me, recording in a notebook entire overheard conversations and the physical characteristics of people I saw.

But here in Hunter's Gap, the land that time forgot, there was nothing to do. I could see only trees and more trees. Cornfields, scraggly-looking farms, hills. I scuffed through the wet grass to the back of the house. A breeze stirred and for a moment, I caught again the faint smell of smoke. In the sunlight, I could clearly see the wooded hill where the lightning had struck rising beyond the orchard. It didn't seem as far away as it had the night before. I stood up on a stump to get a better view.

Aunt Grace's and Uncle Fred's farm was one hundred and forty acres. I had no idea how big that was. An acre might be the size of a mile. Or it might be the size of a city block. I shaded my eyes. The hill certainly didn't seem to be *miles* away. . . . By now I'd waded into the knee-high grass of the orchard, past the rusting hulk of Uncle Fred's abandoned tractor. Above me, clusters of unripe apples hung like tiny green ornaments. The air smelled sweet and warm, like a cake baking in a steaming kitchen. I'd never ventured beyond the orchard. I stood in the sunlit grass and peered into the woods. The farm was not *real* wilderness, after all — not like Alaska or someplace. It was just an old farm in north-central Pennsylvania. If there were bears, they must live high in the mountains. And snakes. . . . I decided not to think about snakes.

I looked back at the house. It seemed still and empty, even from a distance. I didn't want to go back there. But I hadn't left my parents a note. . . . I slapped at an insect angrily. Let them worry.

I thrashed through low thickets and emerged into deeper woods. The ground was covered in a springy mat of pine needles and the silence wrapped softly around me. Gradually, I realized it wasn't really silent — the woods were full of tiny rustlings, the silvery calls of birds, the air breathing in the pines. The silence was like a nest encircling everything, holding each sound like a lovely egg within it. Even my footsteps were nestled within the quietness of the woods.

I kept climbing steadily. I was less sure now. But I reminded myself that this was what it would be like to be on assignment in Central America, hurrying along behind a soldier taking me to a secret, exclusive interview with a rebel guerrilla leader. I wouldn't be sure of where I was going. But something would be waiting ahead of me, something I didn't know about and needed to know. Some truth that might light up the world.

The woods got thicker and changed from pine to a mixture of taller trees that spread a canopy of dappled light and shade above me. I could see birds flickering among the lower branches. I was hot, and when I came to a stream I wished I could drink the cold tea-brown water. But I only splashed it over my face. Out of the corner of my eye I caught a movement on a rock. A quick, slithering shape. I froze. But it was only a few inches long and had tiny legs.

I scrambled up and dried my hands on my jeans. Homesickness lay like a heavy lump in my hollow stomach. How could these woods, with these unknown creatures, ever be my home? I turned my head, saw light through the trees beyond me, and went on. Reporters didn't have homes. They followed after what they didn't know into places that were not their own.

The sudden brightness in the clearing at the top of the hill blinded me for a moment. I pushed through wet grass that brushed my waist, soaking my jeans, and stopped again. The burnt smell was sharp and fresh. I squinted in the glare. And saw the tree.

It rose above everything, a giant white crack against the blue sky. Solitary in the middle of the clearing, dwarfing the forest growth, the white tree was split down the middle. Black, charred wood contrasted with the pale bark so distinctly it looked as though someone had painted it.

The tree had been dead a long time before the lightning struck last night. No leaf clung to the maze of branches. Half of the tree rose into the sky fifty or sixty feet, every twig etched in white against searing blue. The other half lay smashed on the ground, flattening the grass for an area the size of a small house. Whole, the trunk must have been ten feet in diameter. I never knew until that moment how one could stand truly frozen with awe.

And with the awe came also sorrow. I would never see this tree whole. I touched the outer twigs lightly with my fingertips. Perhaps I alone had seen the moment of this tree's fiery division. I pushed deeper in until I was laced around by the branches. There was a sudden piercing shriek so close to me I gasped and stumbled back.

The shrieking came from the impenetrable center of the broken branches. It was impossible to see anything through the latticework of tangled twigs. The screeching increased frantically whenever I moved. Angry . . . and afraid. I worked my way around the outer branches and climbed cautiously up on the broken half of the trunk. My hands turned black from the burned wood, and I felt the warmth. I was touching lightning.

I crawled out as far as I could and stood up, holding tight to a protruding branch. I peered down into the mass below me, and there was the ugliest bird I had ever seen.

It was huge, bigger than a chicken, covered in soot-matted tufts of gray down. Clumps of feathers stuck out unevenly on the wings and tail. Its head was almost bare, comprised of not much more than two great, fierce-browed eyes and a curved beak so sharp and powerful-looking I was sure it could take my finger off. The beak was open so wide I could see the tongue, and the bird lunged awkwardly at me while it screamed. It clung precariously to a branch with oversized, yellow, taloned feet. When I moved closer, the bird lurched at me so violently it toppled, flapping and squawking, into the tangle below. It clawed its way back onto the branch and continued to scream at me.

It might have been the most pathetic thing I'd ever seen. But despite the scrawny neck and naked head, despite the twigs and dirt caught in the ragged down, somehow the bird was magnificent. Beautiful. Brave. The eyes, dark as a dreamless sleep, glared straight into my own. Powerful, unfinished, wild. The bird clung defiantly to its branch and I clung to mine. Sunlight glinted off the knife-sharp beak. To my surprise, when I knelt to straddle the branch, the bird stopped shrieking, and for a long time we were both still.

I don't know how long I sat there. The bird never took its attention from me. If I brushed the hair from my sweaty face or slapped a mosquito, it followed my movement with an alert dart of its eye. Gradually I began to think more carefully. This bird was obviously too young to fly. So it must have been in its nest when the tree was struck by lightning. If it was too young to fly, it would die here. Starve. Or get eaten by something else. But if I tried to rescue it, even if I could get through those jagged twigs which reminded me of barbed wire, I would face a creature who could rip the nose off my face.

It wasn't just that I couldn't do it. I *shouldn't* do it. I had to remain objective. Reporters couldn't get involved in the disasters they came upon. Their job was just to report them. I would simply go home and tell someone about it.

But what if something killed it in the meantime? What if it was already close to starving? I sat up abruptly and the bird hissed at me. Again I looked into those frightened, defiant eyes, and suddenly I remembered the hawk lady. With that thought, I was already scrambling backwards on my stomach down the trunk. I would go home and call her. This bird had to be a hawk or eagle or something like that — what else would be so big? And that's what the hawk lady did: saved hawks. I jumped to the ground and started across the clearing.

And stopped. In every direction, the encircling woods looked exactly the same. I turned slowly around. The bird was silent, but I could feel it watching me from the branches. I was abandoning it. I closed my eyes and took a deep breath. I told myself that this wasn't wilderness. It was Uncle Fred's and Aunt Grace's old farm. I was sure to come upon civilization no matter what direction I chose. I opened my eyes and began to walk, and did not look back at the shattered tree.

The woods no longer felt like a warm nest. Something crashed in the dark undergrowth, and I jumped back with a startled yell, as defiant as the bird had been. My hands were curled as tight as the bird's talons. For a long time I made my way through the sifting, leafy shadows of the woods, slipping down slopes, tripping over roots. I kept going downhill. I twisted my ankle jumping across a stream. Then, all at once, I scrambled down a steep incline choked with thick hemlocks and slid to a stop on a dirt road.

6

I'D ONCE HEARD an investigative reporter on television say that no matter what things *seemed* to be, he gathered the factual evidence before he could trust his story to be true. *Never assume,* he'd said. I didn't realize, when I came upon the trailer set just off the dirt road on a neat patch of lawn, that I was coming face to face with facts that contradicted what I had always assumed to be true. The well-repaired trailer was newly painted a pastel blue, and flowers grew profusely in rock-bordered patches in the grass, on trellises up the side of the trailer, in window boxes and in flowerpots set on the steps. All I felt at that moment was relief.

A man came from behind the trailer shaking the dirt off a bunch of carrots. He was barefoot and wearing only the bottoms of a pair of striped pajamas. But he gave me such an open, welcoming smile I wasn't embarrassed by his appearance. He was very thin, ribs shadowing his white skin, and when he walked toward me he seemed to take care not to crush the grass under his feet. The man's long thin face and his huge, deep eyes reminded me of paintings of old saints in one of my father's art books.

He came up to me as if he'd been expecting me and without hesitation, took my hand. For a moment, I thought he was going to kiss it. But he just smiled again, as if I was the most perfect thing he'd ever seen, and asked, "Have you come to see my flowers?"

I was so startled I blurted, "Yes," and right then, with him smiling at me so beautifully, it seemed to be true. The man's gray eyes were oddly familiar, and all at once I *knew*, but before I could say anything, Rail Bogart came out of the trailer. He stopped when he saw me, flushed as deeply as I must have, and muttered, "Hey, Taylor. What're you doing here?"

"I think she's lost," said his father, without dropping my hand.

"I'm not —" I began, disconcerted. A small girl came out of the trailer flanked by two lean dogs who sniffed at me but didn't bark.

"Who's that, Daddy?" she asked.

"It's Taylor, from school." Rail answered quickly, as if to prevent his father from speaking. He put his arm around him and steered the man toward the door. "You're gonna get all sunburnt out here, Daddy," he said gently. "It's real hot today. Go on in and give the carrots to Dawnie, okay? She's making lunch. You haven't had anything to eat yet."

But Tim Bogart turned back to me, still smiling. "You gotta look after this girl, son. She's lost. You can't just leave people lost when you find them."

I babbled, "I'm okay. Really. I'm just . . . I was up in the woods and there was this tree hit by lightning and a baby bird . . . and I need . . ." I stopped, so flustered that I was out of breath. Rail had the same eyes as his father, but they were frowning instead of smiling. Finally I muttered, "I'm really okay. I just need to know which way to go to —"

"Where's the bird?" asked Tim Bogart, watching me as if he expected me to pull it out of my pocket.

"I . . . I left it —"

"You *left* it?" he said, incredulous.

I turned helplessly to Rail, and he looked resigned. "I'll go find it, Daddy," he said. "Now, will you go in with Cattie?" This time his father went happily up the steps and into the trailer. When he was gone, Rail asked, "Where is it?"

"The bird? You mean — you're really going to go find it?"

"I said I would, didn't I?" He shrugged impatiently. "Dad won't forget about it. He'll just go off looking for it himself if I don't, and then I'll have to look all over creation for *him* . . . so where is it? *What* is it? A robin or something?"

I described the tree and the bird, and Rail's eyes widened. "Well, man," he breathed. "It was that big old sycamore. *Man.* An' it must be a red-tailed hawk — there's been a pair of them nesting in that tree for years. So that's what got hit, last night —" He gave me a measured look, as if assessing me. "Well, you're gonna have to come with me. I'll need help."

"Me?" But he was already going into a shed that was as neatly-kept as the rest of the place, and I was uncomfortably reminded of my assumption that Rail Bogart lived in some rundown old tarpaper shack. Our house was far more rundown than this. He emerged with a burlap sack and said abruptly, "Come on."

By then I had formulated my excuses. "I can't . . . I mean, I really have to get back home . . ." I began, but I was talking to Rail's receding back. I followed a step or two, then stopped. "Do you really need me to help?" I called, frustrated, and Rail paused, watching me with an inscrutable expression.

"You found the baby hawk," he said.

His voice was carefully neutral, but I scowled, torn. I thought about the bird. Alone, clinging to that blasted tree under the hot sky, waiting for its parents to return and feed it. The bird had no nest around it.

It couldn't fly away. I was the only person who had seen it.

"Taylor," said Rail, "if you're coming, we gotta go now. My dad isn't doing too good. I don't want to leave him very long."

It was almost impossible, from the first, to keep up with Rail. He strode up the steep wooded slope without once looking around to see if I was following. I panted after him, growing more and more angry. It was just like in school. He was doing this on purpose. Keeping ahead of me, never letting me forget that he might be better than I was at anything I tried to do. His silence seemed designed to remind me that *I* had abandoned the baby bird, and *he* was going to rescue it.

What incensed me even more was that I couldn't stop thinking about that stupid game. Round-up. About how I'd felt such a wonderfully exhilarating happiness when we ran together. But right now, Rail was making it very clear to me that this whole venture was a nuisance he considered entirely my fault. He made his way with total sureness through the woods, turned sharp left at a boulder as if it was a signpost, headed across a ravine, crossed the stream at a place where three stones lay in the water to step on. . . . I had to follow him. I knew I would never find my way alone.

I tripped after him through a thicket and without warning we stepped out of the woods. The giant white tree rose before us. Rail stopped, staring up as I had earlier. "That tree always made me wish . . . wish . . ." he said softly. Then he shrugged. "Man. Look at it *now*." He went closer, circled the fallen branches and immediately, the screeching started. Rail grimaced. "Yup. Red-tail." He jumped up onto the broken half of the trunk and ran lightly along it until he could peer down into the branches. "Hey," he called soothingly. "Hey. Hey. You sure are a fighter." He knelt and studied the tree. Then he came back along the trunk, jumped easily to the ground beside me, and said, "We're gonna have to get at it from underneath."

"Yeah. Right," I said, eyeing the barbed-wire tangle. But Rail flopped onto his stomach in the grass and wiggled forward. He disappeared almost immediately, but I could hear him grunting, heard the snapping twigs and then a swear word I wouldn't have believed could come from Rail. I swallowed back a giggle.

"I hear you," said Rail, his voice muffled. "I don't notice *you* down here. C'mon, Taylor. You helping, or not?"

I hesitated. War reporters wouldn't think twice about crawling around in the mud and through barbed wire to get their story. It couldn't always be safe. They got killed, too, the same as soldiers, my father said. The only war I'd seen reported was the Gulf War, where the reporters and soldiers looked so clean. But my father had shaken his head. There are no clean wars, he'd told me. With Vietnam, at least they reported the truth of war. This — he'd waved his hand at the television in disgust — this is a lie. If you're going to tell the truth, Missy, you have to jump right into the story, heart and soul and body.

"What do you want me to do?" I asked.

"I'm gonna get under it — okay? You have to scare it so it falls into the sack . . . Taylor?"

"Yeah?" I said weakly.

"Just . . . all you have to do is get out on the trunk and poke at the bird with a stick. Okay? But wait 'til I say so."

It was far more likely the hawk would scare *me* and I'd fall into the sack, I thought grimly, remembering the scimitar-like beak. But I inched along the trunk, wishing that Rail didn't have to witness my awkwardness.

"Distract it," he called.

It wasn't hard to do. The baby hawk lunged at me, its beak gaping, scruffy wings flailing, all the while shrieking so loudly I could hardly hear Rail. I got much closer to it than I'd been before, and I saw a bloody gash on its neck. One of its wings hung crookedly. I could see Rail now, maneuvering among the branches to stand upright.

"Well, now we know it's a female — look at this,

Taylor," he said. I peered farther over the trunk at a denser mass of twigs just below the hawk. Crushed among them was something that looked like a dirty gray rag. "There's the nest," Rail said. "Man. It's all busted to bits. Look at the other chick — see how much smaller he is? That's the male. Wow — how'd this one ever make it out of that mess alive?"

The baby hawk had figured out something was going on. She tilted her head sharply, fixing one wild eye on Rail below her. She hobbled along the branch as far as she could, watching first me, then Rail. She wasn't screaming now, but her beak remained open. I was sure I could see the fear in her eyes. I was so close I saw the pulse of her heart under the gray down.

"Poke her, Taylor," Rail directed. He'd managed to hold the sack open beneath the branch. His arms and face were lacerated with scratches. "Hurry! Hurry!"

I broke off a twig and jabbed it at the hawk. She slashed at it with her beak. I jabbed again and she tumbled backwards, just as Rail wanted, right into the sack. I was so amazed I could only stare, mouth open, while Rail twisted a bit of string around the mouth of the sack. He grinned up at me triumphantly. "Now," he said. "You gotta take her. I can't hold this and climb out of here."

She hardly weighed anything. I pulled the sack up to the trunk, clasping tightly with my legs so I wouldn't slip, and cradled it in one arm. The hawk wasn't struggling, but I felt her heart beating very fast against my skin. "Hey," I whispered to her, the way Rail had. "Hey. Hey. Don't be scared."

"Careful," said Rail, hauling himself up onto the trunk. "She can bite right through that sack."

But I didn't care. I couldn't bear to dangle her in that musty sack. I tucked it more securely under my arm and shook my head, and to my surprised horror, tears stung my eyes. I couldn't even get a hand free to wipe them away. "She's hurt," I whispered. "Her wing —"

I wished Rail would stop looking at me. But a slow smile spread over his face. He surveyed his arms. "I look like I been through a cheese grater," he said. All at once we were both laughing, clinging to the charred trunk with a wild animal in a sack that I was sure could do the damage of twenty cheese graters. Laughing so hard we almost fell off.

I had never laughed like that. The way friends do. I completely forgot that I couldn't stand Rail Bogart, forgot that I'd spent the entire year in Hunter's Gap hating him because we were lumped together and tormented together. I even forgot that it drove me crazy when he got better grades than I did in a place I hardly considered a *school*. And when I did remember, a second later, I gulped through my laughter and met his eyes in confusion. I'd never noticed how many different smiles Rail had; I'd hardly noticed him smile at all, before. Now I saw a smile deep in his eyes, although his expression was serious.

"I really do have to get back," he said. "I'm worried about my dad. Storms set him off real bad — he was up all night."

"I like your dad," I said.

"You do?" said Rail eagerly.

"Yeah. He's the nicest person I've met in Hunter's Gap," I said, and I meant it. Unlike Bitsi and everyone else, Tim Bogart didn't seem to have a mean, ignorant, or gossipy bone in his body. He grew flowers and vegetables and smiled like an angel. I asked, tentatively, "Is he scared of lightning or something?"

"Naw"— Rail looked off into the sky, the way I'd seen him do a hundred times before — "Naw. I think storms just remind him — you know." He glanced quickly at me. "Do you really like him?"

I nodded. His eyes grew soft. "Well, he *is* nice," he said in a low voice. "He just gets . . . I don't know. Turned around. Like he doesn't know where he is. The doctor told me lots of Vietnam vets are like that. Worse, too. Like they're still there. Anything can set them off —"

"Thunder must sound like a bomb," I said.

He nodded, squinting his eyes. "Yup. That's what it was, too. A land mine, in a village. He was playing with a bunch of kids and they all got killed. He didn't even get hurt. Physically, I mean. Then, when he was taken off in an ambulance, the ambulance ran into a mine and *it* got blown up, too, and he was the only one who survived." He turned to me, his eyes bright with puzzlement. "Don't you think that's weird?"

"Like maybe he was meant to stay alive, for some reason?" I asked.

He looked startled for a moment. The hawk inside the sack wasn't moving, but I could still feel her heart against my arm. Then Rail stood abruptly. "Yeah," he muttered. "That's what *he* thinks . . . That's the problem. He doesn't know why. Makes him nuts."

We took turns carrying the sack. "Why doesn't she struggle?" I asked.

Rail shrugged. "You know how, when they train hawks, they put hoods over their heads? It keeps them quiet. I guess they don't get scared if they can't see."

Later, as we were walking down the dirt road toward the trailer, I said, "We should take her to the hawk lady."

"I can fix her," Rail frowned. "I fix up wild creatures all the time — I find lots of hurt things out here. That lady is real mean —"

"Oh, that's just what stupid Kevin says!" I said

scornfully. "For God's sake, Rail. It's what she *does* — she works with *hawks.*"

Rail looked away, stubborn. I followed him behind the trailer to the shed. Inside, he carefully opened the sack in a large wire cage. He had to prod the hawk to get her out. She half-skidded onto the floor of the cage, blinking, and huddled in the corner without moving. She was still panting, and her filthy down and feathers stuck out in every direction.

"She must be thirsty," I whispered.

"She gets water from meat," said Rail. "She wouldn't know how to drink. I'll get a couple of squirrels this afternoon."

I didn't want to leave the hawk. I knelt and peered into the cage, searching for some sign of her earlier defiance. But her eyes were half-covered with a whitish lid and her head drooped. "Will she be all right?" I asked. "When will she fly? When can we set her free?"

Rail squatted next to me. "She's awful scared," he said pensively. "But I'll fix her, Taylor. You'll see. She'll fly. You can tell she's a real fighter." He brushed a cobweb off the wire mesh, but the hawk didn't appear to notice. After a pause, Rail added, without looking at me, "You can help. If you want, I mean. You can come over any time you want."

I stood up quickly. "Yeah. Well. I have to go call my dad now. He must be wondering where I am —"

As I sat by the road to wait for my father, I watched Tim Bogart playing in the garden with his two little girls. Rail waited with me, drawing circles in the dust with the heel of his hunting boot and not saying anything. The little girls squealed with laughter and I saw Tim lifting them both onto his thin shoulders. Rail looked at me. My stomach jumped, the way it did whenever my father zoomed the Chevy fast down a dip in the road. He smiled.

"Why did you chase me, when we had to play that stupid game yesterday?" I blurted.

"I wasn't chasing you," Rail said. "I wouldn't play such a stupid game."

I heard the Chevy roaring up the road. "What were you doing, then?" I asked, standing up.

He looked up at me somberly, his head tilted to one side. "I just wanted to run with you," he said simply.

7

I SAT AT THE KITCHEN TABLE in the sweltering heat and stared glumly at the pile of *Alton Register*s. After four days of desultory searching for some project I could get involved with in Hunter's Gap, some activity worthy of a research essay, I'd come up with . . . nothing. Zero ideas. I read "Dear Abby" through the oil stain in the section my father had used when he'd tinkered with the engine of the Chevy a few days ago. I was desperate. Maybe it was time to write to Dear Abby myself.

I couldn't seem to concentrate. My father always told me I had an investigative reporter's tenacious spirit. Now I felt like I didn't care what happened. But I *did*. That was the trouble. I cared a lot. But it seemed as if there was nothing in Hunter's Gap that would ever make a difference in the world.

I pushed abruptly back from the table and went to find my father in the studio. From the doorway, I watched him at his drawing desk. He drew with bold, black strokes on large sheets of paper, bent over his work as if to thrust all of himself into each line. I didn't make a sound, but I could tell by the way he held his head that he knew I was there. After a while he groaned and looked up. "It's not happening," he said. "It's just not happening."

"What?"

He slammed his hand on the paper. "This!" he complained. "This damned memorial. It's got to be about *them* . . . those *boys*. Going off to war, so eager, so unsuspecting. I want to show them at the moment of betrayal, at the moment they realize that the country they love so much has *betrayed* them. And I just can't *find* it. The image. I have to find it. Do you understand?"

"An image that will shine a light?" I asked softly.

My father reached out his arm, encircling me with his familiar smell. Marble dust, charcoal, sweat, oil, the same as long as I could remember. I leaned against him. "You always understand me," he murmured.

"Dad — will you take me to the library?" I asked. "I can't find anything in those papers."

"Are you still worrying about that writing thing — for that school?" he asked, frowning. He always referred to Porter Phelps as "that school." I nodded. He held me out at arm's length. "Missy, you're already *in* the school," he said. "You don't *have* to do this project — you don't have to prove anything. Your mother —"

"It's not Mom!" I cried. "*I* want to do it. I got a C in English, Dad! Don't you get it?"

"God in heaven, the two of you act as though that grade is the end of the world!" my father said in exasperation. "And no, I can't drive you into Alton today. I have to get some kind of sketch ready to show the town council tomorrow."

"But —"

"Ride your bike in," he suggested brightly. "That's what I did when I was a kid."

"But it's *miles!*"

The phone rang. When my father handed it to me I was so startled to hear Rail's voice I couldn't respond. "Taylor?" he repeated. "It's Rail — from school."

"You don't have to say 'from school,'" I managed to blurt, turning away so my father wouldn't hear. "I know who you are."

There was a silence for a second. "The hawk is real sick," he said finally. "I can't get her to eat. She's breathing funny. I don't know what to do. Can you come over?"

The truth was, I hadn't been able to stop thinking about Rail. For the last four days I'd told myself it was the red-tailed hawk I was thinking about. I had found her, so somehow that made her mine. But I belonged to her, also. Somehow, part of me had remained with the hawk in the cage in the shed, cared for by Rail Bogart. I couldn't think of one without the other.

"Taylor?" Rail said. "You coming over?"

"Yeah, okay," I answered.

I *wanted* to go. But I loitered in the house for almost half an hour, impatient with myself, unable to make up my mind. My father always told me I was just like him — he said I hadn't blossomed yet, and when I did, people would beat a path to my door. But it was wishful thinking on his part. I wasn't the sort of person other people made friends with. I went over the conversation with Rail in my head, detail by detail, convinced he hadn't really wanted to see me and that I'd misunderstood.

But finally I pedaled my bike down the dirt road, slowly, so I wouldn't arrive with my face all red from the heat. I saw him sitting on the steps of the trailer watching for me. He jumped up as soon as I came into view and ran to meet me. "Hey, Taylor," he said. "I've been waiting forever. Did you get a flat tire or something?"

In the shed, it took a few seconds for my eyes to adjust and at first I could only make out a motionless lump on the floor of the cage. I blinked a few times until I could see the baby hawk more clearly. "For God's sake, Rail," I cried softly. "She's almost dead!"

She no longer held her head up. No light reflected

in the listless eyes. Her beak was open, but there was only an uneven flutter of breath at her throat. "I been feeding her just the way her parents would," said Rail miserably. "Squirrel, rabbit, all mashed up . . . she ate good the first day. But yesterday —"

I recognized the same frantic intensity in Rail I'd seen all year at school. "Maybe it's mice," he continued now, desperately. "I mean, maybe her parents only fed her mice. Red-tails won't go for bigger prey if there's plenty of mice around —"

"Rail," I interrupted. "She's *sick.* Anyone can see that. It's not the food. You have to take her to the hawk lady. You can't fix everything."

After a long silence, Rail muttered, "You have to come with me, then."

The hawk never even moved when I picked her up. We put her in a box and tied it to the back of my bike, but we didn't ride for fear the jolting would kill her. Rail pushed his rusty one-speed bike next to mine and for the nearly two miles to the Hunter's Gap Raptor Rehabilitation Center, we hardly spoke.

I wasn't thinking much about the hawk. I was thinking that I was about to see the hawk lady. I was afraid to meet her, the same as when I'd first seen her in Bitsi's store. I was afraid she wouldn't be mysterious and beautiful after all. If I spoke to her, that magical distance I'd felt before might turn out to be something ordinary. . . .

I pushed my bike resolutely across the culvert at

the bottom of the drive. I was a reporter. Truth was more important than magic.

Rail stopped before I did, looking up at the house and barns. "You ever meet her?" he asked.

"Not really —"

He kicked the grass at the base of a fence post. "My dad worked for her last year. When they were building all the cages and stuff . . ."

"Well, she obviously didn't shoot *him*," I said, more caustically than I intended. He flushed and pushed ahead of me up the drive.

The blue Alton State University van was parked near the barn and people were working by several of the large wire mesh cages. Rows of cages were set among pine trees, some attached to sheds. The cages were all shaded by trees and I couldn't see into them from where we stood. Rail looked around the yard, uncomfortable. I handed him my bike to hold, but before I could do anything, the door of the house opened and the hawk lady came toward us.

Even before she spoke, I could see that Dr. Rhiannon Jeffries was annoyed. There was nothing of the vibrant energy she'd had in the store talking to my father. Her long black hair was pulled tightly back in a rubber band. A few strands, streaked with gray, hung damply around her face. Her jeans were filthy and torn, and her shapeless T-shirt was splotched with what looked like dried blood.

Instead of the searching interest I'd seen in her eyes before, the hawk lady's intensity was turned in, opaque and unapproachable. She glanced in irritation first at Rail, then at me, and demanded abruptly, "Didn't you read the sign? Visitors are by appointment only. There are several nesting birds here, and I don't want them disturbed."

There was such a command in her voice that both Rail and I stepped back involuntarily. Rail bumped hard against the box and caught his breath. We looked at each other, Rail's eyes dark with concern. I lifted the lid to look in, and the hawk lady said sharply, "Do you have something in there?"

"That's why we came," I said, with as much dignity as I could.

"It's a hawk," Rail added. "A red-tail. We found . . . Taylor found her. She hasn't fledged, and —"

"You took it from the nest?" the hawk lady barked.

Rail fumbled to untie the rope on the box and muttered, "Yeah, sort of —"

The woman was already walking briskly toward one of the sheds. She said, without turning around, "Bring it in here. And don't make any noise."

"You carry it," Rail hissed at me, shoving the box into my arms. He hesitated as if he intended to wait outside, but I gave him a furious frown and he followed me into the shed after the hawk lady.

She took the box from me and placed it gently on a workbench that ran along the back of the large room. Tools and supplies were piled on shelves along one wall. The other wall was lined top to bottom with small cages, and the shed windows were covered with paper. The woman turned on a light over the work area, but the rest of the room remained too dark for me to see much. We stood uncertainly by the open door.

"Keep the door shut," the hawk lady snapped. She pulled on a pair of thick gloves. "Don't you know better than to take a wild animal from its habitat? No matter what it looks like to you, it's always better to leave a wild animal alone."

There was something fascinating about the contrast of her manner toward us and the careful, gentle way she lifted the baby hawk from the box and laid her on a towel, tilting the lamp so it wouldn't shine in her eyes. Holding one hand firmly on the bird, she ran her other hand over the hawk's injured wing and inspected the gash on the neck under the blood-matted down. To my amazement, Rail slipped past me and stood silently near the bench to watch.

"The wing isn't too badly broken," the woman said, speaking more to herself than to us. "Female — big, too. She's been well looked after by the parents, but she's gotten dehydrated somehow, and she has an infection." She turned suddenly to look at us with narrowed eyes. "When did you find her? Just how long have you kept her?"

"Four days" — Rail whispered. The woman didn't say anything. He added in a low voice — "I fed her right — I've seen plenty of hawks feeding their babies. I cut up a rabbit and mashed it some, and she ate a lot the first day . . ."

"It's illegal to capture a raptor, let alone keep it," the hawk lady said shortly, interrupting him. I could almost feel Rail's flush. But it was the way he suddenly dropped his head, defeated, his hair flipping over to hide his eyes, that did it for me.

No one likes reporters. They're pushy and nosy, and they deliberately try to prod people into reacting. They have to find the truth and they have to tell it, even if no one wants to hear. So they can't worry about what anyone might think of them. What kind of reporter was I going to be if I got tongue-tied every time someone looked at me cross-eyed? I'd better get used to it. I stepped between Rail and Dr. Rhiannon Jeffries and looked straight into her eyes.

"Maybe we should have brought the hawk to you right away," I said. "But you're wrong to say we should have left her where we found her. You never gave us a chance to explain. The tree was hit by lightning and the nest was smashed. There was another baby, but it was dead. She would have died of hunger out there. Or a bear might have got her. Or a snake or something."

The woman stared at me, then burst out laughing. "A bear or a *snake*?" she said. I glared at her.

Rail muttered quickly, "Taylor's from the city. She don't know about wild things."

"Apparently not," the woman replied dryly, raising her eyebrows. She studied the baby hawk lying motionless on the towel, then asked Rail in a more reasonable tone, "When you found her, were there any hawks circling around nearby? Even if the nest was ruined, the parents might have been trying to feed her."

"They wouldn't have been able to reach her," I said, still angry. Rail just shook his head. He was still looking miserably at the floor. "She was caught way down in the branches. Rail had to crawl in underneath. And besides, we could see she was hurt —"

The hawk lady had begun cleaning the sooty feathers with a cottonball and warm water. She leaned close and gently loosened the dried blood around the gash. The baby hawk's eyes were open. Somehow, even though she didn't move, I could tell she was aware of everything.

"I thought I could make her better," Rail spoke suddenly. "I didn't mean to hurt her. I wasn't going to keep her. I wanted her to grow up. We wanted to set her free."

He sounded so bewildered, as if he'd been abandoned by something he'd always been able to count on. When the woman didn't answer him, I added hotly, "We wanted to see her fly. Just like you do."

If I hadn't known better, I might have thought the hawk lady turned away so quickly to hide the tears in her eyes. But I could no more imagine this unpleasant woman crying than I could believe her capable of that light-filled laughter with my father. Still, after she found what she was looking for on the shelf, she seemed more subdued, and when she spoke to Rail, her voice was considerably softer. "You couldn't have fixed her infection without antibiotics, and it's tricky setting a broken wing," she told him, almost kindly. "And it's particularly difficult to do it alone. Come here. You can help."

I had to admire Rail. I'd just about written the hawk lady off. But he seemed willing to shake away his misery, and leaned close over the hawk with his head almost touching the woman's. His hands moved surely, he seemed to know exactly what to do and to anticipate what the hawk lady needed. He parted the thick down on the hawk so she could give an injection, and he held the wing out gently while she examined the break.

All at once, without any discussion, the hawk lady and Rail were working as a team. I stood off to the side — just where a reporter was supposed to be. But somehow, that wasn't what I wanted. In the circle of light over the bench, I watched the woman's face as she worked. Concentration erased all the tension and hostility from her expression, and once she even gave Rail a warm smile when he handed her a pair of scissors before she asked for them. Suddenly she was incredibly beautiful again. She was quieter now, but I felt the same sense of promise as before, elusive as a golden leaf swirling up on a gust of wind.

"You really are excellent," she said matter-of-factly to Rail as he clipped the down away around the gash. "You have better hands than my interns. I take it you're planning on becoming a doctor, or a veterinarian?"

Rail gave her a half-uncertain, half-amazed smile and shrugged shyly. "Naw," he said. "I'm gonna join the Air Force. I want to be a fighter pilot."

Rhiannon Jeffries raised her eyebrows again and glanced at me, but she didn't say anything. I couldn't exercise such restraint. "A *fighter* pilot?" I said. "Rail. You have to fly *military* planes. They're full of guns. You have to *kill* in the military."

He gave me an impenetrable look and shrugged again. "I only want to fly the planes," he said. "I'm not killing anyone."

"But you won't have a choice," I persisted, exasperated. "Not if there's a war. I can't believe you want to join the military, after what happened to your dad —"

I was sorry immediately. Rail looked at me as though I'd stuck my foot out and tripped him. The hawk lady acted as if she hadn't heard anything and continued to sew the gash on the baby hawk's neck. Without a word, she handed the needle to Rail so she could cut the thread and they leaned together again over the hawk. The silence between me and the two of them opened like a chasm.

All of a sudden, I wanted to go home. It always happened this way: sooner or later, I'd say something the other person didn't want to hear. That was why I wasn't any good at keeping friends. Though it wasn't as if Rail was a friend, anyway. We'd spent hours together, but it was only an accident that we'd had anything to do with each other in the first place. I looked at the baby hawk lying motionless on the towel and wished desperately that she would shriek again in defiance. I refused to apologize to Rail. He wouldn't have noticed, anyway. Neither of them would notice. The hawk lady was showing him how to set the broken wing.

"Is there a phone I can use?" I asked loudly.

"In the house," said the woman without looking up. "Just inside the front door."

I called my father. "Give me a few minutes, okay, Missy?" he said, and I knew from his distracted tone it could be as long as an hour. But I had no energy to ride my bike home. I wandered across the yard. The hawk lady's students weren't in sight, although the van was still there. I walked down a path through the pines toward a cage as large as a house. Wood chips carpeted the ground inside, and about twenty feet above me, in one corner of the cage, was a wooden platform. The shade was deep and at first I didn't see anything. Then, up on the platform, there was a swift movement and the flash of a bright, fierce eye. I pressed my face against the wire mesh.

Two enormous brown birds stood close together staring down at me. The dappled light on their feathers glowed. Long, feather-covered legs ended in yellow talons that gripped the edge of the platform as the birds craned their graceful necks to get a better look. I'd never seen anything so fierce and wild-looking in my life. But as I watched, the smaller bird ran its great curved beak in an exquisitely gentle caress down the neck of the other.

I watched, mesmerized. I didn't hear Rhiannon Jeffries come up until she spoke. "Can you see why eagles have been held sacred by human beings since the beginning of time?" she said, her voice behind me so soft I didn't recognize it. "I wonder if we recognize in them our own soul's demand for freedom."

The smaller of the golden-brown birds swooped gracefully from the platform across the length of the enclosure, landing on a low perch not far from where we stood. It cocked its narrow head and surveyed us with a low chirping sound. I had to smile, even through my unexpected sorrow. As large as the enclosure was, it had hardly contained three full wing-beats of the eagle.

I looked at the hawk lady. She nodded. "I feel the same way," she said, reading my thoughts. "I wish they could fly free. But they'll both be here all their lives."

"Why?" I cried.

"They've been damaged too badly. They'd never survive in the wild now," she replied. "See the female? The larger one? She was found tangled in a power line in Wisconsin — she's missing an eye. And the male here — he was shot by a rancher somewhere in South Dakota. I couldn't fully repair his wing."

The smaller eagle strutted back and forth along the perch near us, his eye fixed on the woman. He chirruped again. The hawk lady chirruped back. "He's been with me for years," she smiled. "I brought him here with me . . . He knows who brings the meat."

"Is he tame?"

The woman shook her head. "They're never tame. They're wild creatures. But they adapt, like any living thing. They learn how to live with their circumstances . . ."

She sounded so distracted I thought I'd said something that bothered her, and I asked quickly, "Will my hawk . . . will the red-tailed hawk have to stay in a cage all her life?"

Rail was coming toward us down the path. The hawk lady watched him. Then, as if vaguely remembering that I'd asked her something, she frowned slightly and said, "We'll see. She's too old to imprint on people, so you haven't done her any harm that way. But I don't know how her wing will heal, or if she'll learn to hunt."

"How long will it take —" But her attention was all on Rail. He gave her a lopsided smile when he came up and she smiled back. "She all cleaned up, then? She settled in the cage all right?" the hawk lady asked. Rail nodded.

They walked back up the path side by side. I trailed behind. "Your father is Tim, isn't he?" the woman asked Rail. "If he isn't available, I'd like to offer you a summer job here. I need the fields mowed and the grounds looked after, and some repairs made to the sheds and cages . . . and you could learn something about working with the birds."

Rail's head lifted, and even his shoulders seemed to smile. "I'd sure like that," he said quietly. "Man. I sure would."

"Good," said the woman briskly. "You can start now by preparing some food for the little hawk — the eyas. She might be too stressed to eat yet, but you should try."

Rail followed her toward the shed again. Neither of them asked me to come. I looked desperately down the road for my father. No Chevy, but there was another car pulled up beside the van with two men standing by it. Slowly I scuffed to the shed, hesitated, and went in.

The hawk lady was handing Rail a large plastic

bag from the fridge. "Just make sure to chop them up fine," she instructed. "Then feed her with the glove-puppet — just don't let her see you. She might be too old to imprint, but it's still important that she doesn't associate food with humans. But here . . . you know what you're doing."

One of the students stuck his head in the door and asked for her, and the hawk lady left, brushing past me in the doorway. The woman who had spoken to me by the eagle cage — like the woman in Bitsi's store — had disappeared again. She seemed able to pull one or another of her different selves from a hat, the way a magician pulls out a white rabbit or a rainbow of scarves or a lump of coal, and you never knew which it would be. I wondered if any of them was real.

Rail was inspecting a glove shaped like a hawk's head. He stuck his hand in it and wiggled two fingers so the beak opened and closed, then laid it on the workbench and reached into the plastic bag. "You want to chop?" he asked with a straight face, laying the frozen carcasses of several white mice on a cutting board and handing me a huge chef's knife. I wouldn't, for a million dollars, let him know how close I was to being sick as I began to cut up the tiny, stiff corpses. The label on the bag read "Pro-Team Laboratory Products." Great, I thought. These were lab mice, tortured to death in science experiments. I chopped harder and told myself it was for the baby hawk.

I knew Rail was watching me, but I couldn't look up and meet his eyes. The more guilty I felt for what I'd said about his father, the angrier I got at him. First Rail had taken the hawk from me, then the hawk lady. I knew it was unreasonable to feel this way. But I couldn't help thinking that if I had called Rhiannon Jeffries for help as I'd originally intended, instead of blundering into Rail, I could have met her differently. By myself. She might have asked *me* to help with the hawk, then. I would have done just as good a job. . . .

"Watch out," said Rail. "You aren't supposed to chop off your fingers, too."

"I'm not," I snapped. He smiled a little sheepishly and I put down the knife. "I shouldn't have said that, about your dad," I mumbled.

"Aw —" Rail shrugged and pulled on the hawk-headed glove. I followed after him down the row of cages. Through the door in one, a tiny pair of eyes blinked. I peered in at an owl no bigger than my fist. Rail paused before a cage at the end of the row.

"I want to fly planes because . . . because . . . there's just the sky and . . . nothing. Nothing holding you back," he said with sudden passion. He opened the cage without speaking further. The baby hawk was sitting on a platform, head up, watching us. Rail shut the door quickly and opened a much smaller door on the side. He picked up some of the minced mouse meat with the glove and pushed his arm through. "Anyway," he continued, more calmly, "the Air Force gives full scholarships to college. That's why I gotta get good grades. I can't go otherwise. I know you don't care about grades, Taylor, but you're naturally smart. I'm not."

"What are you talking about!" I cried.

He was intent on feeding the hawk. When he withdrew his arm, the meat was gone. He gave me a triumphant glance. "See? She ate it. Man. She's already feeling better." He closed the feeding door and began cleaning up the workbench. He'd certainly made himself at home here already, I thought sourly as he hung up the glove. He'd see them every day — the hawk lady and my red-tailed hawk. Rail knew all about wild animals, and he knew how to drive a tractor to mow the fields and how to fix things. I didn't. It wouldn't have mattered if I'd met the hawk lady alone or not. I didn't have anything she needed.

"She's really cool, isn't she?" said Rail unexpectedly, eyes shining.

"The hawk?"

"No — her. She's really . . . different. She's not mean. Not really," Rail said. "Man, Taylor. Can you believe she gave me a job? My dad isn't doing that good . . . he can't work much now. An' Cattie's been needing new glasses, an' Dawn's gotta have decent clothes for that summer camp . . . man. This is great."

"Yeah," I answered. No, the hawk lady wasn't mean. Not really. But *I* sure was.

8

WHEN RAIL AND I WALKED across the yard, Rhiannon Jeffries was standing next to the enclosure nearest the house, talking with the men I'd seen by the car. *Talking* may not be the most accurate word, since the larger of the two men was practically yelling.

"You're the one who don't seem to understand, Miz Jeffries," he blustered. "The guy who wrote that letter to the editor ain't the only one riled up — plenty of folks in Hunter's Gap got perfectly legitimate complaints about how you're runnin' this here place . . ."

"Are you referring to the hunters who are trespassing illegally on private property, Mr. Fenstemacher?" asked Rhiannon coolly. "Since you are the policeman in this town, I would have thought —"

The other man interrupted, tapping a folded newspaper in his thin hand nervously. "Well, actually, it's not exactly *private* . . . it *is* state university property, and this program is partially funded by the state . . ."

The hawk lady shot him a look of disdain. "Excuse me, Dr. Williams. Do you want a wildlife rehabilitation program, or a free-for-all with guns? Do you consider that letter a 'legitimate complaint' too? Because if you do, then we seriously misunderstand each other. When you invited me here last year, I was under the impression you wanted me to develop this Center for your department and for Alton University, as a research facility for graduate students. Those students — not to mention the birds — are in danger when they're in the field during the hunting seasons. This may be acceptable to you, but it isn't to me."

The hawk lady appeared perfectly composed. The diminutive man in the tie was getting more and more nervous, glancing at us with a frown, rolling the newspaper into a tighter tube while he gathered enough courage to speak. But Junior Fenstemacher beat him to it. "Speaking of students, Miz Jeffries," he said with exaggerated politeness, "that's a whole 'nother issue, ain't it? Folks in Hunter's Gap don't appreciate a lot of wild college kids running around getting into fights an' drinking . . ."

"I believe that situation was handled last spring

when . . ." began Dr. Williams, but Rhiannon Jeffries smoothly intercepted his words. ". . . When the local men who instigated the trouble at Stovic's Cafe were arrested for drunk and disorderly conduct, isn't that correct? And I hardly think one isolated incident involving two of my interns should be the basis for judging this program's legitimacy."

I'd met Junior Fenstemacher. Besides being the entire police force of Hunter's Gap, he was self-appointed mayor, volunteer fireman, and anything else he could think of to keep his finger in everyone's business. He hired out his flat-bed truck, and had twice helped my father haul blocks of marble from the Vermont quarries down to his studio. Junior also hunted everything that moved. Stuffed into his orange hunting clothes, he looked like a day-glo doughboy. He was crudely jovial with my father, whom he'd gone to school with, snickering at his own idiotic jokes as if he was eleven years old. Last month he'd told my father that now the Jews and blacks were totally running the university in Alton, everyone in Hunter's Gap was going to have to start locking their doors for the first time in history. My father wondered aloud what on earth people of the Jewish faith and African-Americans could possibly *want* from the houses in Hunter's Gap, but Junior had just widened his pink-rimmed eyes and said, "You'll see — you'll see, Bobby-boy," as though he was the prophet of doom, wagging his finger at my father vigorously, the way he was doing now to the hawk lady.

"Miz Jeffries," he said. "That ain't the only basis. This here is not a wealthy community. Most of the local folks depend on hunting somehow . . . fer food, and the revenue that out-of-state hunters bring in here. This here Center . . ." He waved his hand around. "This here place runs right along the state gamelands. When this was Duane MacGaw's farm, he let hunters park right here in the yard. You don't even allow them to walk across your land . . ."

"*University* land," muttered poor Dr. Williams, who looked as if he felt like a Ping-Pong ball batted between the other two.

"Not when I have breeding birds and injured birds, no," said Rhiannon Jeffries shortly. She gave the smaller man a long, level look. "Dr. Williams, as head of the Wildlife Biology Department, I would have thought you understood the importance of a protected environment for a program designed to rehabilitate endangered animals. I have resented the need to police this land simply so that I can carry out what I was hired to do."

I listened to her in amazement. She never fumbled with her words, never lost her cool manner, and spoke in a vocabulary I know for a fact went right over Junior Fenstemacher's bucket-shaped head.

Not that he'd ever let on, any more than Bitsi did. That's the thing about ignorance — you don't even *know* what you don't know.

Junior Fenstemacher took out a cigarette to hide his confusion, lit it, and deliberately blew smoke into the wire enclosure beside him. That's when I noticed the bald eagle. It was standing high up on a platform, watching the movement of Junior's hand with wide, dark eyes. Every time Junior flicked ash, the eagle followed the motion with intense interest.

"I would appreciate it if you didn't smoke," said the hawk lady quietly. Then, obviously expecting her words to be obeyed without question, she continued, "This is an experimental program, Mr. Fenstemacher. The state is cooperating with the university because of a concern over the decline in raptor populations as a result of pesticides, road kill, and so forth. Surely, as a hunter, you understand the relationship between predators like hawks and prey species that you hunt as small game. Both are essential for maintaining a healthy ecological balance. If you ignore this, you'll notice a decline within a few years in many of the species you enjoy killing yourself."

No doubt about it. She was very, very cool. Junior was so befuddled all he could do was puff away on his cigarette. Without warning, quick as the movement of the eagle's head, the hawk lady plucked the cigarette from between Junior's lips, dropped it, and ground it under her heel. Beside me, Rail sucked in his breath. "Man," he whispered, catching my eye. Yeah, I thought. She was as calm and articulate as a reporter standing before a front-line camera.

Junior was livid. Little Dr. Williams unfolded the newspaper with a great deal of shaking of pages and smoothing of creases, and finally he stammered, "Now, Dr. Jeffries, really. Of course we understand what you are trying to do here. When we hired you . . . well, your credentials were simply the best in the country. Your research, your work with raptors internationally, your publications . . ."

Rhiannon stopped him with an impatient gesture, and he blinked very much like the tiny owl I'd seen in the cage in the shed. "Yes, well," he continued bravely. "What I mean is, of course it wasn't to be anticipated when we asked you here that there would be a need to improve our public relations with the local community. But the fact is . . ." He shook the paper apologetically. "The fact is, there *is* a need. The university simply can't afford this kind of bad publicity. This is the third letter to the editor about the Center. You know our program depends on support from the state. It's an election year, Dr. Jeffries. Senator Vinci has always supported environmental issues and allocated generous funding for programs like this, but if he thinks there's too much negative public opinion... not enough community support... well, you see what I mean."

Junior managed to sputter, "You bet there ain't enough community support! Folks here don't appreciate their tax dollars goin' to raise up killer birds ... an' they ain't gonna be shy about letting Senator Vinci know."

The hawk lady turned away in disgust. Dr. Williams reached out a beseeching hand. But with that movement, the bald eagle launched off his platform, swooped to a perch near us, fanned his tail, and shot from under it a thick white stream that spattered a few inches from Junior's foot. Then, with a contented squawk, the eagle proceeded to groom himself with meticulous care.

I never admired anything in the world so much as I admired Dr. Rhiannon Jeffries at that moment. She didn't so much as crack a smile. She even refrained from looking at the eagle. The bird had said it all. There he was, regal symbol of the United States of America, watching Junior Fenstemacher wipe off his shoes. The hawk lady waited just long enough for the significance to sink in, then said with the same perfect composure, "I'm sure you'll excuse me now, gentlemen. I really am very busy."

Dr. Williams seemed to have made a decision. He took such a deep breath his chest puffed out through his jacket. "Dr. Jeffries," he announced, "we are going to develop a public relations program over the summer for the Center."

"*We*, Dr. Williams?"

"You," he said, as firmly as he could, but under her gaze he appeared to wilt a little. "Delegate it to your interns, if you want," he said, relenting. "But I'd like to see a preliminary plan of action by the end of next week . . . outlining the way you intend to educate this community about the program here at the Center. We need to find a way to break down prejudices about predatory birds. This is a rural community, as you know. There are a lot of old beliefs. You need to address this, Dr. Jeffries. If Senator Vinci gets cold feet, we'll have no choice but to close the Center down."

They stared at each other for almost a full minute. *I'll give the little man credit. He did not back down from the gaze of the hawk lady.* Finally, the woman said with scorn, "I won't waste my interns' time on this. They have enough to do with classes, research, jobs, and their own lives. This is a research facility, Dr. Williams. But if you want to turn it into Disneyland, so be it. You are the boss. I'll need money for an assistant —"

"You'll get whatever you need," said Dr. Williams, clearly relieved. "A separate budget for PR, a trained assistant . . ."

"Just make sure you find me someone who can

write a half-decent English sentence," snapped Rhiannon. "I want this whole damned circus documented, and I want a responsible front-page write-up in that rag you call a newspaper."

"Of course. Of course," Dr. Williams agreed hastily. "We'll find someone who can help with whatever you set up, who can write press releases and . . ."

"I'll do it," I said. I don't think I even knew it was my own voice speaking. "I will. I can be your assistant."

My words scattered out into the silence like beads from a broken necklace. I had no idea which way they'd roll. But Dr. Rhiannon Jeffries met my eyes.

"Good," she said softly.

Dr. Williams gave her a puzzled frown. "Well, really . . . that *is* very nice, but — didn't you have someone in mind who could . . . well, perhaps a graduate student who . . . how old *are* you?" he asked suddenly, turning to me.

"I'll be sixteen in August," I said. It didn't matter what he said. I could still hear the hawk lady's soft "good" in my ears.

"Dr. Jeffries . . ." began Dr. Williams helplessly.

Rail interrupted him. "Taylor's great. She's the best writer in the school," he said, looking at Dr. Williams as if daring him to contradict. "And she really *cares* about stuff. The world, and everything . . ."

My mouth hung open in astonishment and embarrassment. The hawk lady smiled. "That's what I want," she told the two men. "Someone who cares about the world and everything. And —" She looked straight at me now. "Someone who is willing to speak up for what she cares about." She gave me another brief smile. "I have no doubt you'll do a good job. Even if you don't know how difficult a job it will be —"

"Oh, I know," I said boldly. "I've been in Hunter's Gap a whole year. The ignorance here is bone-deep." My mother had said that once, and I liked the way it sounded. Junior Fenstemacher didn't, though. He stalked off with a final glare of warning at the hawk lady. What I remembered too late, though, was that Rail had heard me too. Rail Bogart, born and bred in Hunter's Gap. He wouldn't meet my eyes. His face was flushed a deep red. I'd done it again —

Dr. Williams and the hawk lady conferred together for several more minutes. Rail walked away, his hands shoved in the pockets of his camouflage pants. I didn't know what to do. I couldn't call my father again, because Dr. Williams and Rhiannon were standing on the porch of the house and I didn't want to go past them. So I stayed where I was, looking up at the bald eagle who had written *his* eloquent letter to the editor on Junior Fenstemacher's shoe.

I must have been a million miles away, because I

didn't see Dr. Williams leave, and I didn't hear the hawk lady come up to me. "So," she said, "your friend told me you want to be a reporter."

My friend. Right. Not if he stayed around me long enough. "Yeah," I said. "Thanks, Dr. Jeffries, for —"

"Rhiannon," she directed me briskly. "If we're a team, we're going to stand on equal ground. All right, Taylor?"

I couldn't help grinning. "Yeah," I said again.

"And as far as ignorance goes —" she continued, disregarding my uncomfortable glance around for Rail, "as far as that goes, you're right. It *is* in the bones. But to be an impartial reporter, you have to understand that ignorance is in *all* of us. It's nothing more than fear . . . fear of what we don't know, fear that we might have to change. You've got it in your bones. I have it in mine."

"Not like Junior Fenstemacher!" I cried, stung.

"Oh yes," the hawk lady replied. "Just like him."

She looked suddenly tired, and I was afraid to say anything more. And at that moment, my father finally drove up. He jumped down from the Chevy with his widest smile, and it wasn't just directed at me. "Good to see you again, Rhiannon!" he called, striding across the yard. "You're in your proper element, I see. I take it you won't shoot me for trespassing?"

He belted all this out as he came toward us, and I thought I'd shrivel with embarrassment at his last words. But Rhiannon seemed amused. I might have heard wrong, but I thought she even *giggled*. Very quietly. My father threw his arm around me in his usual bear hug. "Well, there, Missy. I was beginning to think you'd moved out. Go throw your bike into the truck —"

No explanation of why it had taken him almost an hour to come less than five miles down the road. But I knew that to my father, an hour was hardly more than a few lines on a sheet of paper or a few chips chiseled from stone. I wrestled my bike over the tailgate. One thing, at least, was clear: I had my research project. I had a subject to write about for Porter Phelps.

What wasn't clear were my feelings about everything else. I felt as if a lifetime had passed since that morning. I looked around for Rail but I couldn't see him, although his bike was still propped against the shed. After hesitating a few seconds, I went to find my father. He was standing with Rhiannon, both of them looking up at the pair of golden eagles.

My father has the sharpest eyes in the world. Not only can he spot something from miles away, but he also has a way of looking *inside* something like an x-ray. He told me that Michelangelo could see living shapes inside a solid block of marble. My father could, too. And not just in marble, either — he could look into people, as well. As if he could see the shape of their deepest dreams. It's how he gets so close to people — he chisels right past the outside, straight into their hearts. He doesn't ask questions that make people uncomfortable or say things they don't want to hear, the way I do. But the biggest difference between my father and me was that he didn't really seem to mind whether he had friends or not, and I did.

"Perfect," my father was saying, his voice no more than a breath. "Perfect." I couldn't tell which he meant, the eagles or Rhiannon. Perhaps he couldn't, either. He bent his head toward hers, touched his hand lightly on her arm, and remarked on something in a low voice. Rhiannon laughed, throwing her head back, and only then did I notice that she'd taken the rubber band from her long hair so it swung loose down her back.

Suddenly Rail appeared beside me, and I was uncomfortably aware that he was watching them, too. There was a space around my father that seemed to draw everything into it. But he didn't overshadow Rhiannon the way he did my mother. Rhiannon was as large as he was, and there was a sort of crackling energy between them, as if the world had to expand to hold them both.

"What do you think, Missy?" my father burst out, turning to me. "Look at those eagles! They're perfect, aren't they! The image I've been looking for." He caressed the eagles with his eyes. "Innocent killers. *Innocent killers* — that's it. The theme for the memorial!"

We all walked back along the path, my father's arm around me. I couldn't help being proud of him, even when he said outrageous things. Somehow he got away with it. Maybe it was because he could pull laughter from everyone the way he pulled beautiful shapes from rough stone.

"You coming with us, Rail?" asked my father at the truck. "I'll drop you off."

"Naw," said Rail. "I'll stay for a while." He gave me a look, as though he was waiting for something. I got more and more restless, standing silently with him by the truck, while my father discussed with Rhiannon when he'd be back to sketch the eagles. More than restless — unsettled. I had no idea what to say. I felt as if we'd been thrown together on a strange and unexpected journey. So did that make us friends? Even if I said stupid things? How did people decide they were friends?

I jerked at the door handle and mercifully, it opened so I could climb into the truck. I'd never in a million years intended to be friends with Rail Bogart. Besides, I'd said enough mean things to him today to make him want to keep a mile away from me. What did it matter, anyway? In less than three months, I'd be leaving Hunter's Gap . . . I hoped, forever.

"Taylor?" said Rail.

"What?"

"You're coming tomorrow, right?"

I watched Rhiannon. She was saying something to my father, her eyebrows raised in playful sarcasm. He was chuckling. She had long ago forgotten about me. "I don't know," I muttered.

Rail stuck his hands into his pocket stubbornly. "Don't you want to see your hawk?" he persisted. My father climbed in beside me and the Chevy's engine roared.

"Taylor?" Rail said. "Come tomorrow, okay? I want to see you."

Maybe that was how people decided.

"Yeah, okay," I answered.

9

THE HAWK LADY WAS MINE. The conviction filled me the moment I woke to hear my mother's voice downstairs in the kitchen. I knew I couldn't have her taking over the work I was going to do with Rhiannon Jeffries. My mother would phone the hawk lady with a hundred questions and suggestions. Arrange appointments for me with the newspaper. Check my notes, help with my research, read everything I wrote, edit it . . .

And my father — I didn't even want him part of it. He would sweep the hawk lady into his own space, and I would never be able to touch her. Right then, I created a secret world in my heart — a high, windy hill where I stood side by side with the hawk lady, our long hair blowing until it mingled together, while above us, circling with a wild cry, flew a red-tailed hawk.

"Melissa! Missy!" my mother called up the stairs, and I scrambled into my clothes and ran down. My father caught me in a hug, half-lifting me from the floor. As always, I was self-conscious hugging him in front of my mother. Her embraces were so uncomfortably awkward I always wanted to pull away. With guilt, I realized she'd driven home late the night before and I hadn't even remembered she was coming. I hadn't stayed awake.

She pushed a box at me across the table, her eyes shining. She was so small and brown; her rapid movements reminded me of a sparrow darting at seeds. She said, "I thought it was time you had some real professional-looking clothing."

I slowly took from the box a taupe-colored linen jacket and a pair of off-white pants. There was a silk blouse, too, of charcoal gray. My mother watched me with restless anticipation. "You can wear it this week," she stated. "We'll go down to the city tomorrow. I was able to set up an interview on Wednesday with Mr. Hawkins at Porter Phelps. I thought —"

"Tomorrow?" I said, stricken. "I have to do another interview? Why?" I looked at my father, crumpling the linen jacket in my hands, but he was carefully mashing bits of toast on his plate into crumbs.

My mother shook the pants out impatiently. "Mr. Hawkins and I both agreed that it would be a good idea — get you focused again," she said. "In view of the difficulty you had last year —"

"It was the stupid *school!*" I cried.

"He wants to discuss the writing project you're doing this summer," my mother continued smoothly. "You can show him your outline and whatever else you've done so far." She stopped when she saw my expression. "You have begun working on it, haven't you?" she asked.

"Ummm —" I frantically stuck my arms into the jacket, but it got twisted around my neck. I thrashed my arms to untangle it.

"You're going to rip it," my mother snapped, straightening the collar. "Melissa, I don't understand. You *want* to go to Porter Phelps. I'm not forcing you to."

I stared at her, wordless. I turned to my father, but my mother leaned between us and angrily snatched his plate away. "For God's sake, Bob, I'll make you more toast if you want," she said. "You don't have to lick the crumbs off your fingers."

He caught my eye with a guilty grimace. "Don't you think another interview is something of an overkill?" he said softly to my mother. She sat abruptly and began folding the new clothes with jerky little movements.

"I'll try them on, Mom," I said, helpless. "Don't put them away . . . I like them —" It was a lie and she knew it, but she laid the clothes down again.

I took a deep breath. I closed the door carefully on the secret world I'd made in my heart. "I do want to go to the city, Mom," I said. "I haven't been there since Christmas. And . . . and I do have something I'm . . . ummm . . . I have an idea for my essay." I prayed she wouldn't ask for details. Between today and Wednesday I could come up with something to make her happy. Anything. It wouldn't matter what, as long as I was left alone. The story I wrote about the hawk lady and the Center was going to make a difference in the world. But it had to be *mine*. No interference. Just me, and Rhiannon Jeffries, and the red-tailed hawk. And —

The phone rang.

"It's Rail," said my father. I grabbed it and went out as far as the cord would reach. "What?" I said.

"Hey, Taylor," said Rail. "What's wrong? You pissed off about something?"

I swallowed. "Yeah. Sort of. My mom wants me to go down to Philadelphia for a few days. I have to interview at this school . . . Porter Phelps? Where I'm going next year? You know." I bumbled along, feeling him get quieter and quieter. He didn't know, of course. He hardly knew anything about me. I hadn't ever said more than a few words to Rail Bogart before the day we'd rescued the hawk.

"Next year?" he said.

"Yeah —"

"Oh." In the pause that followed, I waited for him to say any of a dozen different things, but finally he just grunted, "Well, I was only calling to see if you were coming over today. To the Center. Dr. Jeffries wants . . . I mean, Rhiannon. She wants —"

"I can't," I interrupted. "I won't be back 'til the weekend."

I hung the phone up carefully. Carefully, I sat at the table and ate my cereal. My father looked at me, perplexed. "This is a really good idea, Mom," I said, ignoring him. "Mom. Do you think I should show Mr. Hawkins that essay I wrote — the one on homelessness? Because I really think it should have gotten a better grade."

"And how about the one from last fall — your rainforest piece?" suggested my mother happily. "I thought it was exceptionally well written."

"Sure," I said. Carefully.

My father put his spoon down. He stared at my mother a moment, then said to me, "You have a choice here, Missy. You can change your mind if you want. If you'd rather hang out over at the —"

"I don't think there's a choice," said my mother. My father pushed his chair back suddenly and stood up.

"There's always a choice," he said.

Sometimes I become the Melissa T. Armstrong-Brown my mother thinks I am. It isn't hard to do. It's like walking out of a house and shutting all the doors behind me. After they're all closed and I'm standing outside — then I'm that other *me*. It's really the only way to be a reporter. Reporters have to stand apart.

They have to watch and listen and write what they observe . . . not what they *want*, or *wish*, or *feel*.

"Dad," I said calmly, "if I want to get into a good university, I *don't* have a choice. I need to take Honors classes, and that Advanced Writing program is an Honors class. I screwed up at Hunter's Gap this year. So I have to do the extra work."

I was my mother's *me* all the way to Philadelphia, and during the interview with Mr. Hawkins, and the next morning when we went shopping. My mother bought me more brownish, grayish, tweedy clothes, and I tried everything on and it all fit. I looked at myself in the dressing room mirror, with my mother smiling behind me; I held an imaginary microphone and announced to my reflection: "This is M. Taylor Armstrong-Brown, reporting live from Philadelphia . . ." My mother was very happy.

But that afternoon while my mother met one of her clients and I waited in the apartment for my father to come down from Hunter's Gap to pick me up, the door to the secret world began to blow open. I tried to ignore it. I lay on my mother's bed and watched CNN, but nothing I did could keep those images from spilling through the door. Finally I switched off the television and gazed at the ceiling.

There was the red-tailed hawk clinging to the broken tree and screeching defiance at me. There were her depthless black eyes and the glint of light on her beak. And there was Rail, covered in scratches and dirt, straddling the tree trunk next to me while we laughed ourselves silly. The same laughter came up through me now until I lay smiling broadly at the ceiling. Way off below me on the street, muffled through the walls of the apartment building, I heard all the familiar city sounds. But I wasn't there. I was on that windswept hill, the hawk circling, and the hawk lady was looking at me until the only world I wanted to exist in lay in her eyes. And I knew, all at once, that she was not just my secret. *I was her secret, too.* I sat up quickly and blinked.

My mother had phone books for everywhere. All the big cities, even ones in Europe. And Alton, skinny and never used. I found the number and dialed without really believing I'd hear her voice. But I let the ringing go on and on until, with a clatter and a muttered curse, there she was. "Raptor Center," said Rhiannon, out of breath.

"It's me, Taylor."

I could feel her smile right through the phone. "Well," she said. "I thought I'd lost my assistant already."

"No —"

"Taylor," said Rhiannon. "What's going on? Have you been kidnapped?"

The catch in my throat wouldn't go away. "Yeah.

Sort of," I said. "I just . . . I wanted to see if I could come tomorrow. I mean, if you want me to."

"Of course I want you to," Rhiannon said dryly. "There was another letter in *The Register* today. Williams is having heart palpitations. I haven't got a minute to deal with any of it. I've got three birds overdue for release, and two sick chicks, and the eagle is . . . anyway, it's all up to you."

I hesitated. "It is?"

She snorted. "Taylor, just get here and do your job. Whatever it is. We'll figure something out." I felt the smile again, like something warm brushing my face. "But hurry. The natives are getting restless."

I hung up. The door was wide open now, the wind streaming in over the hill. I jumped up and poked through the fridge, but my mother hardly ever had any food around. There was nothing but a few bottles of Perrier water. I started to dial out for pizza, then for Chinese food, then for Mexican — until I plunked the phone down and went to the window. I prowled in anxious happiness around the small apartment, switched on the television, turned it off, went again to the window, and let the air conditioner blow on my hot skin.

The door rattled. "Let down the moat!" my father boomed, and I flicked open the locks to let him in.

"When are we going back to Hunter's Gap?" I asked the moment he walked through the door. Only then did I know what I wanted.

He gave a puzzled little shake of his head. "You want to go back? You *are* an enigma to me, Missy," he said. He smiled. He'd brushed his hair back neatly in a smooth ponytail and dressed in new jeans. "Nice shirt," I commented, fingering his sleeve. I felt calmer. "Where'd you get this? You went to the Salvation Army without me!" I accused him.

"Well, I didn't think you needed to go now," my father said, studying the contents of the fridge with the same frustration as I had. "Now that you'll be wearing all those fancy grown-up clothes . . ."

"Dad —"

He winked at me, held me at arm's length, and surveyed me critically. "You do look distinguished in these clothes," he said softly. "They're definitely a step up from the good old Salvation Army. But —"

"I know. They're not *me*," I ended for him.

There wasn't time for him to answer because my mother came in the door and insisted we go out to a "civilized" restaurant for dinner before my father drove me back to Hunter's Gap. The menu didn't even list prices. "Mom," I said. "This place serves snails."

"Well, what did you expect?" She laughed. "It's French."

Now didn't seem the time to remind her that I was boycotting anything French because of the nuclear testing in the south Pacific. I even refrained from asking the French waiter anything about it. I'd practice my man-on-the-street interviewing techniques another time. When the food arrived, my father and I rolled our eyes at the same time.

"Don't you say anything," warned my mother. "It's fine European dining." She put the cloth napkin to her mouth and mumbled, "I can practice for next month."

"What's next month?" I asked, searching for something resembling food on my plate.

"Europe," my mother said, without looking at either of us. "The international conference for psychoanalysts. I told you about it. In Germany."

My father put his fork down. "So you decided to go."

"I can't turn it down, Bobby," my mother said. "I thought you'd understand. It's more than just an honor to be invited to give a paper. It's *expected*. If you want to get anywhere."

"I thought you *were* somewhere," my father muttered.

None of us said anything for a while. I pushed the half-cooked vegetables around in the sauce. My father ate methodically. I tried to catch his eye. But he only looked at my mother. "It's for almost the whole month, Anna," he said finally.

"I know —"

I was sure they would make me disappear again. But my mother gave a little shake of her head, took a breath, reached into her briefcase and handed me a package. "It's not more clothes," she assured me. "It's something your father and I thought you should have. Every reporter needs one. You can use it this summer."

I unwrapped the paper and took out a beautiful notebook with covers of creamy supple leather. It was the perfect size for carrying in my pack. I ran my fingers over the leather. "Look on the front," said my mother. I turned it over. My father had tooled the image of a hawk in the corner.

I'd never figured out how my father knows things. I hugged the notebook against my chest. But even through my happiness at being, for that moment, *right there* with my mother and father, the hawk reminded me of my private world and of secrets that were not all my own.

My father and I drove back north from the city all night. I slept on and off, and once we stopped along the highway at a diner. No one was there but the cook and the waitress, having a smoke outside in the balmy night. The cook went in to make us sandwiches and I stayed sleepily in the Chevy.

The waitress wore a short skirt and had frizzed-up hair, but she wasn't as young as she was trying to appear. "That your daughter?" she asked, flashing her eyes at my father. "She's almost grown. Wouldn't have guessed you had a kid that old."

"Ah — she's much older than I am," my father

grinned right back. "She was born old. An old soul." He stayed several minutes, bantering with the woman in his easy, low voice as they leaned side by side against the Chevy. The waitress looked sad when he finally got in, and she leaned her sharp elbows on the open window. "Don't work too hard!" my father teased her as he started the engine, and she waved as we drove off.

We ate our food in silence, but after a few minutes I said, "Dad. I really do want to go to Porter Phelps, you know. It's important to me to get the best grades. I know it isn't to you, but . . . don't you understand?"

He reached his arm over and drew me close on the seat, but he didn't answer right away. The darkness seemed to wait with me. "I believe you feel some strange, driven need to prove you're the best," he said slowly at last. "I guess I understand that, even if I don't feel it myself. But I just don't know if . . . if it's really who you are. In *here*." He tapped his chest. After a moment, he laid his head against mine without taking his eyes from the road. "I just don't want you to lose yourself, trying to be the best. Always pushing for it. You can lose all the joy. Like your —"

"Like Mom."

His arm tightened, and for a long time we drove without speaking through the summer night. Sometime around two in the morning, we pulled up by the dark house in Hunter's Gap. I got out and stretched, breathing deeply of the warm, cricket-filled air. My father chuckled and gave the large rounded fenders of the Chevy an affectionate pat. "Well, she came through again. Got us home safe."

The moonlight spilled over the old truck. "She looks like one of those women — you know, Dad. That sculptor you like so much. What's his name? Henry Moore. Those big women he carves," I said, following his pat with my own.

"See, Missy?" said my father, reaching in the back for my bags. "That's what I mean. Your mother wouldn't see the truck that way. She just worries that it's not safe. It's hard to see the beauty in front of you, if you're trying to control the future all the time." He paused and sighed. "But it's part of how hard she tries. I never knew anyone who tried as hard as your mother. It's one of the reasons I fell so much in love with her." He was almost talking to himself, but he smiled at me. "The future will come soon enough, Missy," he said. "Don't focus on it so much you miss seeing what's right here with you now."

I couldn't fall asleep. I held the leather-bound notebook against my cheek on the pillow. The leather was as soft and warm as skin. In the darkness, I ran my hand over the design tooled into the front cover. Red-tailed hawk, wings outstretched, beak open. I could almost hear her wild cry circling overhead as I stood on the windy hill.

10

THE EARLY MORNING MIST was beginning to burn off the long grass as I pushed my bike up the drive toward the Raptor Rehabilitation Center. I looked eagerly toward the house, hoping to see the hawk lady and hoping Rail had not arrived yet. I wanted time alone with Rhiannon. The story I would write — the story that could save the Center — had to be the best work I'd ever done. And it would be. I could *feel* it. A restless excitement filled me. This was the beginning of my career. I was going to shine a light in Hunter's Gap. It was only a small corner of the world, but I was going to make a difference.

A car passed me halfway up the drive. By the time I dropped my bike in the yard, Rhiannon was already talking to a man in a Pennsylvania state trooper's uniform who was opening the back door of his car. "Must've just happened," the trooper was telling her. "Back there on the interstate by the White Buck exit. Feathers still flyin' around when I come up. Those tractor-trailer rigs catch 'em, you know . . . they don't have a chance."

He pulled out something wrapped in his leather trooper's jacket and handed it carefully to Rhiannon. All I could see was a mass of speckled gray feathers and a round, flat face marked with concentric bands. Rhiannon pulled back the jacket. "My God, Ray," she breathed. "It's a great *gray* — an Arctic gray owl. I've never seen one this far south . . ."

As she spoke, she was hurrying with the bundle toward the shed, the trooper following. "Anything more I can do for you, Dr. Jeffries?" he asked, holding the door open.

"Rail! Rail. Bring a towel. Here —" Rhiannon took the towel Rail handed her in the shed and transferred the owl to the workbench. "Thanks, Ray — no. I've got a helper here." She paused to give the trooper a dry smile. "Unless you want to arrange this damned visit from Senator Vinci for me. I've already wasted hours this morning on the phone."

The trooper rolled his eyes. "Tell me about it," he sympathized laconically. "They've doubled up on all our shifts for that day. You'd think he was royalty. So he's really coming out here to watch you let that eagle go? Well, good luck. See you on the big day, then."

By the time the trooper had closed the door, Rhiannon and Rail were already bent over the injured owl. "Thank God the neck isn't broken," Rhiannon said, filling a syringe. "Usually are, when they get sucked into those rigs . . . here. Put your hand over his back like this . . ." She leaned closer over the owl, murmuring, "There. That should keep him quiet. God. A great gray. You're seeing a rare thing, Rail. All the way from the Arctic —"

They worked together under the lamp, Rhiannon and Rail and the owl held in the circle of light, while I sat on a stool at one side. I balanced my new notebook on my knee, opened it to the first clean page, and began to record everything. I described the owl, the equipment, the procedure of pinning the broken wing and suturing the torn leg. I marked in the margin where I would need to do further research. Arctic gray owl. Pinion feathers. Boreal forest. Castings. But the more detailed and accurate I made my notes, the farther away I felt from the circle of light over the workbench. After a while, I put the notebook down and watched Rail's hands.

I couldn't see his face. But his deft fingers cut away the blood-matted feathers, gently swabbed the wounds, held out the broken wing while Rhiannon inserted the steel pin. He didn't lose his focus, rarely spoke, and never faltered. I knew from the way he held his shoulders that he would have that familiar fierce frown of concentration. But there was something different about his manner, now. With Rhiannon, he didn't seem afraid. Suddenly I felt terribly lonely, as if a bus had just pulled away and I was left standing alone in the darkness.

I picked my notebook up and read what I'd written. My words seemed to have nothing to do with what I was watching. Rhiannon smoothed the owl's ruffled breast feathers and said something in a voice too low for me to hear, but Rail nodded. He followed her caress with his own, his hand so gentle I felt suddenly that I was intruding, and looked away from him to the bird. The owl's speckled feathers shivered slightly as it breathed. Rhiannon filled another syringe.

"Antibiotic," she said. "Want to do it this time?"

Rail tapped the syringe with his finger, the way Rhiannon had done earlier, and pushed the needle under the owl's skin while the hawk lady held the feathers apart. When he had finished, he turned his face slightly toward Rhiannon and I saw his shy smile of triumph. She took both his hands and held them between her own, looking at him intently. "Don't you dare join the military," she said. "Don't you dare waste these hands." Even in the shadow where I sat, I saw Rail's flush of pleasure.

The phone Rhiannon wore clipped to her belt buzzed and with an impatient exclamation, she answered. "Yes . . . yes. I'm sorry I didn't get back to you. I had an emergency to . . . no. No, certainly not. The Senator is welcome —" She listened, cradling the phone against her shoulder in order to help Rail wrap gauze around the owl's leg. They communicated with gestures and glances until she hung the phone again on her belt. "Damn!" she spat. "I knew this would turn into a circus. This publicity stunt better keep Williams off my back. Rail, finish up here — put him in Number Eight cage. It's clean. And have these other guys been fed yet?"

"I was chopping stuff when the owl —" began Rail, but Rhiannon gave a dismissive wave of her hand. "It's no problem. Just get it done. I've got to go attend to this absurdity."

I stumbled off the stool to reach her before she left. "Can I help? I mean, do you want me to do anything?" I blurted. My notebook fell to the floor. Rhiannon frowned, poised on her way out the door. "Oh, Taylor," she said. "Yes. I forgot. Look, I don't really have time . . . just go into my study and look through that pile of newspapers. Make a list of anything that seems likely between here and Alton. I don't know . . . community groups, camps, local organizations. Anyplace where we could offer a program with the birds —" Her last words were lost as she hurried out.

I picked the notebook up and brushed it off. If the hawk lady had physically pushed me aside, I wouldn't have felt worse. All the anticipation I'd had on the way to the Center that morning was gone, flattened out of me like a deflated balloon. I stuffed the notebook into my pack. I was not going to be able to write a story about this place. I was no reporter. I couldn't even come close to maintaining any objectivity. The closer I tried to get to the hawk lady, the further away she seemed to be.

"Hey, Taylor. Could you stand on the other side? I gotta sweep here," said Rail, pushing a broom around my feet. I stepped back and watched him sullenly. He swept up a pile, leaned on the broom, and said, "Man, that owl was so cool. Hey, you wanna see your hawk?"

"She's not mine," I snapped.

He was quiet a moment. Then he said, in a puzzled voice, "Well, okay. *The* hawk, then. But you found her. I thought you'd at least wanna see her —"

"If you're going off to medical school someday, you better stop saying 'gonna' and 'wanna,'" I said scathingly. "You sound like a —"

We stared at each other.

"A redneck. I know," Rail finished softly.

"Yeah. A redneck. That's what you sound like." I zipped up my pack with a vicious tug. Rail began to push the broom again in short jabs around the workbench. I wished, unreasonably, that he would stop and look at me. Understand everything I was feeling, read the unhappiness in my eyes without my having to explain. The way a best friend would understand.

I turned abruptly to leave. "I guess I am a redneck," Rail called after me just before I opened the door. I paused unwillingly and he continued, "You think I don't know that? I know what it looks like to everyone . . . a Bogart, wantin' to go to college. I know I'm not smart like you, Taylor, an' I don't know how to talk like —"

I threw my pack on the floor. "Why do you keep *saying* that!" I cried. "You're better than me in *everything*! Do you just want to hear me say it? The way Rhiannon always does?"

He flushed deeply and took a step toward me. I wouldn't have minded if he'd hit me. But he was breathing hard and for a moment, horrified, I thought he was crying. "That isn't the way it is at all, Taylor," Rail said. "Man. I thought you'd understand."

I felt as chopped up and raw as the mound of half-thawed mouse meat Rail was preparing to feed the birds. He worked silently, his hair falling over his eyes, thunking the knife down on the board. After a moment, I heaved my pack over my shoulder and pushed open the door.

"Too bad you won't get to see the hawk fly free like you wanted to," Rail said conversationally, as he stuck his arm through the feeding door. "Rhiannon says she's healing up fine. So once she learns to fly and hunt, we can let her go."

I looked back at him sharply. "What do you mean?"

Rail picked another gloveful of meat from the bucket and continued feeding, talking to the wall in front of him. "Rhiannon says it'll be best to wait and release her during the October hawk migrations. So you won't get to see her. You'll be away at your fancy school."

I stalked across the yard. This was definitely not going to work. I would just have to think up another subject to write my essay on. I was so furious I didn't even notice the Chevy pulled up near the house. I almost bumped into my father carrying an armful of drawing materials toward the large enclosures.

"There you are!" he greeted me cheerfully. He'd been working all morning and was covered in sweat and dust, his T-shirt draped around his neck. He put down his things, wiped his face with the shirt, and pulled me against him. "Yuk," I said, making a face.

"I know," he smiled ruefully. "I finished up that little black marble piece outside this morning. It's hellishly hot."

"You worked in the sun without your shirt on?" I said. "Mom told you to stop doing that. She thinks you'll get skin cancer."

"Your mother listens to too many of her neurotic patients. They're all paranoid about something or other," said my father.

I saw Rail emerging from the shed. "Dad?" I said quickly. "Dad, can you run me home? Please? I need to —"

But it was too late. Rhiannon was coming toward us, and my father turned away from me to meet her. I don't know how they touched without touching. But they did. They only stood talking, but the space between them was more intimate than any touch.

Rail hesitated when he saw us. I don't know if it was because of me or because of them. But in either case, seeing him watch them made me furiously angry — angry at Rail because I'd been so mean to him, angry at my father for making Rhiannon laugh, and angry at Rhiannon because she wouldn't let me get close to her. I escaped into the house, went right through the kitchen and into the room beyond.

My father always claimed you could understand everything about a person by looking at the things they kept in their house. There was plenty in this room to look at. But it wasn't going to help me understand Rhiannon. I could almost hear the busy rustlings of secrets, as if behind the hundreds of books on the shelves were stories still too alive to rest in their pages, as if under the frayed edge of the big red Persian carpet was hidden the dust of journeys too difficult to sweep away. I went slowly through the room, stepping around haphazardly placed furniture, cluttered piles of books and boxes overflowing with papers. Arranged on every surface were rocks, animal skulls, turtle shells, feathers, carved wooden bowls inlaid with delicate shells, rough clay pots with ancient-looking designs . . . it reminded me of the museums I'd been to on school trips from Dressler Academy. Tapa cloth from Samoa hung on the walls along with carved masks from Africa. On the top of one bookcase a bronze Indian Buddha head stared down at me. Smooth Inuit carvings of seals and walruses weighted down stacks of papers on a desk dominated by a computer. Even if I hadn't been familiar with these things from looking through my father's art books, I would have known the room contained objects from all over the world.

I pushed past the couch to look out the tall window behind the desk. My father was sitting on an upturned bucket near an enclosure with his drawing board on his knees. Beyond him, I could see Rhiannon pushing a loaded wheelbarrow. Rail came up to her and they spoke for a moment. I turned away. And saw the photograph.

I could easily have missed it. It was black and white, overshadowed on the wall by a bright, large oil painting. I leaned across the desk and stared.

A woman stood on the top of a hill, the wind blowing her hair across her face. She wore a bulky wool sweater and knee-high rubber boots. From her up-flung arm, encased in a heavy gauntlet, a magnificent white falcon was just lifting free. Its powerful wings were spread, its talons barely touched the woman's arm, and the graceful, snowy head faced into the wind. The woman seemed to be lifting free as well, her whole body aligned with the upward flight of the white falcon. Some trick of light on the camera lens made everything seem to pulse with an internal glow.

I reached out and ran my finger over the woman's face, as if I could brush away the hair that hid her from me. With my movement, I knocked a pile of papers to the floor. Underneath them was a much smaller photograph, framed in silver. Feeling like an intruder for the second time that day, I picked it up and held it cupped in my hand. It was a picture of a little girl, hardly older than a baby, with curling dark hair that looked like mine had at that age. There was a watchfulness in her eyes that captivated me, but although I didn't put the photo down, the child's gaze seemed so unguarded I covered it with my other hand. Stenciled lightly in the bottom corner was a date: June 1982.

Rhiannon came into the room. Guiltily, I put the small photo face-down on the desk and gestured to the photograph of the woman with the white falcon. "Is that you?" I was about to ask, but even as I opened my mouth, I changed my question to, "What kind of bird is that?"

"Gyrfalcon," Rhiannon answered shortly, but I hardly paid attention. At the moment I'd looked again at the photograph I'd seen what I had not noticed before: the woman was pregnant.

Rhiannon snapped on a light and picked up a pile of newspapers from the floor by the couch. "A little difficult to look through these in the dark," she commented.

"I —"

"Taylor. We have to have a list of scheduled events together before that damn Senator's visit," she interrupted. "You've got to find places, call them and arrange for us to give a program — here. Rail had some suggestions. There's a nursing home around here, and some Lutheran church camp, and something about a fireman's club —"

"The Fireman's Picnic. It's in August," I said, my face burning. Naturally Rail had suggested all the places I had disregarded as not being important. "I didn't think —" I began.

"Taylor, I *need* you to think. You're my assistant." Rhiannon sat on the couch and shoved aside some books. Reluctantly, I sat next to her. "What's wrong?" she asked brusquely.

I was so startled I blurted the truth. "I thought you wanted . . . I thought I was going to work with you. But Rail . . . he's better than . . ."

She gave me a penetrating look. "This isn't about better," she said finally. "It's about doing something you told me you'd do. As for Rail — he needs someone to give him a chance at getting out of this place. I thought you knew about his situation."

"I only know what Bitsi says," I whispered, miserable. "She says Rail is more like an adult than Tim. She says —"

"Well, she's right for once," Rhiannon said. "She does care for that family. Tim Bogart and her son were best friends."

"Bitsi has a son?" I gasped, incredulous.

"Arnold," Rhiannon nodded. "He and Rail's father were drafted together. Arnold was killed in Vietnam six months later. I'm not sure which one was luckier."

I stared at her. "How do you know all this?"

"Old Bitsi told me," she said, standing up.

"You mean Mrs. Bitsi?"

"No — Old Bitsi," Rhiannon said. "Told me when I hired Tim last year."

"But Old Bitsi doesn't talk to anyone!" I cried. I thought about Bitsi and Old Bitsi with a son. I wondered if Old Bitsi had stopped talking after his son died. "Wow. Poor Old Bitsi," I said. I looked at Rhiannon in wonder. "How'd you get him to talk?"

She frowned. "I didn't 'get' him to. He wanted to tell me. He cares about Tim and he was worried about Rail."

I gathered up the pile of *Alton Register*s and started to leave the study. Rhiannon glanced up from something she was reading, a pair of glasses slipping down over her nose. "Taylor, I *am* counting on you," she said firmly.

138

I deposited the papers on the seat of the Chevy and thought I never wanted to see a newspaper ever again. I went to find my father. He'd moved to a smaller enclosure and was drawing, his T-shirt wrapped like a turban around his head to keep the sweat from dripping onto the paper. He reached out his free arm without pausing in his drawing and pulled me close. "Just give me half an hour more?" he asked.

"Okay," I said. I leaned on him the way I had when I was little, when he would draw me a bedtime story, unfolding the story picture by picture in front of my eyes. Under his pencil now, a small, delicate hawk was emerging with a grasshopper in its mouth.

"Pretty thing," my father murmured, shading one tiny, taloned foot. "Caught that bug right in front of me. Very obliging." In the enclosure, the little kestrel was perched a few feet away, watching every move of the pencil.

Under the drawing were other sheets, already filled, and my father lifted his arm briefly so I could pull them out. One sheet was covered with the golden eagles. Another caught a barn owl in sleepy repose in the dappled shade. And another . . . Rhiannon. Pushing the wheelbarrow. Pulling a broken branch off the top of an enclosure, her hair falling loose from its braid. Rhiannon standing, arms folded, looking directly out from under her dark brows. Even in the unfinished sketch, my father had captured the quick, impatient frown and the laughter shadowed by sorrow that she kept hidden behind her eyes.

My father took the drawing from me. "A rare bird —" he said quietly, slipping it with the others underneath again. I moved a few feet away, out of his reach. "Anna's coming home tonight," he added without looking up. "I want to get as much drawing done as I can before we go home, because she'll be here for the rest of the week."

I nodded as if it made sense. But it didn't, of course. My father didn't stop working just because my mother was around. I scuffed slowly down the path through the trees and found myself near a row of long, high enclosures running out from the back of the shed. These cages were more isolated than the others, shaded near the shed by thick trees, but open at the far end with a clear view of fields and sky. I made my way cautiously through the pines. The first cages were empty, the doors to the inside of the shed closed. But in the last one, perched on a low branch, was the red-tailed hawk.

She faced out through the pines toward the open fields. Threads of sun drifted over her through the breeze-stirred shade. The hawk turned her narrow head and looked at me, her eyes under the fierce line of her brow as bright as the sky. I took a few steps closer to her and as I did, she hopped to a perch level with my face only a few feet away. For several minutes neither of us moved.

I was so close my breath stirred the wispy feathers around her beak. Although I stood so near, the hawk appeared utterly solitary. In the darkness of her eyes I felt my own aloneness. I was no longer a girl. She was no longer a hawk. In the vast space between us we met as a single being, connected by the heart of solitude.

A sparrow flickered in the branches. Quick as the catch of my own breath, the hawk swiveled her head to follow the movement. I stepped back, stumbling on a root.

"Hey," said Rail, voice soft as the insect-dancing air. "Hey, Taylor. Don't jump. I just came to find you . . ."

He came up beside me and the hawk let out a shriek, beating her wings and flapping awkwardly to a perch at the far end of the enclosure. "Isn't she the most perfect wild thing?" Rail whispered, reverent.

"Yeah," I whispered back. Rail sat crosslegged on a root and I didn't know what else to do but sit next to him. The words I wanted to say pushed in my throat, but I could not make my voice obey. If I said "I'm sorry" aloud, it would make *real* all the mean, horrible things I'd spoken. I told myself they weren't that important to him, that he'd probably forgotten about them anyway. But I was wrong.

Rail flicked a twig toward the cage and the red-tailed hawk turned her head sharply in the direction it fell. "How come you were so pissed off with me, back there?" he muttered, jerking his head toward the shed. "I wasn't doing anything to you."

"It wasn't you."

He scowled. "Well, man, Taylor. You sure acted like it was me."

I snuck a look at him. He was glaring at his boots, as if they were going to jump up and bite him. I noticed how old and worn they were, the cracked leather patched with duct tape. I took a deep breath. "It's just that . . . I like her so much —" I trailed off helplessly and stared away from him.

Rail stretched out his long legs and re-tied his boot laces, even though they'd seemed perfectly all right to me. "Yeah, I know. Me, too," he said finally. He caught my eye, flushed. "Man, Taylor. It's not a contest."

Suddenly I was sure Rail understood more than I'd even had the courage to admit to myself. The warm afternoon air shaded by the pines, the musky scent of new-mown hay, the contented preening of the baby hawk all wrapped around me like a balm. I smoothed my hand over the needle-carpeted earth. "Rail . . . I'm sorry," I said.

He gazed smiling out through the trees toward the fields. Above us, the sun shone like a thousand tiny doors opening among the shadowed branches. Beyond the trees, we both heard the sound of Rhiannon's delighted laugh. Into the silence that followed, I asked, "Did you ever . . . do you know why your mother left?"

He didn't answer for a long time. Then he said, "Well, sure — she ran off with Tom Barker. I thought everyone knew that."

"But" — I took a deep breath — "was he the *real* reason?"

Rail poked a twig deep into the earth. "Naw," he said. " 'Course not. It was my dad. He's just . . . he's just real hard to live with. He don't mean to be, though."

"But she left *you* with him."

His face darkened. "I'm not saying she done the right thing. There was just two wrong things, and she had to decide between them." He paused. "I dunno. Maybe it would have been worse if she'd stayed . . ."

Rhiannon's laughter came to us again, and I caught a glimpse of her walking with my father toward the eagle enclosure. Rail stood suddenly, slapping pine needles from his camouflage pants. "It's no use worrying about that kind of thing, anyway," he said, glancing at me sideways as he made his way out of the pines. His eyes seemed to hunt for something in mine. "You don't ever know what anybody's gonna decide to do. And whatever they do, you can't hardly ever figure out why, either." He stopped abruptly. "So, you calling those places I told Rhiannon about — find out if they want a bird program?"

"Yeah, I guess."

He began walking toward the yard, but before we got there, he mumbled over his shoulder, "Well, I hope you do write something about this place. They really might shut it down . . . it could make a big difference." He threw an unexpected grin at me. "And besides, I want to keep this job. And the baby hawk — what would happen to her?"

"Okay," I said.

"You could write a really great story," he added. "Besides —"

"Rail. Give me a break. I said okay. I'm going to write it."

"Besides," he said, as if I hadn't spoken. "It would mean we could work together all summer."

11

My father and I stayed up to wait for my mother's arrival. My father had four *Star Trek* videos stacked by the television and was settled back happily sprinkling cayenne pepper on his share of the popcorn. I made a half-hearted attempt to go through some of the newspapers, my notebook open on the couch beside me, but it was difficult with the USS *Enterprise* about to blow up at any moment. At eight-thirty the phone rang. My father sighed, pushed the pause button, and left Captain Kirk trapped in mid-"Beam me up, Scotty."

"Annie," he said into the phone, smiling at me, "Where are you?"

There was a long silence. Too long. By the time my father said softly, "All right," and replaced the receiver, I was already slumped back in the cushions. He didn't say anything for a moment, just punched the button so Captain Kirk could return to his ship.

"She's not coming, is she?" I said.

"Tomorrow night," my father shrugged. "Some crisis with a patient. She's at the hospital."

Well, I thought. It wasn't as if it was the first time. I shoved the newspapers to one side. "Well," I said, as brightly as I could, "now you can go draw at the Center tomorrow."

I wished I hadn't said it. Because what I meant was — now *I* could spend another day there, too. Underlying the familiar disappointment was an unfamiliar sense of reprieve.

My father sighed and switched off the video. "I did want to get some more drawings done, actually. So it's just as well. This way I won't be so distracted when she does get home —"

He never got angry, no matter how many times she did it. And I always pretended I wasn't angry. But this time, I didn't have to pretend so hard. This time, all I could think of was being able to spend another day at the Center. With Rhiannon. I glanced guiltily at my father just as he glanced at me. We both looked away. But I'd seen the same thought in his eyes. So now we had a secret from my mother that we couldn't even talk about with each other.

The next day at the Center had a sour quality, as if I had stolen something to get it. My father was unusually quiet, too. I looked for Rail, but there was no rusty bike propped against the shed. Rhiannon was busy with a group of students and she only waved absently to us from a distance.

Feeling dispirited, I watched my father go off toward the enclosure with the golden eagles. He didn't stop to talk to Rhiannon and she didn't look in his direction. But there was something so deliberately studied in their *not meeting*, I felt a dull twinge of irritation. I had no energy for working, and once in the amazing study, I plunked the newspapers on the couch and went immediately to look at the photograph of the unknown woman and the white falcon.

I wished with a sudden ache that I *could* tell my mother what I was doing. I wished I could show her the red-tailed hawk and the eagles, and I wished I could make her understand the desire to see them fly free. But she would be impatient with fantasies. She would see saving the Center as a Project, something to be worked on with a goal to be achieved. Through the window, I watched Rhiannon. On her wrist perched a ghostly-looking barn owl. She was stroking her finger down its white breast and talking to the students. I turned resolutely away from the window and the photograph. My mother would be right. I was getting lost in a fantasy. The only thing that was going to help save the Center or get me into the Advanced Writing program at Porter Phelps was an objective approach and hard work.

I opened my notebook to my meager list of community groups and resumed my search with new determination. I began with this morning's *Register*, but the first thing I came across, on page two, was a letter from a "Concerned Tax Payer" in Hunter's Gap.

My father says any newspaper that prints anonymous letters to the editor lacks moral fiber. He believes that if you want to say something, you should have the courage to sign your name to it. But I could understand why the "Concerned Tax Payer" wouldn't want to sign his or her name. Who would want to admit to composing something as barely literate and ignorant as this letter?

"Senator Vinci better pay attention to us tax payers," the letter threatened. "Hunters pay taxes too. But after all those hawks and eagles are let go there won't be nothing left to hunt. Them birds kill anything that moves. I seen one peck the eyes out of a calf what was alive. What's next, Dr. Jeffers? Maybe you should leave while you're ahead. Or are you going to take our hard-earned tax dollars and rebilitate wolfs and mountain lions too? How about rattle snakes?"

I took the paper and went out to find Rhiannon. She was looking over my father's shoulder as he sketched. "Have you read this?" I asked in disgust.

She took the paper, frowning. My father watched, sketching quickly as he looked up at her. She read for a few minutes, and I thought her face seemed to lose color under her sun-brown skin. She thrust the paper back at me. "I've had this kind of trouble establishing raptor centers in other rural places. It's not the first time I've been asked to leave," she commented. Her face was carefully composed and she spoke evenly, as if she were in a lecture hall. "This attitude is no more than the echo of very old fears. Primitive humans survived by hunting. Other species of hunters were a threat..." She looked sharply at my father. "What are you doing?" she demanded.

My father had drawn Rhiannon's face as she'd read the letter. In those few seconds, he'd discovered behind her expressionless calm the inexplicable presence of grief, and with a few sure lines had exposed it on a clean sheet of paper. In one swift motion, Rhiannon took the drawing from him and ripped it in half. "You're welcome to draw the birds," she said in a cold, still voice. "But I never agreed to be a model for you. Please don't do it again." And she walked away, tearing the drawing again as she went.

My father showed no reaction. He just pulled out another sheet and, looking intently at the eagles, resumed his drawing. Stunned and mortified, I went slowly back to the house. The more a mystery Rhiannon was, the more I yearned to know her. I stared at the photograph of the woman and the falcon, but I couldn't see past the windswept hair covering her face. Then I looked for the photo of the little girl. But that picture was gone.

I looked everywhere for it, even through the drawers in the desk. I only found more papers, letters, and a professional journal with an article by Rhiannon. The short blurb listed her degrees, her publications, all her accomplishments. But it wasn't *her*. The real Rhiannon had something to do with what my father had drawn, with the woman on the hill . . . and with the picture of the little girl.

My mother came home that evening and for three days, neither my father nor I went to the Center. At first he spent time with her, but gradually the chill crept between them and he disappeared into his studio. My mother and I were alone. She didn't have anything to do in Hunter's Gap; she'd hardly really moved here. All her books, her computer, everything was in the city. On the phone, she always made a point of promising that we would have plenty of "special" time together when she got here. So when she was home, I felt compelled to spend all my time with her. But if I went out for a minute, I'd often come back to find her sneaking a look at something in her briefcase or picking up her messages from the phone. She'd always smile apologetically with a guilt that mirrored my own, and we'd sit around for another hour without knowing what to do or say.

"Don't let me interrupt you, if you want to work

on your essay," she said to me, on the third day. "Are you finding enough material? You chose a pretty specialized topic — community environmental programs. Are you finding programs like that around here? Recycling, or something?"

"Yeah," I mumbled. "Something like that. There's a few . . . I mean, they're starting some. Anyway, I have lots of stuff to work with. Really, Mom. Don't worry. You're not interrupting. I'm okay."

Once, we went down to the studio to find my father. He was on the phone, trying to arrange with Junior Fenstemacher a time to go to Vermont to pick up the marble block for the Vietnam memorial. He rolled his eyes at us, a comment on Junior, and continued to negotiate. My mother looked idly through the pile of drawings on his drafting desk while we waited.

"He told me he was going to use eagles for his theme —" she remarked, studying the top sheet for a few moments before turning it over.

Too late I remembered the drawings of Rhiannon. My mother paused, holding the sheet of paper, head cocked to one side like a small bird listening for something stirring underground. "What an interesting-looking woman," she said.

I glanced at my father uncomfortably. "It's just Dr. Jeffries," I said. "She lets him draw the eagles. At the Center. He only went over once or twice. To draw. She —"

"It's all right, Melissa," smiled my mother.

She left the morning Senator Vinci was due to arrive at the Center. Even before my mother had turned the car from the drive out onto the road, my father rumbled the Chevy up to the house and shouted for me. We got to the Center just as Rhiannon and Rail were lugging one of the large transport crates out to the van. Two students held the back doors open.

Rhiannon gave me a sardonic smile. "Well, Taylor. Ready to report on the three-ring circus?" But despite her words, the hawk lady seemed excited, almost eager. Her interns joked with her and laughed. The grounds of the Center were neatly mowed and trimmed, and the sky rose over it all in an unbroken arc of blue.

"I sent the Senator and his henchmen down to the site already," Rhiannon told me. She closed the doors of the van. "If we're really lucky, they'll get lost . . . Here, Ryan — you drive. Tamara, you have the equipment box?"

"There's the TV people," Rail called. On the road past the drive, a white Channel 24 van slowed, then drove on. "Well, look at that. They're following directions," Rhiannon said. "All right. Come on. I don't want the eagle in that box any longer than he has to be." She started to get into the van.

"Come with us," my father said. He'd been leaning against the Chevy, one foot propped on the front fender. Now he opened the door with a flourish he normally reserved for me. "A special occasion deserves a special vehicle. Short of a limo, you can't beat a 'fifty-five Chevy."

I didn't think she would. But one of the students said, "Go on, Dr. Jeffries. It's too crowded in the van with the crate, anyway." Without a word, Rhiannon climbed in and slid across the seat next to my father. After I got in, then Rail, we were all squeezed practically in each other's lap. I stared nervously straight ahead of me, Rail on one side and Rhiannon on the other. I wished I'd ridden in the back. But I also wanted to stay like this forever.

My father drove for twenty minutes down the river road that ran along the high, wooded bluffs by the Susquehanna River. The wind rushed in the open windows as the Chevy roared over the rough road. My father bent his head toward Rhiannon and said something I couldn't hear. When she laughed, the sound filled the cab and streamed out the windows like a rippling ribbon. Her whole body moved with laughter beside me. My father drove with one arm draped over the wheel, the other propped out the window. The sun gleamed on his muscular neck and shoulders. The wind whipped in and blew Rhiannon's dark hair over my father's arm. It was beautiful. I stared down at my hands.

"You going to the Firemen's Picnic?" asked Rail suddenly.

"You mean me?"

"Man, Taylor, who else would I mean?"

I was tongue-tied. Was he asking me to go *with* him to the picnic? Or just wanting to know if I was going? All of Hunter's Gap would be out on the school grounds in mid-August for the annual Fireman's Picnic. Bitsi had told me about it. There were games, music, fireworks, food, even some rides. She also told me the Firemen's Picnic was just an excuse for "them big overgrown boobies" (she meant the volunteer firemen) to mess around with fire. "Every year those guys come moochin' around here collecting donations for them nasty fireworks," Bitsi had said. "You know what I tell 'em?" She always gave me a chance to guess what she was going to say, so she could correct me when I was wrong. "You told them to raise money for a worthy cause like AIDS research, right, Bitsi?" I'd answered, to oblige her. She'd glared at me. "That ain't a worthy cause an' you know it, young lady," she'd growled, her jowls quivering. "No, I told 'em they *knew* what they could do with their fireworks." She'd looked immensely satisfied at recounting this incident, but somehow I'd missed the punch line. You could only expect so much from Bitsi.

"Taylor?" Rail jabbed me with his elbow. "Earth to Taylor — you there?"

"Sorry —"

"So, you going?" he persisted.

"I don't know," I mumbled, distracted. I glanced at my father. His hand was half on the gearshift, half resting on Rhiannon's knee. I looked away quickly. I was tense and jumpy, and I wished we would get to where we were going.

"We'll all go," said my father unexpectedly.

"I hate fireworks," I said.

Rail said sadly, "You do?" and at the same time, Rhiannon asked, "Fireworks?"

"Sure," grinned my father. "Hunter's Gap's big gala event of the year. One of the pleasanter memories from my childhood —"

"Mom's going to be home then," I interrupted darkly. "She hates fireworks, too."

My father had both hands on the wheel now. He shook his ponytail back and leveled a look at me. "Your mother will have just spent the entire month with a bunch of cigar-smoking psychiatrists," he stated. "She'll need some fun. And she can meet Rhiannon. And Rail."

"I didn't know about the fireworks," broke in Rhiannon, worried. "We hadn't opened the Center by last August. They have it on the school grounds? That's too damn close to the birds. The fireworks will drive them nuts."

"It'll drive my father nuts, too," said Rail suddenly. We all looked at him. He flushed. "That's why I wanted you to come," he muttered to me. "Dad wants to go. Cattie and Dawn've been bugging him to — they're too little to understand about him and noise. So I thought you might help me with him. He liked you a lot."

I never knew having a friend could be so complicated. No wonder I'd never been involved with other people much. Now, between knowing Rail and Rhiannon, I hardly recognized myself as the same M. Taylor Armstrong-Brown who had only a few weeks earlier been looking forward to the last day of school at Hunter's Gap. Now I'd have to go to the Firemen's Picnic, where I'd be seen by every single person in Hunter's Gap . . . there I'd be with Rail Bogart and his sweet, crazy, flower-planting father, and my own father with my mother the psychopath on one side and the shotgun-toting hawk lady on the other. Well, whatever Rhiannon thought, today was not going to be the final word in three-ring circuses.

"Missy?" said my father. I looked into Rail's anxious eyes. "Sure, I'll go with you," I said, and I was surprised at how soft my voice sounded.

We turned down a dirt road that ran between cornfields, and ahead I saw a black limo looking incongruous parked in the weeds under the trees, flanked by two state troopers' cars. Around the Channel 24 van milled a group of busy people. Rhiannon glanced in the rear-view mirror at her students following in the university van. "The eagle's under

enough stress," she growled. "Drive over there —"
She pointed toward an open place some distance away,
and my father motioned out the window for the students to follow. We bumped over the rutted road,
but by the time we'd pulled up, the television people
were already hurrying toward us. Behind them,
more slowly, came five men dressed in suits and ties,
picking their way carefully over the uneven ground.

"Open the door, but don't bring the crate out yet,"
Rhiannon told the students, and then she was surrounded by the television crew, who clamored eagerly at her to stand where they could get shots of
her meeting Senator Vinci. They apparently didn't
observe that Rhiannon held neither television nor
senators in high esteem. She kept them several feet
away from the van with a furious gesture and a glare
from her dark-browed eyes. "Keep back!" she
snapped. "This is a wild creature. He's not here to
entertain you."

"Dr. Jeffries, could you just tell us —"

"Would you mind stepping over here, Dr. Jeffries,
to meet Senator Vinci?"

"Dr. Jeffries, would you mind letting the eagle out
over here, so the camera crew can —"

Into this melee of voices and movement, another
car pulled up near the van and the nervous figure of
Dr. Williams emerged. Rail muttered "Uh-oh" and
Rhiannon, true to form, turned her scathing look on
the head of the Wildlife Biology Department. "The

public relations are going very well, as you can see," she said sarcastically. "The problem is, I may have a dead bald eagle before long. He's either going to get cooked in that crate, or this mob" — she gestured toward the television crew — "will have him stressed to exhaustion. You know the first twenty-four hours are crucial in a released animal's life, and if he's too exhausted to hunt —"

One of the men in suits came forward, hand outstretched, a wide smile on his face. "Dr. Jeffries, we all have the best interests of the eagle in mind. Please let the television crew know exactly where you'd like them to stand, and I'm sure they'll be happy to do so."

"Dr. Jeffries . . . Senator Vinci," Dr. Williams mumbled the introductions unhappily. Rhiannon shook the Senator's hand abruptly. The Senator had the widest smile of any human being I'd ever seen. His teeth seemed painted, they were so perfect. He leaned toward Rhiannon and whispered something to her, and whatever he said made her relax enough to actually smile. The television interviewer was making sneaky little movements, each one bringing her closer, as if she intended suddenly to thrust the microphone right between the Senator and Rhiannon. But the Senator waved her back in his pleasantly calm way. "I'm sure Dr. Jeffries will be happy to talk to you later, after she's made sure the eagle is safely released."

"But we need a close-up of —"

"Use your telephoto lenses," the Senator said, testily.

I stood with Rail and my father next to the Chevy. "Well, the Senator has good taste. You can tell he likes her spirit," my father remarked in a satisfied voice. "Look at him. He knows a worthy soul when he sees one. He's not going to let anything happen to her program."

He might have been right about Senator Vinci. But Rhiannon had alienated the entire television crew by now, and poor Dr. Williams was running damage control, trying to placate them with an ineffectual promise of "touring the Center" afterwards. I watched the reporter closely. She was a lean, glinty-eyed woman wearing too much makeup and an insincere smile. She barely respected the Senator's request, pushing as close as she could to where Rhiannon was working.

But finally everyone seemed content or resigned to where they were. The camera crew had reset their equipment, the Senator was back with his aides, the troopers leaned against their cars in the shade drinking coffee. Rhiannon's students carried the large crate to an open spot at the edge of the bluffs, left it with Rhiannon, and came back to the van. I propped my notebook open on the hood of the Chevy.

A light, warm breeze ruffled the leaves of corn. Beyond the bluffs the river shimmered like a polished silver band under a pale blue sky. Rhiannon went to the edge of the bluff and stood a moment, surveying the scene around her. Only a few dozen feet lay between her and the group of people, but somehow she appeared completely alone. A silence fell over the group. Then Rhiannon turned.

"Taylor," she called.

I went immediately, as if I had been waiting for her call, past the camera crew and the students with their binoculars, past the Senator and his aides, who were holding their suit jackets over their arms in the heat. For a moment, Rhiannon and I stood side by side on the rocky bluffs that dropped away more than a hundred feet to the river. In the crate, the eagle chirruped softly and scuffled his feathers. Rhiannon smiled at me faintly. I felt the distance between us just as I had with the red-tailed hawk, as if that space connected us in our solitude. If we had been eagles, our flights would have matched wing-beat for wing-beat along parallel rivers of air.

"I thought you'd want to release the eagle," Rhiannon said at last. She stepped away from the crate.

I bent to unlatch the door, careful to stand to one side so the eagle wouldn't see me and be startled. I drew the door back and joined Rhiannon. We waited. I could feel the group of onlookers waiting behind us. There was a heavy "thunk" as the eagle jumped off his perch, and the dry rasp of his feathers dragging against the floor of the plywood crate. And then he walked out into the sunlight.

The eagle blinked, tilting his head first one way, then the other, his dark eyes scanning the open sky. He shook himself, took a few steps, and then, spreading his powerful glossy wings, he lifted into the air and sailed out over the bluffs. An updraft caught him and he rose, hanging suspended a moment before turning in a long, graceful sweep over the river. He circled over the water, then swept back inland above the trees, his shadow racing ahead of him across the cornfield. He glided low over the delighted camera crew, who were turning in circles, trying to follow his flight. With three lazy wing flaps the eagle crossed the river, gave a few high-pitched chirps, and disappeared over the trees on the far side.

I hadn't been aware of moving, but I must have followed the eagle as he passed over us. I found myself poised at the very edge of the bluffs. Suddenly Rhiannon was beside me, her arm around me, pulling me gently back. "Wait until you've grown in all your feathers," she said.

She didn't take her arm away and for a moment, oblivious to everyone behind us, I leaned against her. The sky seemed flat and empty. "Why do I feel so sad?" I whispered.

"Because you've allowed a piece of yourself to fly

away, too, I think," Rhiannon said quietly. "I know. I feel it each time."

"But it's gone. It won't come back."

She was silent. I could hear the voices of the camera crew. "I don't think we can lose ourselves like that," she said at last, pensive. "When you release something from your heart, it takes you with it. Out there" — she waved her hand toward the river and flickered a smile at me — "into the wild blue yonder."

The reporter had reached us now and Rhiannon, resigned, patiently began to answer questions. Senator Vinci shook her hand on camera and told the reporter how important programs like this were in preserving the environmental health of a state with as much wild land as Pennsylvania. "That eagle is more than a beautiful symbol of America," the Senator said. "He is the measure of how well we care for the land that our children and our children's children will inherit. He carries their future on his wings."

I don't think he'd rehearsed it. His words came spontaneously, and he was looking into the sky over the river, not into the camera, as he spoke. Rhiannon seemed, for once, at a loss for words. The Senator's speech didn't need an answer.

12

FOR A WEEK after Channel 24 aired the story about the Senator and the eagle release, Rhiannon was besieged with phone calls from representatives of every public function under the sun, all wanting her to bring an eagle to their events. "I'm not a damned entertainer," she growled after the first five or six phone calls, one of which was from a father requesting that she come "perform" at his son's sixth birthday party. By the end of the morning she'd turned off the ringer on the phone. She even refused to listen to the messages piling up on the answering machine. If the shotgun Rhiannon was reputed to have had been anywhere handy, I was pretty sure she'd shoot the phone off the hook. At lunch on the first day, I heard her call up old wimpy Williams, as she referred to him, demanding to know whether he wanted her to be a social debutante or a wildlife biologist.

For most of the week I monitored the phone calls, took messages, made program arrangements with the Kiwanis Club of the Greater Alton area, the Bitter Creek Nursing Home, and the Lutheran Summer Day Camp for Disadvantaged Children in Hunter's Gap. In between, I struggled to turn my notes into an outline for my essay. But although I forced myself to work, the list of facts growing in my notebook became a tedious irritation, unwieldy and meaningless. I spent hours in Rhiannon's study, gazing into the vibrant landscape of the photograph and letting the wind blow in off that hill in my secret world, rich with the enchanting scent of something I couldn't quite recognize.

Rail didn't show up for two days, and Rhiannon was gone one day picking up a wounded goshawk that had been found near the New York border. My father came and went. If Rhiannon was not at the Center, he didn't stay to draw for long. But when they were both there, the place seemed more alive, as if the day was always on the brink of revealing a magical promise. It became more and more difficult to spend any time at home in the deserted house that my mother hated and my father hardly lived in.

One late afternoon, as Rhiannon was getting ready

to transport a saw-whet owl for release in the swampy woods near the creek, a car came up the drive and stopped in the yard, blocking her truck. A squirrelly-looking woman got out, notebook in her hand, her eyes darting around as if grabbing everything up to store for future use. "Jan Weltz, reporter for *The Register*," she announced in a preemptive manner, sticking out her hand.

"I thought I told *The Register* I wasn't interested in giving an interview," Rhiannon said, positioning the owl's crate carefully in the back of the truck and ignoring the reporter's hand. But the woman scooted right in under Rhiannon's elbow, so Rhiannon had to move around her. For a moment, I thought Rhiannon was going to shove the reporter aside. "This is the person I'm entrusting with the story of the Center," she said, indicating me with a nod of her head. "I don't like reporters. They can't seem to understand what really matters. If you'll excuse me —"

The reporter sucked in her cheeks. "*The Register* is a highly responsible paper —"

Rhiannon stopped, hands on her hips, and leveled a look at the woman. "When my assistant has written a story, I'll submit it to your editor."

"It's unlikely they'll publish a story by a high school student," said the reporter huffily, making it sound as if I had a disease.

"I'll take my chances," Rhiannon said abruptly,

and got into the truck. The reporter spun her tires in the gravel when she left. "Weaselly creature, wasn't she?" Rhiannon commented.

"Squirrelly," I said.

With a snort of laughter she started the engine.

"Rhiannon," I said. The engine idled and she waited. "Maybe I can't write the story the way you want," I said in a low voice. "Maybe it won't be good enough."

"Do you believe it won't be good enough?"

I looked at the ground in confusion, remembering the C in English and the pages filled with scribbled notes that I couldn't form into any shape.

"Because if you do believe that, you better tell me now. I need the story. Do you want me to get that reporter back here?"

"No," I whispered.

"Good," she said. She shifted the truck into gear. "Because I meant what I said. You're the one I trusted with this story."

"But why?"

"You needed to do it," she answered simply. "And I needed to work with someone I knew."

I watched her drive off down the road. We'd never met before the day I'd offered to be her assistant, I thought. So how could she say she *knew* me? But suddenly I remembered the day my mother and I had driven past Rhiannon on the road — the day our eyes had met. I realized, all at once, that what had startled me so much was the *recognition* I'd seen in hers.

My mother called late Friday night. "I think I'll stay down here for the weekend after all," she said. "Then I can come home for a few days before I go to Germany without worrying about my work. I can spend the whole time with you. How would that be?"

"Okay," I said.

"How's the essay coming?"

"Fine," I said.

"This really is a bad time for me to go away, isn't it?" my mother worried. "I'd like to proofread that essay for you before you send it off to the school. I know how good you can be, sweetie . . . I just want to make sure something this important is the best you can do. At Porter Phelps —"

"Mom, it's fine," I said.

"I suppose you could fax it to me —"

I shoved the phone at my father as he came through the door, shook my head at him violently, and ran up the stairs to my room. Lying on my bed, I opened my notebook to a clean page and wrote across the top, "WHO GETS TO HUNT IN HUNTER'S GAP? Tax dollars and hunting rights-of-way are at the center of a dispute between the community of Hunter's Gap, Pennsylvania, and the state-funded wildlife program at the Raptor Rehabilitation Center there. Dr. Rhiannon Jeffries, Director of the Center, said . . ."

I stopped. The door inside me swung wide open, the wind streamed in off the hill, and the white falcon dove straight through me, down my arm, out the pen, and onto the page. "I trusted you with the story," Rhiannon had said, but the words I began writing now were not forming a story. They had nothing to do with facts. I was not reporting. I was flying along currents of dream-words, my wings beating powerfully in time with my heart, each beat a word that carried me further into the limitless sky.

My mother promised to come home four days before she left for Europe and her conference. "She won't be home 'til Wednesday, right?" I asked my father. "Late Wednesday," he said. So on Tuesday, when Rhiannon and I, Rail, and four birds of prey were scheduled to give our debut public program at the Bitter Creek Nursing Home, I would be safe from my mother's eye.

"What would have been so bad if she just came to watch?" Rail asked, as we cleaned out the transport crates the day before.

"She would have come to watch *me*," I said.

We were working at the back of the main barn, hosing down the crates and scraping them clean of dried droppings. It was a gray afternoon, and thunder rumbled from a distance. Rail glanced at the sky.

"Will you have to go home if there's a storm?" I asked.

He flushed. "Naw. I dunno. He's been a little better, now that they changed his medication."

"You really worry about your dad a lot, don't you?" I said, scrubbing the hinges.

"Well sure. Don't you worry about your parents?" he answered sullenly, as if I'd caught him doing something foolish.

"Yeah. My mother," I grunted. I had to stick my head inside the larger crate, on my hands and knees, to get at the back wall.

"What?"

I sat up. "My mother. I think she's going to leave my dad." I blurted it out. I hadn't intended to. Rail put down the hose, the concern in his eyes startling me.

"Man, Taylor. Really? What'd your dad do?"

"Do? He didn't do anything," I replied defensively. "It's not him. He hates it that she's gone all the time. He's always trying to get her to stay." Rail began drying the crates with an old towel, his back turned, but I knew he was listening. I continued impulsively. "She's really unhappy. *I* make her unhappy. I'm not turning out the way she thought I would. I mean, I used to be really good in school the way she was . . . but now I'm —" I stopped, confused. I couldn't say *what* I was now. I turned the hose on full blast inside the crate. "It'll make it a lot easier for her when I'm away at school. She won't have to come to Hunter's Gap at all, then. There's nothing for her here."

Rail took the hose from me and turned it off. My jeans and sneakers were sopping. "Is that why you're leaving? Because it's easier for your mom?" asked Rail quietly.

"No!" I snapped. "Because there's nothing for *me* here, either. Give me the hose —"

"It's all clean," he said. "You know, Taylor, I'm not the only one who doesn't think you should leave. Rhiannon wants you to stay, too."

"That's ridiculous!" I stumbled on the hose, sat abruptly on the wet crate, and felt like crying. Rhiannon only wanted me around so I could write her story. But I couldn't even seem to manage doing that. Rail coiled the hose and sat on the smaller crate.

"No, it's not," he said calmly.

"You don't understand," I said miserably. "I can't even write up a simple story about the Center. That's all she wants me to do. I thought I'd be able to. But I can't. Here. Look at what I've written — go ahead. Read it." I yanked the notebook from my pack and thrust it at Rail. He took it, but looked hesitant. "Read it," I insisted. "You'll see."

I started lugging the crates to the yard, ready for the birds we would take to the nursing home. Each time I went back for another one, Rail was still reading, leaning against the barn with that familiar frown on his face. When I'd hauled the last crate to the yard I stayed there, sitting on the steps of the house. Rhiannon wasn't around. A few drops of rain pattered in the dust.

Rail came around the corner of the barn and walked toward me, the notebook in his hand. "This isn't an essay," he said, handing it to me.

"I know. I told you."

He squatted down and looked at me. "Man, Taylor. It's the most amazing thing I ever read. It's incredible. I didn't know you could write like that. How'd you make the words fly along that way?"

"I didn't —"

He moved up to sit on the steps next to me, stretching his legs out in the dust. He held his face up to the cool drops and closed his eyes. Without opening them, he said, "Well, I think she'll love it. I think it's just the way Rhiannon would want you to write about this place." He paused, then added thoughtfully, "I bet she knew you would, too. The minute she met you." He gave me his lopsided grin. "Anyway, she doesn't like reporters, remember?"

"But I *am* a reporter. At least, I want to be. I *thought* I wanted to be —" I said sadly, but I was filled with an unaccountable elation at Rail's words.

The rain fell harder. I stood up, stuffing the notebook in my pack. "I'm going to get soaked riding home," I said. I paused looking at Rail. "You know how much you want to get into the Air Force? Well, that's how much I want to get into that Advanced Writing program. Maybe it is a fancy school . . . but that's the only way I'm going to get into the best university. And that's what I *want*."

Rail walked with me across the yard. After a few minutes, as I got on my bike, he said slowly, "I'm not sure I do want the Air Force anymore. It doesn't seem to mean the same thing it did before. I don't know why. I feel like I'm all upside-down or something."

"Yeah," I said. "Me, too."

The next day, we carried the equipment through the back door of the Bitter Creek Nursing Home in the pouring rain, leaving the birds in the truck until we set up. The Activities Director bustled us into a hot, airless room dominated by a huge television. "My God," Rhiannon growled under her breath, stalking around the room. The Activities Director looked offended. "You'll have to turn that off," snapped Rhiannon. "The birds have extremely acute hearing — the television will frighten them. And *that* —" She was pointing to a bird cage near the window in which a number of canaries flittered around with high-pitched chirps. "That will need to be covered. These are birds of prey. They *eat* canaries."

I rolled my eyes at Rail and he grimaced. This wasn't starting well. And it got worse. Nursing assistants began wheeling the elderly residents into the room. To my astonishment, I saw Betsy Warren and behind her, shadow and cohort as always, was Cindy. Betsy's eyes got round when she saw us. "What're *youse* guys doing here?" she asked. The old woman in the wheelchair she was pushing moaned and bobbed her head, and Betsy immediately leaned over and wiped the spittle off her mouth. I was as startled by Betsy's gentleness as I was by the sight of her in the first place. "She don't hardly like comin' out of her room much, but she's real excited to see this," explained Betsy. "Ain't you, Missus Johnson?" She smoothed the old woman's hair and pushed the chair past Rail, eyeing us both with wary curiosity. Cindy was arranging a blanket over an old man in another chair, cringing and silent as always, sneaking looks at us from her pale eyes. She had an ugly bruise on one cheek, as if she'd been hit, but I couldn't imagine who would pick a fight with someone who couldn't say two words for herself.

Betsy finished settling Missus Johnson and came up to me again. "So you work here?" I asked her, stupidly. I couldn't think of anything else to say. Evidently she couldn't, either, and left the room. Rhiannon glanced at Rail and me. "Someone you know?" she asked as she strode past us toward the door.

"Oh . . . just from school. Not really —" I said quickly, embarrassed.

"She's my cousin," said Rail at the same time. I stared at him.

"You're kidding. *Betsy?*"

He shrugged. "I told you the Bogarts are related to everyone around here. Yeah. She's some kinda cousin."

The door shut sharply behind Rhiannon. "We better go with her," I said with trepidation. I hadn't liked the look on her face. I knew that Rhiannon was capable of a sort of reckless perversity and could easily cancel the whole event right then and there, whatever the consequences with Dr. Williams might be. She didn't care about anything but the birds.

She was fuming when we reached her out by the truck. "The birds are going to cook in that room! And what was that woman thinking of, with those silly canaries! These are wild raptors, not circus animals!"

"She didn't know," Rail said reasonably. "You just gotta tell her. The Activities lady is real nice, Rhiannon. She's one of my mom's . . . she used to be my mom's best friend."

"It's supposed to be an educational program," I added cautiously. Rhiannon glared at both of us.

Rail persisted. "You could just take the eagle in. He's from South Dakota. So he wouldn't mind the heat."

To my surprise, Rhiannon suddenly threw her

head back and laughed. "You two are wonderful," she said. "My students take everything I say so seriously. If I were with my interns, we'd probably be halfway back to the Center by now."

"I take you seriously," I protested.

Unexpectedly, she put her arm around my shoulders and hugged me. She felt so different from my mother. Strong and soft. No hard edges. I fit against Rhiannon's body perfectly. Then, self-conscious, I glanced over at Rail standing apart, looking off into the sky. Rhiannon saw him, too, and reached out for him with her other arm. And there we stood, three of us hugging in the pouring rain, and that's how Betsy Warren saw us when she stuck her head out the door.

"Youse guys coming?" she called. "We got everyone set up in there. They're all waiting."

I pulled sharply away from Rhiannon, flustered, and we carried the crates in one by one and set them on a long table in front of the elderly men and women. I had another surprise. Hulking in shapeless majesty behind the tiniest, most ancient-looking woman I'd ever seen was Bitsi in a flowery, tent-like dress. I mumbled something after Rail greeted her, and Bitsi pinned me with her ever-snooping eyes. "I told Ma I'd come in today, when I heard you was all mixed up in this," she announced with satisfaction. She leaned forward and shouted into the tiny woman's ear. "That there's Bobby Armstrong's girl — you remember Bobby, Ma? Gracie and Fred's nephew?"

The old woman had no teeth when she grinned. But her eyes were as bright as Bitsi's. "That boy who went to jail?" she shrilled at the top of her voice.

All around me, the old faces turned toward us. Betsy's eyes had gone very round again. I caught Rhiannon's look. There was a barely suppressed grin on her face. "Yes. That's my dad," I shouted right back at Bitsi's mother. "And I'm proud he did."

The tiny woman put out a hand so thin I thought the bones might poke through the onionskin-like flesh. She tapped my arm. "You don't need to shout so loud," she admonished peevishly. "I ain't *that* deaf. An' you sure as heck *better* be proud of yer daddy, young lady. The Bible says you gotta respect yer parents. And he done the right thing, besides. That war weren't no good fer nobody."

"My ma and me don't always see eye to eye," commented Bitsi in a stage whisper, leaning toward me.

"I heard you, Belinda," said the tiny woman smugly. "Don't think I didn't. I kin read yer lips, anyhow." She picked at my arm again. "You say hello to yer daddy fer me. Bobby Armstrong. Yup. He'll remember me. I sent him a Christmas card when he was in that jail. You see? My memory's sharp as a tack. I told him he done right. The only time the good Lord meant us to kill was if'n we was *hungry.*" She settled back in the wheelchair with the same self-satisfied expression I'd often seen on Bitsi's face. Except Ma Bitsi was so tiny she almost disappeared amid the blankets piled around her. From the pink and blue crocheted depths she added, "Like them birds there. They're the Lord's creatures, doin' what the Lord made it natural fer them to do."

Rhiannon was holding a goshawk on her leather glove by now, the tether draped over her wrist. The goshawk surveyed the room with savage red eyes. One of the canaries cheeped in its blanketed cage. Faster than a gasp, the goshawk swiveled her head toward the sound and half-crouched on the glove. The Activities Director blinked. Rhiannon smiled — a little wickedly, I thought. "This is a female Northern Goshawk," she began in a deceptively soft voice. "She's an accipiter, one of the most fierce and efficient hunters in the raptor family. She lives primarily in —"

"Them's the kind of birds kilt my chickens," said a bent, sinewy old man sitting propped among cushions on a couch with his cane held over his knees. He raised the cane like a shotgun and pointed it at the goshawk. The bird crouched again. "Used to shoot 'em," nodded the man.

"Please don't wave that around," snapped Rhiannon.

Ma Bitsi peered around the edge of her wheelchair

at the old man. "You'd get a nice fat fine fer that now, Duane MacGaw," she said contemptuously.

Rhiannon began again. "Over the last fifty years, many species of raptors have been added to the endangered list. They are protected by federal regulations . . ."

"Damn liberal government," spat the old man.

"Is *he* some relation of yours, too?" I whispered to Rail.

Rail grinned. "Dunno. Probably. Hope so. He's kinda cool."

Rhiannon carefully returned the goshawk to her crate and Rail helped her get the next one ready. Betsy sidled up to me and said, "Will you get the hawk lady to talk louder? Some of these old folks can't hear so good."

Somehow we muddled through a half-hour presentation. When Rhiannon took the big turkey vulture from his crate, Duane MacGaw thumped his cane on the floor and muttered, "Ugly ol' bald thing. Damn carrion eater."

"Humans are carrion eaters, too," I pointed out to him. "You eat meat you didn't kill yourself that's been sitting around for days, just like vultures."

Rhiannon snorted with laughter, started to say something, but tiny Ma Bitsi chimed in. "You're an ugly ol' bald thing yerself, Duane MacGaw," she stated. "But you're wrong about him eatin' meat, young lady. He don't have no teeth left to eat with, do you Duane?"

"No more'n you do, Shirley," the old man replied complacently.

By now, everyone who could hear was giggling, even the Activities Director. Bitsi leaned toward me again. "Don't pay them any attention. My ma's been like that with him since long as I can remember," she said in disgust.

Betsy reappeared next to me. "When's she gonna take the eagle out? Cindy really wants to see the eagle," she asked.

"Soon, I guess," I said. I looked over at Cindy, who sat in a corner holding the hand of a woman who slept with her mouth wide open. Cindy's other hand covered her bruise. "What's wrong with her?" I asked. "It looks like someone punched her."

Betsy chewed her ragged fingernails and glanced with furtive worry at Cindy. Suddenly she blurted in a low voice, "Someone did. Her stepdad. I thought he stopped, but she come in this morning lookin' like that . . . he musta started again . . ." She clapped her mouth shut, then mumbled, "Don't you dare say nothin'."

"But you *have* to say something!" I said, incensed. "You can't know about something like that and not *do* anything! Report it to the police. Can't you call Junior Fenstemacher or something?"

"Junior *is* her stepdad," hissed Betsy, looking desperately as if she'd wished she'd never said a word. For a moment, wordless, we stared at each other.

"Taylor. You helping?" Rhiannon spoke and I half-jumped away from Betsy. Rhiannon reached in for the golden eagle, the star of the show. When she brought him out on her wrist, the old people stirred. Even Duane MacGaw seemed properly in awe. Sunlight poured in through the rain-streaked windows and shimmered like watered silk over the bronze feathers. Rhiannon stretched out the eagle's left wing to show that only half of it was there.

"Sometimes, even though a wound can heal, the damage is so severe you can never fly again," said Rhiannon, speaking to the eagle and laying her head briefly against the crest of his wild head.

In the silence that followed, Rhiannon took the bird around the room. Although she'd said he wasn't tame, he was calm and obviously used to people. But the most amazing thing happened when she came to Duane MacGaw. The old farmer put out a hand bent as a claw and ran it down the glossy feathers on the eagle's wing. "You just got arthritis like me," he said, almost gently. "It can happen to the best of us."

I could barely speak on the way back to the Center. Even Rhiannon was subdued. The road reflected the sky where the potholes were filled with water and she avoided each one with an almost grim concentration. Only Rail seemed cheerful. "I think it went real good," he said.

For me, everything had turned upside down. Hunter's Gap was full of people who were not what I'd thought them to be. Bitsi had had a son and still had an old mother she didn't get along with. Once Bitsi had been my age, and people had called her Belinda, and what had she dreamed for herself then? I thought about Betsy Warren, smoothing away an old woman's spittle and grieving over her frightened friend. And Junior Fenstemacher, first citizen and moral watchdog of Hunter's Gap, with hands the size of hams. And old Duane MacGaw, whose chicken farm was now home to the birds he'd once killed, and who found in a wounded eagle something he could connect with —

I sat between Rhiannon and Rail. By now, it would be difficult to compile all the facts I knew about them both. But each fact, as I thought it, seemed to drift down like a single feather fallen from a flying falcon. I could pick the feather up, I could hold it in my hand, but the falcon was farther away than before. No matter how many feathers I found, it was not the bird. Only the flight was the bird. And flight was not a thing you could hold in your hand.

13

My father stood in the doorway of the kitchen. "Junior can't haul my stone next week," he announced. "Something's come up. He said he could take me up this evening, though. We would get the block tomorrow and I'd be back tomorrow night."

My mother continued to wash the dishes. My father came up behind her. He didn't touch her, but stood breath-close and still. I shoved my chair back noisily. "Marble stone or granite?" I asked, pushing into their silence.

My father bent his head and laid his mouth against my mother's neck. "Marble," he said, caressing the word along her skin. "Marble lasts forever. Unlike our fragile, momentary lives . . ." He finished his words with an embrace, wrapping himself around my mother so she was engulfed. "I didn't say I'd go," he murmured. "Tomorrow's the last day before you leave, Annie."

My mother pulled out of his arms. "Tell him you'll go, Bob. How will you work without your stone?"

When Junior arrived, I looked at his huge hands and the pillow of a belly that hung over his belt, and edged away from him. "You ain't comin' up with your daddy this time?" he asked me in his usual jocular manner.

"I'm busy," I said.

My mother and I followed my father out of the house. "Let's haul rocks," grinned my father, clapping Junior on the shoulder and throwing his overnight bag in the cab of the flat-bed truck.

Junior nodded to my mother and winked at me, thrusting his florid, sweaty face close. "Don't you let that hawk lady work you too hard," he warned, his smile more like a leer. "Ain't good fer a girl, being too much around a woman like that."

I didn't answer. My father pulled me into a bear hug. "Keep your mother company, okay, Missy? She needs to relax. Don't let her work. Promise me? Do something fun together." I nodded, feeling his eyes locked with my mother's over my shoulder. "See you tomorrow night, Annie," he said softly.

Later, as we sat together on the steps in the gathering summer dusk, my mother asked, "Who was Junior talking about?"

"Rhia — Dr. Jeffries," I said reluctantly.

My mother was quiet awhile, gazing at the fire-flies that danced over the weeds in the garden. The darkness was a perfect setting for her. She perched in it like a small, watchful owl, listening for the rustlings of what she could not see. "I hardly feel part of this place," she mused at last.

Because you're never here, I thought, and looked away guiltily.

"Oh, Melissa," murmured my mother. "The whole world is about to open up for you. It's wonderful. You'll love Porter Phelps. It'll almost be like going again, for me, to have you there —"

I felt like a traitor. She looked so tentative, next to me on the step. As if at any moment she might lift up and glide away on tiny, silent wings into the night. "Mom, did you ever have something . . . something you wanted more than anything for a really long time . . . and then, you *didn't* want it? And you didn't know why?"

"No," she said. "I've always wanted what I wanted. Why?"

We sat for a long time, quiet. We were like the two bright stars that shone over the barn roof. They looked only an inch apart. But they must have been light-years in distance from each other.

I woke early and lay in bed, trying to think of something my mother and I could do together. All I could think of was the Center. I hugged my pillow. My tailored, self-contained mother . . . meeting the vital, expansive, and completely unpredictable Rhiannon? No. I didn't want to see the contrast.

The phone rang. "Taylor. You gotta come over right now," Rail cried. "Rhiannon wants to take the red-tail into the field today. She said she's been flying the length of her cage all week, so she's ready. She said —"

"I can't," I said.

"But Taylor —"

"I can't," I repeated, sharply. I glanced at my mother. She had her laptop open on the kitchen table, but she looked up and caught my eye. "I have to go," I muttered into the phone.

My mother was signaling. I put my hand over the mouthpiece. "Melissa, if there's something you want to do, go ahead," she told me. "I have a lot of work to get done."

"But Dad made me promise not to let you work."

She waved my protest away. "To tell the truth," she admitted, "I'm glad your father isn't here to play watchdog today."

I made the mistake of looking back before I turned my bike out onto the road. My mother was standing in front of the empty house, watching me go.

Later, I sat wedged next to Rail in the back of Rhiannon's truck on the way up through the fields behind the Center. Whenever the truck lurched, I was thrown hard against Rail. I shoved myself tighter into the corner. After a few minutes, Rail asked, "You pissed off or something, Taylor? You haven't said hardly a word since you got here."

"I'm just thinking," I said.

He stared off into the sky. But this time, I saw a thin white trail across the blue. "Hey, look at that," breathed Rail, craning his neck to follow the trail. "An F-16! Man!" He turned to me, eyes bright. "A Fighting Falcon! Must be good luck!"

"I thought you didn't care about the Air Force anymore," I said.

He sat back and studied his hands. "I dunno. I'd probably get stuck on a base in New Jersey or something. I probably wouldn't go anyplace."

He looked so dejected that I said, "It's not like the Air Force is the only way to go somewhere. I mean, look at Rhiannon. She's been all over the world —"

"Naw, it's not the same," Rail said passionately. "I want to *go* somewhere. I'm not just running away."

I scowled. "What do you mean, running away?"

He met my eyes squarely. "There's a difference. You can tell. Sometimes people *go* someplace, and sometimes they just run away. I seen it happen."

Rhiannon veered off the dirt track and parked by an open field. She and Rail carried the crate with the red-tailed hawk to the middle of the field and set it by a pole with a perch about six feet off the ground.

186

Rhiannon knelt next to the crate and Rail came back to the truck, fiddling with something in his hands. The July heat had broken and the morning was sweet and cool. A breeze stirring in the evergreens that surrounded the field lifted Rhiannon's long hair so the dark strands seemed to weave with the whispering grasses and the light played over her face. I could not imagine someone so beautiful and strong running from anything.

Rail came up beside me. "We have to wait a few minutes, to let the hawk settle down a little," he said. He was tying one of the thawed white mice onto a piece of leather that looked like a big cat toy. "It's a lure," he explained. "We didn't feed her yesterday, so maybe she'll be hungry enough to fly."

"I thought she'd want to fly."

"Naw. It's scary for her, just like it'd be for us to step off into the air. The cage has been kinda like a nest — she hardly knows what to do with all this space around her," said Rail, handing me the lure. "Here. Rhiannon said you should do it."

I took it gingerly. After Rail explained what to do, I walked across the field and dropped the lure ten feet from the post, playing out the long cord attached to it as I continued on toward the edge of the woods. I crouched under the trees and watched Rhiannon open the crate and set the red-tailed hawk up on the post. My hand tightened on the cord. Rhiannon stepped back and made a gesture to me. I jerked the cord.

Nothing happened. The hawk sat hunched and ruffled, turning her head in agitation back and forth to survey the unfamiliar openness around her. I tweaked the cord again. The hawk shook herself, lifted her tail, shot out a white stream, then settled back on the perch in sleeker form. This time, when the lure jumped in the grass, she swiveled her head sharply toward the movement. I pulled again.

She struck so fast I gasped. A streak of brown, and the impact almost tore the cord from my hand. But she must have come down too hard because, with a wild flurry of wings, she tumbled off the lure and flipped on her back. She scrambled up, beak wide open, and I jerked the cord again. The lure bounced away. With a sharp cry, the hawk flapped unevenly into the air, the tether on her leg snaking out behind her. With an ungainly pounce, she pinned the lure securely under her talons. She spread her wings out, lowered her head, and tore at the mouse. The cord shivered in my hand with each twist of her head and she screamed when Rhiannon walked up.

Rhiannon allowed her only a few mouthfuls before capturing the hawk and placing her again on the perch. "Make her work a bit harder this time," she called over to me. I dropped the lure farther from the perch and pulled the cord in violently, so the lure bounced along the ground. The hawk lifted perfectly and came toward me in a low, graceful swoop, crying her wild hunting call. When she plummeted toward the lure, I didn't have time to step back. She hit, skidding three feet from me, talons spread. The force of her impact burned the cord across my fingers. She thrust her open beak at me, glaring ferociously, her outstretched wings covering the lure. I couldn't move, as if she had pinned me, too. Without taking her eyes from me, she tore the mouse away with one swipe, gulping half of it.

It seemed as though I crouched there forever, within touching distance of the red-tailed hawk. Bright specks of blood beaded her curved beak. I heard the soft rip as she tore at the mouse. The mottled feathers on her breast rose and fell with the beat of her heart.

Rhiannon allowed the hawk to eat the mouse before throwing the blanket over her and picking her up again. The tether attached to her leg was tangled slightly and one broad brown-banded feather drifted to the ground. I held it on the palm of my hand. "It'll grow back," Rhiannon said. "But she'll have a gap in her tail until her first molt next year."

"Why can't we just let her go now?" I asked.

We were walking so close together our shoulders touched. Rhiannon shook her head. "She's still too young. She needs a lot more practice flying and several more lessons in hunting. You saw how she bounced around out there. But she's big — she might be ready near the end of the summer . . . still, it'll be better to release her closer to the fall migrations."

"Where will she go then? Will she ever come back?" I felt the loss already, the touch of it feather-light in my heart. I brushed the still-warm tail feather across my cheek.

Rhiannon knelt to put the hawk in the crate, and I knelt beside her. "Anywhere. She could go any-where. Maybe no farther than New York — maybe as far south as Texas or Mexico," she said. "If she survives, she'll be back . . . but we won't know where. Once we let her go, she's a wild creature. You won't see her again."

"Like the white falcon —"

My words came unbidden. The impact of her eyes on mine was as sudden as the hawk striking the lure. I was pinned under the intensity of her look. "What white falcon?" she demanded.

"The one . . . in that photograph. I asked you about it before."

She relaxed slightly. "Oh. Yes. The gyrfalcon."

"It's you, isn't it? In the picture?" We were half-hidden in the nest of long grass, and the summer field murmured around us. Her eyes never left mine. I could dare to ask.

"Yes," she answered. "A long time ago. In Scot-land." In the crate the hawk rustled and thumped

around restlessly. I still dared. "Who's the other photograph? The little girl?"

She gave me a wary, biting scowl. "You really *are* a
nosy little reporter, aren't you?"

Tears burned my eyes. I looked down at the grass
I was braiding, but my fingers fumbled and the
grass tore. After a moment, Rhiannon reached out
and took both my hands between hers.

"I wasn't trying to be a reporter —" I whispered.

"I know."

"I just want . . . to know you," I mumbled.

Rail was coming toward us across the field. Rhiannon pressed my hands once and let me go. "The little girl was my daughter. Ninian. She died thirteen
years ago," she said quietly, standing up.

I lagged several steps behind as they carried the
crate between them to the truck. *Ninian.* The name
seemed to hum between us, an invisible tether that
bound Rhiannon's sorrow to a longing that rose up
in me so powerfully I felt its ache through my whole
body. I drew the brown feather across my face, the
touch of it as soft as the touch of Rhiannon's hands.

In the back of the truck on the way to the Center,
Rail said enthusiastically, "Didn't she do great, Taylor!"

"What?"

He contemplated me. "The *hawk*," he said, with
extreme patience.

"You wouldn't even know her wing had been broken," I replied. Rail's hands lay on his knees, sun-browned except for a few pink lines of healed scratches. I remembered how those hands had appeared in the circle of light over the workbench the day we'd brought the baby bird to the hawk lady. "You fixed her, Rail," I said. "Just like you said you would."

He flushed. "I don't know who fixed who," he muttered, but he smiled at me through his embarrassment.

Rhiannon had to go to Alton, so she offered to drive us both home. Before she dropped us off, she pulled in at Bitsi's Gas and Lunch. "Let's celebrate a successful maiden flight," she grinned. "We'll charge it to the university. All those tax dollars can go for a candy bar or two. Get whatever you want," she said merrily as we went through the door. "But don't tell Bitsi about it," she added in a stage whisper.

"Don't tell Bitsi *what*," demanded that personage herself from her throne by the door. She appraised Rhiannon suspiciously. "I heard you was bringing them birds to the church camp next," she said.

Rhiannon raised her eyebrows. "I have such a busy schedule, I can't keep my engagements straight," she said. "Ask my social secretary."

"Yeah," I told Bitsi. "Are you going to be at the church camp, too?"

"I'm everywhere, young lady. Junior Fenstemacher has nothing on me." I thought she almost smiled and just in case, I smiled back. But at that moment, the door opened and Betsy Warren came in, followed by Kevin, whose last name I could never remember, and Rail's unacknowledged cousin, Al Schumman.

To be fair, if it had just been Betsy herself, everything would have been all right. She gave me that prissy little wave that I now knew was meant to be friendly. But she was trying to impress Kevin, as usual. "Hi, Missy," she said. Rail came down the aisle toward me with a handful of candy bars.

"Hey, Bets," he said. Then, to me, he asked, "You like this kind? You pick anything out?"

Kevin gave a sneer meant for the benefit of Betsy. "Hey, Rail 'n' Missy. Bets said she saw youse at the nursing home," he said. "So — you guys going out now? Told you they were —" He turned to Betsy, who giggled.

"Lay off," said Rail.

My face was burning. Rhiannon was watching us. Kevin shoved past me so I was jostled hard against Rail, who put a hand on my arm to steady me. "You okay, Taylor?" Rail asked, narrowing his eyes at Kevin.

"Hey! No necking in Bitsi's store, you guys. Right, Bitsi?" Kevin, said, loud enough for all of Hunter's Gap to hear. I yanked free of Rail's hand. "Let *go* of me!" I hissed at him. For a horrible moment, I caught Rhiannon's eye. Betsy piped up, "Oh, Kevin, don't be such an idiot! Missy, Kevin don't mean —"

"Just shut *up*!" I snarled. I spun around, pushing Rail away, and slammed out the door.

The worst of it was that Rail didn't say anything when he got into the truck. Even when Rhiannon dropped him at the end of the dirt road, he only grunted, "'Bye, Rhiannon. Thanks. See you, Taylor." He jumped down and started walking, his hands in the pockets of his camouflage pants.

I laid my head on my arm in the window. Rhiannon reached over and stuck a cassette into the tape deck. The truck was filled with loud music. "Jimi Hendrix," she announced, thumping the steering wheel in time to the beat. After a moment, she thrust an old shirt at me. "Here," she said. "Wrapped a Cooper's hawk in it the other day, but it's mostly clean." She raised her eyebrows. "Music too much for you? Had this tape forever — thirty years. Damn. I'm *old*."

"You're not old," I gulped, wiping my nose on the shirt. Through the noise, I could feel Rhiannon waiting. Not the way my mother waited for private information you might let slip by accident, but just waiting in case I needed anything. "He'll hate me forever," I whispered.

She switched off the tape immediately. "I don't

think so," she said. "You'd have to do something pretty awful to lose his friendship."

"It *was* awful," I said. She didn't say anything. I scrubbed my nose savagely. "It's better if I'm alone," I burst out. "I've never had friends. People like me don't have friends."

"Nonsense," said Rhiannon, pulling into the bottom of our driveway and stopping. "Rail's your friend."

I hesitated. "It's just that . . . well, he's not the kind of friend I thought I would have."

"What kind of friend did you think you should have?" She'd pinned me again with her gray eyes, and even through the awful, sick shame, I didn't want to drop my eyes from hers. "We don't get to choose people very often, Taylor," continued Rhiannon. "People come into our lives as they are — that's about it. And we certainly don't get to pick the people we love. It just *happens* to us." She glanced up toward the house. My father's Chevy was parked in front of the barn. I couldn't see my mother's car. Rhiannon turned away and said, "We can't force love to happen when we want it, and we can't stop it from happening when we don't want it. But when it does happen, no matter who it is, it's the most precious gift we ever get in this life. Don't turn it away."

I didn't want her to drive me up to the house. Before I got out, she took my hand briefly and said, "Rail's not your only friend. I'm your friend, too."

I wished I could throw myself against her. I wished she could hug me forever. But I could only nod, still sniffing, and she drove off. I went slowly to the house. It was empty. My mother was not home. But I could hear the radio in the studio. My father had come back early from Vermont.

I whacked the weed-tops in the neglected garden with a stick as I went down the path. Suddenly I wanted my father's comfort more than anything in the world. He understood everything, even when I could not explain. And I couldn't explain anything ... neither the short, intense conversations with Rhiannon that never seemed quite complete, nor how unsure I was of my feelings for Rail. I pushed open the door of the studio.

My father was whacking at a stone harder than I'd whacked at the weeds. Sparks flew from his chisel. After a few minutes he put down his mallet and pushed up his goggles. "You promised me you'd stay here with Mom," he said abruptly without greeting me. I stared at him. He waved his hand toward the house. "She left a note. Her work's lying around all over the place. She said you were at Rhiannon's and she was doing some errands."

"She said I could go —"

"Of *course* she said you could," said my father coldly. "But since she's leaving tomorrow for almost a month, I thought you might, just for once, manage to get along with her."

"But I wasn't . . . we *were* getting along!" I cried, shocked. I searched his face with disbelief. But he had shut himself away from me. "Is she coming home?" I whispered.

He looked at me strangely. "She'll be back for dinner." He picked up the mallet again, then put it down. "Were you at Rhiannon's all day?"

"Yes, but —"

"Missy, I really needed you to stay here with your mother today. I wouldn't have gone to Vermont otherwise." He sighed and sat down on a stool, holding out his hand to me. I didn't move. "Look, Missy. I understand what it's like to want to be around someone you admire so much. Rhiannon is an amazing woman. I remember what it's like to have a crush —"

"What are you talking about!" I screamed. In a rage, I slammed out the door, then spun around and yanked it open again. "You just feel guilty because *you* didn't stay here with Mom!" I spat. "And I'm not the one in love with Rhiannon. *You* are!" I ran out of the barn, but not fast enough to miss seeing my father's stunned face.

14

I WAS LOSING EVERYONE. Rail. My father. And now my mother. She was beginning to make the break. She'd be back from Europe only two weeks before I had to go off to Porter Phelps ... enough time to pack the few things she had in the house and get me ready for school. After that, she'd never be back. As we waited in the airport lounge for her flight, my father was clutching her so tightly against him that I was sure he knew it, too.

My mother kept smoothing her clothes. "How do I look?" she asked for the second time. Her tailored suit was as drab as the linoleum in the airport bathroom. When her flight was called, she barely said goodbye to me. My father watched her until she disappeared down the ramp. She turned at the last moment and their eyes met. But I'd already lost her.

For the next couple of days, it rained. The leaf-choked gutters my father was always promising to clean spouted waterfalls down the sides of the house. I spent hours in my airless room, reading listlessly on my bed, which I never made and which got grayer and more disheveled every day. I hardly saw my father. Sometimes he roared out in the Chevy and was gone for hours. He'd return with no explanation and barely a greeting, shove a bag of soggy hoagies in the fridge for me, and disappear into the studio. On the third day, the phone rang.

"Taylor, where the hell are you?" demanded Rhiannon.

"I'm . . . I didn't —"

She said bluntly, "You have a job to do. I was counting on you." She paused. "You just disappeared."

Her voice changed with her last words, and there was something in it that both drew me and frightened me. "I'm coming right now," I said.

By the time I pushed my bike up to the Center, I was dripping wet and Rhiannon met me at the door with a towel. "I would have driven over to pick you up," she said. "You didn't give me a chance." She gave me a T-shirt to change into. It was unwashed and it smelled of her — of grass, wind, and blood, and of something undefinable, familiar, as if I had put on some memory of hers. "Almost fits," I said, and when she smiled, the sadness filled me like hunger. I followed her around all morning.

Before lunch, I helped her repair the loose wire mesh on one of the enclosures. I was doing what would have been Rail's job, and right at that moment, I fiercely wished him to stay away forever. I held the wire against the post and Rhiannon reached above me to tack it on. Her body was warm against me. She did not poke me with her elbow or step on my foot the way my mother would have.

"I miss my mom," I said in a low voice.

"I keep forgetting about your mother. I've never met her," Rhiannon said softly, and let me lean against her.

"She's never home," I said.

She made a pile of cheese sandwiches for lunch. "I didn't know you were a vegetarian," I said happily, my mouth full.

"Ridiculous, isn't it? For a falconer?" she mused. She was looking out the kitchen window, her back to me. But in a moment she turned, brushed my hair lightly with her hand as she went by, and said, "Go put your writing skills to some use, and get working on my story." Her voice sounded like a door closing.

As I sat at her desk in front of the computer, I saw the photograph of the little girl. It had been propped against a pile of books facing the window, as if to give those dark, watchful eyes a view of the open sky. Ninian. Long ago, Rhiannon had held this little girl in her arms, played with her, laughed and danced with her. . . . Quickly, without thinking, I turned the photo facedown. Rain streaked the window and I shivered. Turning to the computer, I began to transcribe the notes I'd made from my reading. The development of raptor centers in the United States. The role of raptors in the environment. The effects of farming on raptor populations. Raptor rehabilitation programs in Canada, Russia, Scotland, developed by Dr. Rhiannon Jeffries. . . .

I stared at the computer screen so hard my eyes blurred. I blinked, turned my head away — and then I was on my hill, the hawk calling above me, my hair blowing across my face. I picked up my pen and began to write, the notebook a familiar weight on my lap, my pen flying along effortlessly. In the words I wrote, all the things I didn't understand began to make sense. There were no facts. There was only the mystery and lure of sorrow, of joy, of all the hawk lady made me feel. Each word drove its truth through me with the certainty of the hawk's strike.

The phone rang. It was Rail. "Hey, Taylor. Didn't think you'd be there. You working on the story?"

"Sort of," I managed to say.

"That's great —" He paused. "Will you tell Rhiannon I can't come over 'til tomorrow?"

After I hung up, I sat for a long time. The notebook

201

now felt like dead weight. I looked at what I'd written, pages and pages, and swallowed. Nothing. It was useless. I couldn't do the one, simple thing Rhiannon needed from me. It eluded me as surely as Rhiannon herself. I closed the notebook and went out into the rain.

"Was that Rail?" Rhiannon called across the yard. "Is he coming? I thought he'd be here by now."

She came up to me as she spoke. I shook my head and looked at the ground miserably. "What is it?" Rhiannon asked.

"It's just . . . he was so nice —"

"And?"

"Why do I feel so angry at him?"

She laughed a little. "Because he *was* so nice. After you treated him badly."

I muttered, "That doesn't make any sense."

She snorted and strode toward the shed, pushing the damp hair out of her face. "Since when does human nature make sense? That's the trouble with reporters — they try to make sense of why people do things. They spend their lives chasing their tails." She went into the shed and I followed.

In the dim stillness, with the cages full of resting birds around us, I whispered, "I just like him so much —"

Rhiannon turned around to face me. "*There's* your sense," she said, almost fiercely. "That's the only sense you'll find in anything."

I couldn't tell her I didn't want to go home. I couldn't tell her how the empty house would suck out little bits of me until I felt just as hollow and empty inside, or how the sound of my father's radio in the studio made me want to whimper with loneliness. Finally, after a supper of more cheese sandwiches, Rhiannon leaned back in her chair and studied me for several minutes. But she didn't ask me anything, in the end. She just said, "You better get home, Taylor. If it's clear tomorrow, come early. We'll give your hawk another hunting lesson."

I suppose I slept. I woke before dawn, my sheets sour and damp with the white morning mist. I lay listening to the steady drip-drip from the trees. After a while, I heard the kitchen door open downstairs and the sounds of my father rustling around. I lay stiffly until he left the house, and felt there was nowhere in the world I could feel comfortable other than with Rhiannon.

When I arrived at the Center, mist was still pooled in the hollows of the hills but the sun was clearing the air of the last moisture. Rail's bike was on the ground near the shed and I paused, but before I could decide what to do, he came out of the house. As if nothing had happened between us, he called in excitement, "Hey, Taylor. Guess what! We're gonna fly the hawk with a live lure. We gotta —"

"A live lure? You mean — *alive?* So she can kill it?" I was so taken aback I forgot my uneasiness.

"Man, Taylor," said Rail with exaggerated patience. "What do you think hawks *do?* She's been pouncing on the meat we feed her in the cage for days — haven't you seen her? She won't survive if she don't learn to hunt and kill. She's sure ready to learn."

I followed him into the shed, feeling stupid and apprehensive. Those pathetic little lab mice were going to be killed anyway, I thought, and —

"What's that?" I demanded, staring at a wire crate on the floor.

"That's the rabbit. I trapped it yesterday," said Rail.

I refused to sit with Rail in the back of the truck, where I would have to see the rabbit who crouched exposed and motionless in the crate. At the last minute, as Rhiannon was coming out of the house, my father arrived. He barely looked at me.

"Thought you'd changed your mind," Rhiannon commented shortly, climbing into the cab.

My father slid in next to her. "Lost track of the time," he mumbled. "Worked all night. But I want drawings of a hawk hunting —"

I sat tensely next to them. They didn't speak again, but in the restive silence between them, I felt the presence of unspoken things. They did not pay much attention to each other, but I was sure that if I hadn't been there, they would have talked. I wedged myself tighter against the door. Once, Rhiannon glanced at me across my father, started to say something, but caught his eye and stopped. I looked away.

In the field, Rhiannon set the hawk up on the perch. The morning sun gleamed on her feathers. There was nothing ungainly or uncertain about her today. Her wide, wild eyes seemed to flash with a tense anticipation, as if she could sense that something about this was different from all the other times she'd stood on the perch. Despite myself, I felt a current of the same excitement run through me. My father propped his drawing board on the hood of the truck. I sat on the ground with my back to him.

The red-tailed hawk faced in my direction. Rhiannon stepped back. The sun, just rising above the trees beyond, lit them from behind. Rhiannon raised her arm in a signal to Rail and at the same instant, the hawk rose into the air. Each outspread feather shone translucent in the new light. She appeared to be rising from Rhiannon's arm. With her shrill hunting cry, the hawk swooped low over the grass, her shadow racing along a golden shaft of sun.

The released rabbit darted across the field, then froze against the ground when the hawk's shadow passed over. But the hawk screamed again and the rabbit leaped forward, twisting its elongated body through the grass in an evasive effort. Legs extended, talons spread wide, the hawk struck.

She didn't kill it. The hawk clamped the rabbit's hindquarters in her talons and they tumbled together through the grass. For a moment all I could see was the grass thrashing in a brown blur. A shrill wailing filled the air. I thrust my fists over my ears but I could not close my eyes. Then the rabbit broke free, still wailing, and with a sick, lurching motion tried to escape. Straight toward me it ran, hindquarters dragging, and I clearly saw the white-rimmed eyes and open mouth before the hawk plunged again.

She was so close I heard the thud of her impact, the rasp of feathers and the snap as the rabbit's neck broke. The hawk mantled her kill, thrust her head out and screamed. Once again I was staring into her eyes. Her wild challenge sliced through me as surely as her beak went through the flesh of the rabbit. I clutched the grass as if my fingers were talons.

When Rhiannon approached, the hawk screeched and lunged, but the leg-tether prevented her from flying away. Rhiannon dropped the blanket over her, Rail came running with the crate, but even after the hawk was inside, I couldn't move. Right in front of me, Rail scraped the bloody remains of the rabbit into a clear plastic bag.

"Man, a couple more kills like this an' she'll be an *expert*! Taylor — wasn't she amazing?" he exclaimed.

I was afraid if I moved I would vomit. Rail squatted next to me, the plastic bag dangling a few inches away. "You okay, Taylor?" he asked, concerned.

"Get *away* from me!" I croaked. Rail stumbled back and gave me a look that cut right through my heart. I managed to get into the truck and sat there while Rhiannon and Rail loaded the crate and equipment. But only my father and Rhiannon got in with me. Rail walked off down the track by himself, hands in his pockets. I refused to look at him when we drove past. My father glanced in the rear-view mirror. "Kind of a long walk," he remarked.

"He'll be all right," said Rhiannon.

I stared stonily out at the fields and woods as we bumped down toward the Center. I wished fiercely that I'd never rescued the baby hawk — that I'd left her where I found her, to let nature take its course. Reporters weren't supposed to get involved. And this was why. The lightning that struck that huge white tree might as well have struck me. I felt as much an orphan as the hawk.

"I always thought the human world was so *flawed*," Rhiannon was saying to my father. "I believed only the natural world was perfect. I wanted it to be perfect. Even the killing."

My father drove over the ruts, his eyes more on Rhiannon than the track. " 'These hunt, as they have done, But with claws and teeth grown perfect,' " he replied softly.

"I know that poem, too," she said, smiling. Then she sighed. "It took me a long time to accept that there aren't two separate worlds — the natural and the human. And animals make mistakes, too. They have to learn, just as we do. They can make a real mess of things —" She paused. Her voice dropped. "The only difference is, that little hawk will learn a lot faster from her mistakes than I ever learned from mine —"

Once again, I felt the tug of an inexplicable longing, as if something behind her words was trying to find its shape within me. I shook the feeling off. "What about the rabbit!" I demanded. "What mistake did *it* make? It didn't even have a chance! Not like in the wild —"

"In the wild, your little hawk would have been long dead by now," snapped Rhiannon impatiently. "You chose to interfere. You can't step back now and make judgments. Your life and hers are entwined. If you want her to survive, it has to be on *her* terms. You can't be squeamish. You accepted those terms when you rescued her."

I refused to answer and did not look at her. Somewhere behind us, Rail was walking alone. I'd interfered in his life, too, ever since the day we'd met by accident. "Stop the truck, Dad. I want to get out," I said. My father braked without question and got out to open the door for me. For a moment, he drew me wordlessly against him, holding me tight. His arms trembled. "I'll be back," I whispered.

I saw Rail first. When he caught sight of me he stopped, hesitated, then continued walking toward me. "Hey," he said when I reached him.

We walked side by side for a few minutes. Every time I thought I knew what I wanted to say, my throat clamped up like a trap, catching my words. Finally I choked out, "I don't know why I said all those horrible things to you. I didn't mean to."

"Yes, you did," Rail said bluntly. "You're embarrassed by me."

"I am not!" I cried.

He stopped, glaring at me stubbornly. "Yes you are, Taylor. I'm sick of it. You think I'm just an ignorant redneck, like you think about everyone else in Hunter's Gap. Well, maybe I am." He paused, then started walking again. Without looking back, he added, "I'm really *glad* you're leaving to go to that fancy school."

"I *hate* that school! I don't *want* to go!" I screamed after him. I stood on the track, unable to follow. After a moment, he turned and came back. His eyes had become dark and unreadable and he walked up to stand very close to me.

"I don't know what it feels like to be a redneck, Taylor. I only know what it feels like to be *me*. I wish you could just . . . see *me*," he said.

He was so close I wondered if he could hear my heart thudding. I whispered, "I do. I do see you. I mean, maybe I didn't . . . before, but —" I looked at him desperately. "I'm really sorry, Rail. Because I really . . . I like you a lot."

Maybe it was an accident that my hand brushed his. We were standing so close. But it wasn't an accident when he took my hand and held it. "Man, Taylor," Rail said. "I like you, too. I like you a whole lot."

209

He didn't drop my hand as we walked. I didn't know where to look — at him, or at the ground, or at the fields. My heart was stuck high in my throat and it was hard to breathe evenly. But Rail kept talking calmly. "The first time I shot a deer, I only wounded him," he told me. "It was awful. I was twelve. My dad made me track him 'til I got him. I didn't want to. I couldn't stand to see what I'd done. But my dad said you couldn't ever abandon something you'd hurt, 'cause it would stay with you forever."

I was getting my breath back and getting used to the warmth of Rail's hand. He gave me one of his inscrutable looks. "Anyway, I never wounded anything since. I practiced and practiced, on tin cans and things, 'til I could shoot perfect." He smiled. "See, that's what the red-tail's gonna do. I bet she won't make the same mistake twice."

We were in sight of the Center now. The blue university van was pulled up by the barn and Rhiannon's students were working around the enclosures. I pulled my hand from Rail's. But he seemed to understand. He just said, "I'm real glad you came back to find me, Taylor."

By the time we reached the yard, the heat had cooled from my face. I was even able to say, in a halfway normal voice, "I'm glad I found you, too." Like the red-tailed hawk, I wasn't going to make the same mistake twice.

15

I WAS EXHAUSTED. I fell asleep early, and was wakened in the morning by my father sitting on the edge of my bed with a cup of coffee, a plate of donuts, and the newspaper. "You used to do this for Mom," I smiled, sitting up groggily and slurping the coffee.

"Your mother wouldn't stoop to eating donuts," my father replied. "Only croissants for her."

Suddenly I was crying, cuddling up under his arm the way I had as a little girl. "I'm sorry, Dad. I'm sorry," I sniffed.

He leaned his head against mine. "You aren't the one who needs to apologize, Missy," he said. He rubbed his chin on my hair and continued in a low voice, "I know what things look like to you right now. I wish . . . I wish you wouldn't worry so much.

I know it's hard to understand, but facts don't always add up to the truth."

"What *is* the truth?" I asked, muffled in the darkness under his arm.

He held me away from him so he could look into my eyes. "The truth is," he said quietly, "the truth is, I love your mother very much. Absolutely. Okay?"

I fingered the sheet. "What about Rhiannon?" I persisted.

"Rhiannon and I are good friends. Like you and Rail."

My father shifted to get more comfortable and the plate of donuts upset, rolling sugar over my dingy sheets. One bounced across the floor. My father caught it, inspected it, then took a huge bite of it.

"Yuk," I growled.

He grinned a powdery grin. "We really have to do something about this gourmet diet of ours," he said, wiping his hands on my sheets. "We'll get spoiled. Why not rough it for a while, and cook?"

"I hate cooking. So do you."

"Ah — but have you ever cooked for someone else? An appreciative appetite? Someone who will thank you not only for your culinary creation but for the effort you put into it?"

I giggled. "Yeah, right. Who? You? Is this your way of conning me into cooking for you?"

My father stood up and brushed the powdered sugar off his jeans. "Actually, I was thinking of Rhiannon," he mumbled. He gave me a sheepish smile. "Well, why not? What's wrong with that? She's our neighbor. She's a friend. She's getting pretty stressed about what might happen to the Center. Read today's paper . . . She could use a night out."

"We're not exactly what I would call a night out," I commented.

"You could invite Rail —" began my father reluctantly.

"No," I said quickly. He looked at me and I dropped my eyes. We wanted Rhiannon all to ourselves. Unsettled, I read the editorial headline in the paper my father had folded open. "Are Senator Vinci's Environmental Enthusiasms Misplaced?" I bit my lip. "Do you think the university will close the Center down? Would Rhiannon leave?" I asked.

My father gazed out the window over my desk into the morning sun. "Rhiannon?" he said at last. "Sure. She could leave. At any minute."

"You mean — even if the Center stays open?"

He shrugged. "Sure."

"But why?"

"She's a leaver. I don't think she stays anywhere for long," said my father. He picked up my empty coffee cup and the plate of donuts and left.

I dressed slowly, staring at the newspaper editorial.

Senator Tom Vinci, who is up for reelection this fall, pours so much of his energy and political clout into developing state-funded environmental programs that some people are beginning to question his priorities. In Pennsylvania's rural areas, where a growing unemployment crisis is draining large amounts from the state's limited welfare budget, some citizens are voicing complaints about how their tax dollars are being spent. "The state should be funding employment programs, not saving wild animals. We need jobs. *Work* is the endangered species around here," said one disgruntled resident in the tiny township of Hunter's Gap . . .

I sat down and reread the editorial twice, feeling chill despite the warm morning air. It was almost August. In two weeks, my mother would be home. I had no essay for Porter Phelps. And I had no story for Rhiannon.

I opened my notebook and leafed through it. More than half the pages were filled. But not with anything I could send the school, and certainly not with anything that would raise community consciousness about what Rhiannon was doing. And anyway . . . did it matter? If Rhiannon was going to leave either way? As for that school, I didn't even —

I stood abruptly, folded the newspaper and stuffed it with my notebook into my pack. I *had* to write that story. I'd promised my mother and I'd promised Rhiannon. Whatever those words in my notebook were, I couldn't let them get in my way. I was a reporter, and I had a commitment. Unbidden, I remembered what Rail had said after he'd read my notebook: "How'd you make the words fly like that?"

I couldn't have answered him now any more than I'd been able to then. The words came as if a wind blew them straight from inside me onto the page. Might as well ask me how I make my heart beat, I thought sourly, clattering down the stairs. I paused in the kitchen with an impatience born of determination. "I'll be gone all day," I announced.

"Okay," said my father, without looking up from the mail. He had tracked marble dust across the floor of the kitchen. I grimaced.

"Don't make me vacuum the house before Mom gets home," I said. "It's your mess. She'll have a fit. You better clean up."

"Sometimes," said my father gravely, "I cannot tell you from Anna, you sound so much alike."

I looked in the fridge. "There's no food," I complained.

"I'll get more," he said.

"Can we call Mom when I get home tonight?"

"I'm going out," he grunted.

"Where?"

He looked at me over the page of a letter. "Out," he repeated.

At the Center, I found Rhiannon distracted and short-tempered. A copy of *The Register* lay open to the editorial on the kitchen table. When I walked in, I saw Dr. Williams nervously sipping tea while Rhiannon dressed a scratch one of her interns had gotten from a goshawk. Rhiannon was trying to attend to both, and she barely concealed her irritation. "I'm handling the newspaper coverage. I thought we'd agreed on that," she told Dr. Williams. "The reporter *The Register* sent out didn't care two hoots about this place."

"She's supposed to be impartial," Dr. Williams ventured.

"I don't *want* an impartial story!" Rhiannon exploded. The intern scampered out the door. "I want a *sympathetic* story. That's the *point*. Did you think those letters to the editor were impartial?"

"Well, then, where is it?" asked Dr. Williams.

"Where is what?"

"Your sympathetic story. We need something. Soon. I mean it, Dr. Jeffries . . ."

"Oh for God's sake stop calling me Dr. Jeffries," Rhiannon snapped, but her voice was tired. She put her arm over my shoulder. "Here's my story. We'll have it to the paper in —"

"A week," I blurted.

After Dr. Williams had gone, Rhiannon said, "Don't worry. Just get it done as soon as you can."

"A week," I repeated stubbornly, frightened at the unfamiliar dullness of her voice. For a moment, she had reminded me of my mother. I went in and sat at the computer. This was getting ridiculous. It wasn't as if I hadn't written research essays before, I thought. At Porter Phelps, I'd be writing several a term. I sighed, pulled the chair in, and began. I wrote for three straight days. I forced every word out. Once, Rail poked his head around the study door. "Hey," he said. "Come on. Take a break. You haven't watched the hawk fly all week. You gotta see her — she's doing great."

"No," I muttered.

"Man —"

I slammed the chair back. "Can't you see I'm *busy*!" I yelled. Even the printer seemed to be moving at a snail's pace. I practically ripped the page in half taking it out. "I have to get this done," I said. "I've got to. Rhiannon's being pestered by Williams, and we need more community support or the senator's going to cut back on his funding . . . and besides, I have to get this thing done for that school or my mom'll . . ."

"Oh. That school," Rail muttered.

I didn't answer. Rail picked up my notebook. "*This* is what you should send them," he said, hefting it in his hands.

"That isn't anything," I snapped.

"It's *you*. And if that school was worth anything, they'd see that," he said quietly.

By the time Rail, Rhiannon, and I took the bird program to the Lutheran Summer Camp, I had finally finished the essay. I saved everything on a disk and printed out a copy. If I edited it that night and rewrote it the next day, I'd be able to send it off to Porter Phelps before my father and I went to Philadelphia to visit his friend Dan for the weekend. But after the program at the camp, I was so tired I dragged home and fell asleep on the couch surrounded by my books and papers. I was vaguely aware that my father came in and put a blanket over me. He leaned down and stroked my forehead with his stone-roughened hand. "How many times have I seen your mother asleep under her work?" he murmured, half to himself, and gathered up the papers.

My father stopped in Alton on our way back from the city. "Tonight's the night," he announced, pulling into the supermarket. "Time for our dinner party." From the carefully casual way he said it, I knew he'd been thinking about it the whole time we were in Philadelphia. I pushed the cart while he tossed things at me with cheerful abandon. "Your aim stinks," I said, picking up a box of pasta from the floor. Finally I pushed the cart beyond his reach. He was embarrassing, like a little brother.

"Don't you think you should've asked her *first*?" I said, grabbing the tomatoes from him before he could toss them. "I mean, before we buy all this food?"

"It's an Alice-Through-the-Looking-Glass dinner," he said merrily. "We'll do everything backwards. Food first, then invitations."

Usually my father grew more and more temperamental as he got more involved in a big sculpture. One of the reasons she'd agreed to move to Hunter's Gap, my mother said, was because it was a big enough place to escape my father when he was working. But for the last week, my father had been in a restless good humor, sometimes acting as if he were a million miles away, sometimes bubbling over with his huge laugh. "Are you going to show her what you're working on?" I asked him suddenly, stopping the cart in the frozen foods aisle.

He cocked his head, considering. "Maybe I will," he said.

Rhiannon, to my surprise, agreed immediately to come to dinner. My father grinned as I spoke to her, while he chopped zucchini like a pro. "Are you sure?" I asked into the phone. "I mean, if you're busy —"

"I'm sick of cheese sandwiches," she said.

I couldn't concentrate. I almost chopped off my fingers slicing onions. "Aren't we making an awful lot?" I asked once, viewing the pile of food on the counter. My father had hardly eaten a thing in the last week. But now we had enough for an army. I kept peeking out the window to see if Rhiannon's truck had turned up the drive yet. When she finally did arrive and I met her at the door, I was speechless. I'd never seen her in anything but dirty jeans and torn T-shirts. Tonight she was wearing a skirt — a long, shimmery-red skirt that flowed around her like a flame, with designs embroidered in blues and golds and blacks. Her hair was loose, the rich darkness of it giving off a musky, far-away scent as it swung heavily around her shoulders. I could hardly look at her.

"Aren't you going to let her in?" my father said, coming up behind me. I stumbled on my own feet as I stepped back.

She seemed to avoid looking at my father, smiling at me almost apologetically. "I vowed to give all my nice clothes to the Salvation Army if I didn't wear them at least once a year," she said. "So you see — you've given me an excuse . . . and you've deprived someone of this . . ." She flicked the red skirt with her fingers and somewhere, hidden in the folds, I heard tiny bells tinkle.

"Lucky us —" said my father softly, catching her with his eyes. I sat stiffly at the table, tongue-tied, while my father put the spaghetti on to boil. Rhiannon made the salad. They moved around each other in the kitchen as if they were part of the same dream.

Incredibly, the dinner my father cooked for Rhiannon was edible. But it was their talk I couldn't get enough of. It wasn't so much *what* they talked about — the places they'd traveled to, the music they liked, what they'd done in the sixties, their ideas about books and science and art — because those were things I'd always heard my father talk about with his friends. But somehow, between him and Rhiannon, their stories seemed to glow. Something larger than each one of us seemed to fill the room with a life of its own, woven from their laughter and their words into a glimmering, gold-threaded magic carpet flying us all to a place beyond our imagination. Rhiannon and my father never left me behind. Not for a single moment. I never felt myself disappear.

By the time my father had burned the garlic bread, and by the time Rhiannon had splattered tomato sauce over her white blouse and swore so vigorously my father practically choked with laughter, I had relaxed enough to join their spaghetti-noodle–sucking contest with complete confidence. After dinner, my father piled the dishes in the sink and cried, "And now for the dance!"

I groaned. "Not your *records,* Dad . . ." But Rhiannon was delighted. My father pulled out his ancient LPs with the ridiculous names: Sly and the Family Stone. Nitty Gritty Dirt Band. Cream. I sprawled with disgust on the couch. My father grabbed Rhiannon's hand and they bounced around the room, flapping their arms and screaming with laughter. The floorboards shook, the needle on the stereo skipped, and I wondered if such joyful activity had ever taken place before in this old house. Certainly it hadn't since we'd moved here . . . and suddenly I thought of my mother, so small and quiet, so far away. For a terrible moment, I couldn't even bring her face to mind. It was if she'd drifted away into deep space and I had only just noticed her absence. My father was right here, stomping up the dust on our own special planet with Rhiannon.

But I didn't have a chance to think more. My father caught my hand and hauled me up, Rhiannon took my other hand, and they whirled me into the heart of their dance. It was more wonderful than flying. I was the wind swooping over the crest of a hill. I was a wild pair of wings beating along rivers of air. I held tight to Rhiannon's hand and she smiled into my eyes, and at the next whirl she pulled me close. I wrapped my arms around her, buried my face in the heat of her dark hair, and then with another whirl my father caught us both. We jumped around and stomped in a circle until, gasping for breath and laughing, we fell on the couch.

"I used to be able to do that all night," said my father morosely.

"We're old, I tell you," Rhiannon said, and they doubled over in laughter. I was pressed between them in the cushions. I closed my eyes. I never wanted this to end. I wanted always to be surrounded by their great, romping warmth. I wanted always to be part of them. And I wanted my father to love Rhiannon forever.

I caught my breath and sat up. The phone rang into my already-ringing head. My father went into the kitchen. "What is it?" Rhiannon asked. "Do you have the hiccups?" I shook my head. The record had ended, the room was too quiet, and I was terrified that my thoughts would show on my face. But Rhiannon was warm next to me on the couch and without meaning to, I nestled closer. She smiled and brushed her lips across my forehead, and I remembered I hadn't kissed my mother goodbye. Then she stirred, reached over idly and picked up a framed photograph from the table next to the couch.

I felt her whole body stiffen. She gazed at the picture for several minutes. "How old were you here?" she asked at last.

I took it from her, frowning. I'd never liked the photo. My mother was holding me on one arm, her other arm tucked around my father's waist. She was holding me gingerly and I was perched so precariously I'd always wondered why I hadn't fallen off. She looked as though she didn't know what to do with me. "I don't know. About two, I guess," I said. I turned the photo over. The date was written in my mother's handwriting. June 1982. "Yeah. Not quite two."

Rhiannon was still studying the photo in silence when my father came back into the room.

"Who was it?" I asked.

"Anna," he answered, reluctant.

I jumped up. "Dad! That was Mom? Why didn't you let me talk to her? Is she coming home?"

"She only had a few minutes. She was at a pay phone," he said. He gave me a perplexed look. "And of course she's coming home. She said to be sure to tell you she loves you —"

I turned away, disappointment made more bitter with guilt. The magic carpet lay in a tattered heap. Rhiannon and my father seemed all at once uncertain what to say or do. They did not ask me to come to the studio. There was a wary tension between them, and although I felt it, I followed them anyway. Ahead of me on the path in the summer dark, they walked so close together their shapes were indistinguishable from each other.

In his studio, my father switched on the small light over his drawing desk. The huge blanketed form of the marble block was in the room beyond. Rhiannon said softly, "You don't have to show it to me. I can wait until it's done."

"No. No, I want to," he said.

But he didn't come any closer and he didn't turn on any more lights. He gestured to me. I hesitated. It was always a ritual, when my father finished a piece: I would unveil it for my mother. "It's all right — go ahead," he reassured me. I pulled the blanket off and stepped back.

In the half-light, the pale marble seemed to shimmer as if it was not solid at all, but a shape formed of mist. But even in the mist, the carving had begun to take on definition: an up-flung eagle's wing, a suggestion of talons, a curved beak still half-buried in stone. Below the eagle was a boy in uniform, his face not yet carved, one arm flung up in the same direction as the eagle's wing. He was stumbling. In the soldier's other hand, tensed as a taloned foot, he clutched a gun.

Rhiannon laid her cheek against the cool marble and closed her eyes. With one finger, she traced each feather in the eagle's wing. Slowly she moved around the block, trailing her hand, then stopped. I heard her quick intake of breath. My father did not move. "I had to do it," he whispered. "All those dead boys — they all had mothers. The face wouldn't leave me —"

I knew before I looked. I squinted, trying to make out my father's work. Behind the stumbling soldier boy, the body of the woman had not emerged fully from the block. But her head was complete. Every feature in her face held grief. Rhiannon might have destroyed the drawing, but my father had kept inside him the shape of what he had seen in her face. Suddenly Rhiannon put out her hand and lightly touched her stone counterpart's cheek. Her eyes met my father's across the dark room. Then she took the blanket and draped it gently over the unfinished sculpture. She smiled at me. "It appears your father has caught me, just as you caught the red-tailed hawk," she said.

"I didn't catch her — I rescued her," I said.

"Ah —" she answered, once again gazing past me to my father. "Is that what you're trying to do?" she asked him.

16

I RODE OVER TO THE CENTER early the morning after our dinner, but Rhiannon was gone. Ryan, the graduate student entrusted with looking after the Center while she was away, just shrugged when I asked. "Oh, she does this sometimes," he said, hardly looking up from his work. "She just takes off. She gets calls from all over the place. I don't know when she'll be back. Maybe she just needed to get away."

By the time I rode my bike back to our house, the August temperature was over 90 degrees. I sat in the stuffy kitchen, half-paralyzed by the oppressive heat, and listened to the cicadas buzzing in the trees. I thought about calling Rail. I stared moodily at the dishes from last night's dinner piled in the sink. The spatter of sauce Rhiannon had got on her shirt was congealed to a hard crust on the stove.

"She just takes off," Ryan had said. It echoed my father's earlier words: "She's a leaver . . ." I didn't know where Rhiannon had been before she came to Hunter's Gap, and someday she would leave here and go someplace else. Restless, hungry, I opened the fridge and stood gazing into it. As soon as it was open, I was no longer hungry. The cold air was not refreshing. I slammed the door shut. I wanted something so much my whole being ached. But what? What? All I knew was that Rhiannon made me long for *something*.

I scuffed down the path to the strangely silent studio. It was dim inside, but when I switched on the lights, my father growled, "Turn them off." His voice came from behind the block of marble. He was sitting on the floor, his back against the sculpture, gazing at nothing. I sat beside him and after a moment, he sighed and put his arm around me, pulling me close. We sat without speaking for a long time, cooled by the white marble, our backs pressed against the half-carved figure of the grieving woman with Rhiannon's face.

After a while, my father said, "Why don't you call Rail? Go swimming or something."

"I can't," I said. I wished I wanted to. My father sighed again and nodded.

Rhiannon returned two days later with no explanation. She was brusque and distant, and as I stood in her study nervously watching her read through my essay, I felt even farther from her than during the days she'd been gone. In her hands, the pages I'd once imagined would shine a light and make a difference in the world, or at least in Hunter's Gap, seemed pitifully insignificant. She looked up at last over the tops of her glasses. "Is this what you sent off to that school?" she asked.

I nodded. "I know it isn't that good —"

"Nonsense," Rhiannon said abruptly. "It's quite skillfully written. It'll do very well for the newspaper. And the school will love it."

What she said might have been accurate. But she wasn't speaking the truth. Because the truth, as I knew very well, was that something vital was missing from my essay. Rhiannon said again, "It'll do fine. Let's send it off to *The Register* and make poor wimpy Williams happy, shall we?" With a kind smile, she handed me an envelope, and I felt as empty as the words on the pages.

At Bitsi's, I balanced the envelope for a moment on the lip of the mailbox, waiting to feel something. Anything. Relief. Anticipation. The sense of accomplishment my mother was always telling me I'd have when I did something well. But as the envelope addressed to "Editor, *The Alton Register*" slid into the box with a soft thunk, I still felt nothing but empty. Two-thirds of the summer lay in that envelope at the bottom of the mailbox. In a few weeks I'd be away at a school I no longer cared about. I wouldn't be here to see the red-tailed hawk fly free in October. I never thought about being a reporter anymore. All in all, I hardly knew M. Taylor Armstrong-Brown. I might as well have signed a different name to the story I'd just sent out into the world.

"Hey, Missy. Hey, Miz Jeffers. Youse hot enough?" I spun around to see Betsy Warren getting out of a hideous pink car. She gave me a sly smile that, I knew now, was her friendliest greeting. "I got my permit!" she announced proudly. From the passenger side her mother emerged, nails and lips painted the same nasty pink. I could excuse Betsy a lot, seeing that. "Ma's gonna let me drive to the Firemen's Picnic. Youse guys going?"

"Wouldn't miss it," said Rhiannon, straight-faced.

"You goin'?" Betsy said persistently to me. "You gotta, Missy. The games is the best part — you can win prizes. Me an' Cindy won three stuffed bears last year."

Rhiannon gave me a wink as we got into her truck, but by the time she'd turned up our drive, she was serious. "When exactly *do* you leave for that school?" she asked.

"August 28," I said, but there was nothing real in those words for me.

Rhiannon dropped me by the house and was about to drive off when my father came up the path from the studio, bare to the waist, marble chips stuck on his skin with sweat. "Yuk," I grimaced.

"I share your sentiment," he replied, but he was looking at Rhiannon, his hand on the open window of her truck. "Missed you," he said matter-of-factly, as if he was commenting on the weather. She didn't answer. He glanced at me. "Missy and I had plans to go swimming . . ." he began.

We didn't have any plans I'd been aware of. Rhiannon seemed strangely unable to speak. She just nodded without really looking at him, and ten minutes later we were in the old Chevy rumbling down the road toward the river. We passed Rail riding his bike toward the Center. "Come on," my father called out the window, skidding to a halt and loading Rail's bike into the back before he could do more than protest hesitantly, "But I gotta finish mowing that field —"

"Oh, get in, Rail," said Rhiannon. "He won't take 'no' for an answer. I don't want you mowing today, anyway. You'll faint in the heat."

On the cool packed mud of the riverbank, shaded by thick trees, my father stripped to his underpants and slipped into the slow current like a pliant, white otter. "Yum," he grinned, rolling over and over in the water. Rhiannon stood watching him, her face unreadable, hands hooked in the pockets of her jeans. After a few minutes she took them off and waded in after him, her t-shirt billowing up when she swam.

Feeling ridiculous and uncomfortable, I walked

downstream and went in fully clothed. The river folded over me like a cool balm. I floated on my back, staring up through the trees, hearing Rhiannon's low laugh as she talked to my father. Something brushed softly along my side and I gasped, thrashing the water as I tried to find a footing on the slippery bottom. "Man," said Rail, aggrieved. "It's only me. What'd you think it was — a shark?"

The water only came up to my waist and my shirt stuck to me like another skin. Rail dog-paddled around, snuffling the water and brushing my legs when he came too close. "Don't," I said, stepping back.

He glanced over at my father and Rhiannon. They were swimming close together, their bodies ripply-white under the surface of the green shadowed river. Rail looked quickly away. I dove so sharply I scraped against the pebbly bottom. I kicked hard toward deeper water. But when I came up, gulping for air, Rail had followed. "Man, Taylor. What's wrong with you today?" he complained.

Rhiannon and my father were floating past us farther out in the river. The sun sluiced over their sleek heads. Their voices drifted with them. Rail followed my eyes. "They sure get along good," he said reluctantly, as if he thought he should comment.

"They're just friends," I snapped.

He didn't answer. He was sweeping the palm of his hand back and forth over the surface of the water, barely touching it. He flicked drops over my arm and I shivered. "My mom used to laugh a lot, when I was little. Like Rhiannon," Rail murmured.

"I don't think my mother has ever laughed," I said.

We floated on our backs and when I began to drift away, Rail caught my hand. Two dark specks circled above us in the narrow strip of sky between the trees. "Red-tails," breathed Rail. We watched until the hawks disappeared.

"Once she's free, I'll never see her again," I said. "And even if I do, I won't know her —"

Rail's shoulder pressed warm against mine, our heads only a few inches apart. The hot afternoon was still, the river was still, and over us all hung an uneasy spell of enchantment. In two days my mother would be home, and as unreal as that felt now, I knew it would change everything. So I did not want to leave the river, or to let go of Rail's hand, or to lose the sound of my father's and Rhiannon's voices eddying around on the current like the first fallen leaves of autumn.

My mother did return. We picked her up from the airport and she slept all the first day she was back. She woke the morning of the Hunter's Gap 35th Annual Firemen's Picnic and immediately a silence began to buzz between us like an angry hornet. I didn't know when it would land and sting. In the bedroom, she sorted through the dirty clothes my father had thrown in a heap on the floor. She yanked each article out separately. "Didn't either of you do any laundry while I was away?" she said.

"I washed some stuff out . . ." I began unhappily.

"Here's his best shirt. For God's sake, it's covered in spaghetti sauce! What on earth was he doing!" She flung it savagely toward the hamper. It fell short and I picked it up and buried it at the bottom. My mother shoved an armful of clothes at me. "Take these down and start the washer. God. I didn't think I'd have to come home to *this* —"

I crammed the laundry into the machine, listening to the thumps coming from upstairs. Two days earlier, my mother had been in Europe presenting a paper and speaking at a prestigious conference. Now she was in Hunter's Gap doing my father's dirty laundry. And mine. I remembered the food going bad in the fridge, the trash overflowing with pizza boxes, my never-washed sheets . . . I took the stairs two at a time, but I was too late. I stood helplessly in the doorway while she stripped my bed, hating that she had to touch the dank gray things I'd slept in for the last month. That's when the hornet stung.

"They'll have rules about things like this at Porter Phelps, Melissa. They don't tolerate sloppiness," said my mother grimly, yanking the pillowcases off.

"If you want to go ahead and throw away every opportunity out of stubborn laziness, the way you did last year at school —"

"I wasn't stubborn and lazy!" I cried.

"And I want to read that essay," she suddenly shot at me, gathering up the armload of sheets. "Right now."

I swallowed. "I don't have it — I mean, I already sent it off."

"Surely you kept a copy."

My father appeared in the doorway. I looked at him hopelessly. "I'll print it out tonight . . . it's on Rhiannon's computer . . ." I stammered.

"What does Rhiannon have to do with anything?" demanded my mother, pushing past my father.

"I'll get it tonight, Mom. I promise. I did write it. It's good. You don't have to worry. I'll get it after the picnic . . ." I followed her downstairs, my voice coming out in jerks, until my father put his hand on my arm to stop me. For a moment we all stood looking at each other in the kitchen. I'd never seen my mother's face so worn and colorless. She was almost dwarfed by the pile of laundry.

"I'm not going to the picnic," she said finally. "I have to go down to the city tonight. Just tonight — I'll be back tomorrow afternoon —"

"No," said my father.

For a month I hadn't felt that familiar, stomach-tensing chill rising from the unvoiced struggles between them. For a whole month, I hadn't once begun to disappear. Now my heart twisted and turned like a rabbit running from a hawk. I begged desperately, "Mom, please come to the picnic. It's only for a few hours. Please."

But even then, we didn't go as a family. She followed in her car as my father chugged the Chevy into the parking area by the school. The field where I had run on the last day of school was a mass of people moving slowly between makeshift booths, barbecue fires, and the platform where a raucous band played. The smell of frying meat and humanity was overwhelming. I caught my mother's eye anxiously, wishing I hadn't made her come, but for the first time since she'd been home she smiled at me. My father, as usual, had already become the center of a group of men, most of whom had beer bellies and wore baseball caps and slapped my father on the back and called him "good ol' Bobby Armpit." My father reached out and drew my mother against his side, fielding each joking remark with one of his own. I wandered off, trying not to be obvious as I looked around for Rail. I felt as if I'd been rubbed raw by sandpaper, and I wanted his calm presence and his steady voice. And all at once, as if hearing my wish, he was beside me, holding out a sticky-looking blob on a stick. "I was watching for you," he said. He never seemed to mind admitting what I couldn't even admit to myself. I took the blob gingerly.

"Thanks," I said. "What is this? It looks like it's covered with that fly paper Bitsi hangs in her store."

"Man, Taylor. You're welcome," Rail grumbled. "Just eat it. It's a caramel apple. Haven't you ever seen one?"

I licked at it, uncertain of what to say next. The spell of that afternoon on the river seemed to hold us both even now, its bond at once disturbing and intimate. I held the apple out to Rail. "You want a bite?" He grabbed it with his teeth and tore a big chunk away, his mouth bulging, his eyes smiling at me.

"Where's your dad?" I asked, although I meant Rhiannon, and he answered both the spoken and unspoken with a nod, still chewing vigorously. I looked in the direction he had gestured. The crowd was thickest around the booths and food, but at one side of the field people had begun to lay blankets on the grass to claim a spot for watching the fireworks. I saw Rhiannon talking with Tim Bogart while Rail's little sisters tugged impatiently at his hands. Even from a distance, I could tell Tim had his angelic smile. There was something at once protective and dependent in the way he stood close to Rhiannon, and I was reminded of the two golden eagles standing together in their enclosure. "Your dad looks like he's okay," I remarked hopefully, but Rail flushed.

"Yeah —" he said, hesitated, then grunted, "C'mon," and set off through the crowd toward them. I went without looking back at my parents.

Rhiannon drew me the way the brightest star might draw someone sailing in the night. I followed Rail, winding my way between people throwing base-balls into baskets and squirting water pistols into jars, between grills with sizzling sausages and ma-chines spinning pink cotton candy. I didn't see Bitsi and Old Bitsi until I'd almost plunged my caramel apple into Bitsi's sofa-sized stomach.

"Melissa Armstrong!" she snorted, shielding the frail Old Bitsi with her bulk. "Don't you got eyes in yer head? You got any idea what it's like fer some-one my age to fall on the ground?"

"Sorry," I muttered, trying to keep my eyes on the direction Rail was going. Bitsi's sharp little eyes fol-lowed mine and she leaned closer to me, holding me by the arm with one massive hand. "You ain't gonna find a better one than that boy," she whispered loudly. "He's just like his daddy was when he was a boy, afore he got messed up by them Commies. But that there *woman* —" Bitsi jerked her head toward Rhiannon. "You watch yerself with her. She got more of a mess hidden inside her than Pandora's box. You don't want none of it to come out."

I opened my mouth, outraged, but Bitsi was al-ready lumbering on, Old Bitsi trailing like a thread-bare shadow. I stared after her. There had been no hostility in her voice, just concern. Slowly I pushed past a knot of people watching a clown twist bal-loons into animal shapes, past a small, jerky merry-go-round without any music, until I saw Rhiannon making her way toward me. I didn't care that all of Hunter's Gap could see; I went right up to her and she put her arms around me. "Things a little rough?" she asked.

"My mom came home," I said, unnecessarily, because she already understood. I looked up at her. "I wasn't sure if you'd come —"

"I said I would," she said shortly. "Rail's worried. I'll try to persuade Tim to leave before dark . . . I want to get back to the birds before the fireworks, too." She shaded her eyes with her hand and studied the edge of the field where the fire trucks were parked. "That damn Junior wouldn't budge an inch. Said the fireworks had always been set up on that end of the field . . . said it never bothered Duane MacGaw's chickens when it was his farm."

"Junior Fenstemacher's a bastard," I blurted.

Rhiannon raised her eyebrows. "That might be a bit harsh —" Then she shrugged. "I threw tarps over the most exposed enclosures. It'll keep out the flashes, anyway . . . Where are your parents?" she asked suddenly, and I pointed. She didn't do more than glance but later, after we'd reached Rail and his father, I saw her watching them through the crowd. And in a few minutes my father came toward us, a big grin on his face, his arm around my mother's stiff, narrow shoulders.

The games had begun. And not just on the field,

where screaming people raced around balancing raw eggs on spoons and a woman in tight jeans clutched piggyback to a fat man as they thundered around an obstacle course. On the blanket my mother spread out, it seemed to me that five people were playing some kind of game as well. The only ones who didn't play were Tim Bogart and the two little girls. I didn't know the rules, but somehow I had to play. It was like walking a balance-beam blindfolded.

"Melissa talks a lot about you," my mother said to Rhiannon.

I had hardly ever mentioned Rhiannon to my mother.

"I've enjoyed having her help out this summer," answered Rhiannon, even though I hadn't helped out much at all with the work at the Center.

"She's been so busy working on some secret project, I've hardly seen her all summer," teased my father, although he was the one who'd holed himself up in his studio day and night. They were all looking at me, as if everything they said to each other had to pass through me first. I squirmed on the hot blanket.

"We've been teaching the hawk to hunt," Rail said suddenly, and I glanced at him with gratitude.

"What hawk?" asked my mother.

"The one I found . . . the red-tailed hawk . . ." I stammered. I'd told her so little, and she'd remembered nothing.

The crowd around us erupted in applause for the winners of the game that had just ended. From the band platform a man with a cowboy hat announced the sack race, holding up a giant purple teddy bear that was to be the grand prize. Betsy Warren materialized from the crowd, towing Cindy. Betsy's face was as pink as her mother's car. "Hey, Missy. Hey, Rail. Youse guys doing the sack race?" She practically squeaked in excitement.

My face burned. Rail rolled his eyes. "Man, Bets. Get outa here. No way we're doing such a stupid thing."

The little girls yanked at Tim's hands. "Can we, Daddy? Can we?"

"That sack's bigger'n both of you together," laughed Tim, but he let them go.

"So what happened to Kevin?" I asked Betsy.

"Oh, he's around somewhere," she said dismissively. "I wouldn't do the sack race with him for a million dollars. Cindy's my best friend — we always do it." She wrapped her skinny arm around Cindy and steered her in the direction of the starting line.

My father leaped up and grabbed my mother's hand. "Come on, Annie!" he cried. "I always used to win this race. Let's go show them that Bob Armstrong hasn't lost his magic in the sack!"

My mother's face went white. Rhiannon stared into space, pretending not to have heard. Even Tim looked a little startled behind his perpetually saintly smile. My father frowned down on us, hands on his hips, as if he couldn't believe what he was seeing. "Okay, then, Missy'll be my partner. She won't let me down."

"Oh yes I will," I growled.

My mother said quietly, "Rhiannon will be your partner. I'm too short for you, anyway. You'd only lose."

It was as if the three of them, my father, my mother, and Rhiannon, were locked in an invisible wrestling match just under the surface of their words. I knew my father couldn't possibly care that much about the stupid sack race. But he stubbornly held out his hand to Rhiannon. With a sting of disappointment, I watched her reach up to take it. She rose to meet him lightly, so perfectly matched to my father, so beautiful and strong. She laughed a little self-consciously.

"Mom. Mom. She really doesn't want to. You race with Dad," I pleaded, but my voice came out weakly and I knew I didn't even mean it. Being with my father and Rhiannon was like being caught in an elemental force — a storm, or the current in a river, or a hawk's plunge. I didn't *want* to stop it. I wanted to be part of it.

"Relax, Melissa. It's just a game," said my mother, but her smile made me want to cry. She smoothed the blanket out and I slid closer to her until her bony shoulder dug into mine. Rail knelt on the other side of me and Tim stood so he could watch the girls. The burly man with the cowboy hat slapped a number on everyone's back and handed them a thick burlap sack and twine. Betsy and Cindy were giggling so hard they'd practically fallen over before the race began. Tim clapped in delight and cheered his daughters, who were the only people as far as I could see who didn't look ridiculous.

Rhiannon and my father each stuck one leg into the sack, and my father tied it around their thighs. He put his arm around Rhiannon's waist, and she put her arm around his, and they hopped to a starting line drawn in chalk-dust on the grass. My father pointed something out to Rhiannon, bending his head close to hers. I could hardly bear to watch. It felt as if a burning stone lay in my stomach. But no one else seemed to notice. All around me, people were shouting joking encouragement, clapping and cheering the contestants on. Even my mother stood up with Tim to see better. Rail and I sat on the blanket without saying a word.

"Hoo-ee!" yelled Tim when the burly man waved the starting flag. The sack-racers lurched and staggered in a frantic rush down the field. Rail's little sisters hopped along like tiny crickets and Tim clapped furiously. But no one could match my father and Rhiannon. They led from the start, their bodies perfectly synchronized, almost graceful in the clumsy sack. When the little girls bounded into my father's leg he scooped them up with one hand and steered them toward the finish line, then fell in a laughing, tangled heap with Rhiannon. The girls screamed in triumphant excitement as they clambered over them across the line. The giant purple bear almost engulfed them as they ran back to Tim.

"I tried to win the prize for you, Annie," my father called, limping back red-faced from exertion. "Those girls of yours are just too fast," he said to Tim. He flopped down on the blanket and nestled up to my mother as if Rhiannon no longer existed. My mother ignored him and only seemed interested in talking to Rhiannon. I wanted to kick them all. My father was acting like an idiot. My mother was pretending to enjoy herself. Rhiannon. . . .

Rhiannon was unrecognizable. Her voice was flat, polite, and disconnected. "I did read Melissa's essay, yes," she was saying in answer to my mother's question. *Melissa.* I stared at her. I wasn't even *me.*

"Let's get something to eat," said Rail, jumping up and pulling me with him before I could protest. "C'mon. They probably have tofu dogs someplace around here . . ."

"Good luck on that," said my father with a wink.

Rail tugged my hand and made me come. "What's *wrong* with them!" I fumed, barely out of earshot. "*Melissa.* Rhiannon called me *Melissa.*" I was almost tripping over my own feet. I yanked my hand away.

"I'm *coming!*" I said savagely. "Why can't my mother ever mind her own business! I *told* her I'd print out that stupid paper! What does she have to ask Rhiannon for?"

"She's jealous," said Rail simply.

"You're crazy." But I felt a jump of fear, and looked back at my father.

"No, I'm not," he said stubbornly. "Just think about it. You've spent the whole summer with Rhiannon. Your mom doesn't even know her. She's jealous of you spending time with her."

"Of *me!*" It took my breath away.

Rail was loading up on soda. "Sure. Man, Taylor. Anyone could figure that out. I mean, I'd be jealous if you started hanging out with . . . with Kevin, or something."

"*You!*"

Rail looked at me, his arms full of soda cans. "Taylor, your brain must be fried in the heat. Come on. Let's go back."

I trailed reluctantly after him over late afternoon shadows that lay like bars across the field. The sun hung deep behind the hedgerow separating the school field from the hills of the Center. The games were over, the band was taking a break, and over where the fireworks had been set up I saw a group of boys skulking around the fire trucks. Rail paused, worried. "Rhiannon said she'd try to make Dad leave before dark," he told me.

"He still seems okay —"

"He always seems okay, until he flips out," Rail said abruptly, threading his way through families and couples on blankets. Near our own spot was a ragged rug with a man and woman playing with their baby. "Hey there, Rail," said the man, looking up.

"Hey, Buck," Rail answered.

"Cousin?" I asked a few steps on.

"Uncle. My mom's side."

There was a sharp explosion, like a gunshot. Rail dropped all the soda cans. Near the fire trucks, a few people clapped and yelled. My father came to help pick up the soda. "Scared you?" he chuckled. "They must have set one off to test it."

Rhiannon sat alone on the blanket, her knees drawn up under her chin, her arms wrapped around them. "Where's Mom?" I asked. My father handed me some cold cans and my skin broke out in goosebumps. "She was looking for you," he said. "She had to go. She wanted to get down to the city before jet lag caught up to her. She said to —"

"She left without saying goodbye?" I whispered, stricken.

My father looked suddenly beaten. "I know. I know," he said, tired.

"Where's my dad?" Rail asked, an unfamiliar frantic note in his voice. "Rhiannon, did you see where my dad went to?"

Another firework went off, the bright flash searing the sunset sky. My father frowned. "He went to get hot dogs for the girls," Rhiannon said, but she'd stood up, too, and was searching the crowd. She looked at my father. "I thought they weren't going to set those damn things off until after dark."

Two more explosions, one after the other. A brilliant spiral of green pinwheeled over the hedgerow, hissing sparks. "Shit!" said Rhiannon. A second later, another explosion, this one like a giant red flower blossoming against the dying sun. It burst open over the hill beyond the field, instead of over the crowd. The fireworks were aimed toward the Center. Rail stood motionless beside me, but when the fourth explosion went off, with a flurry of whizzing sparks, he cried in anguish, "Dad!"

The two girls were running toward us, clutching hot dogs and giggling in delight when another explosion wheeled into the twilight sky. Behind them was Tim. In his arms he clasped the baby belonging to the young couple Rail had spoken to a few minutes before.

He backed slowly away from the suddenly silent crowd, both arms wrapped tightly around the wailing baby. Two firecrackers went off at once, striking across the sky, and I could smell the acrid smoke. Tim froze, crouched low, his trembling body shielding the baby. The baby's mother whimpered. Tim didn't move. The woman darted at him, but all at once Old Bitsi pushed through the crowd and caught her arm. I heard his voice, low but distinct. "Don't grab at him, Sophie. You'll make it worse. Don't you worry none. He ain't gonna hurt her. Here, Buck, keep holda Sophie . . ."

It all felt like slow motion. The two little girls, frozen, staring at their father. My father sprinting toward the fire trucks, waving his arms and shouting for Junior. The silent crowd, the frightened wail of the baby. Tim was muttering something frantically, over and over, but I couldn't hear his words. And Rail, walking slowly toward him, putting each foot down as if the ground might blow up under him, saying: "Hey, Dad. Come on. The baby's okay. Come on. It's only the fireworks, Dad. It's Hunter's Gap . . . that's where you are, Daddy. See the school? See?" Tim, still muttering, moved back warily with each step Rail took, and Rail kept repeating, "No, Dad, nobody's dead. There's no dead children. The baby's okay. You gotta give her back . . ."

It wasn't hard to imagine the dark field strewn with land mines and the bodies of children. I caught my breath when Rhiannon walked past Rail right up to Tim. I watched each place she put her foot down.

At first I couldn't hear her. But when Tim slunk back she followed. She put her hands out to him, begging. "Give me my baby. She's mine, Tim. Give her to me. I need my baby." With a furtive, desperate look up into Rhiannon's face, Tim suddenly relinquished the baby. He wrapped both arms over his head and sank to the ground. Rhiannon handed the baby to Old Bitsi and then I couldn't see because the crowd closed in. I heard Bitsi's indignant voice scolding, "Get back, you fools. Can't you see he needs space? Rail, honey, you let Old Bitsi get your Daddy to the car . . . don't worry. He knows what to do. You go find your sisters." A moment later, Rail and my father emerged from the press of people and came toward us.

"C'mon. We gotta go with Dad to the doctor," Rail said, taking the girls' hands. His voice was steady but his dark eyes were huge and scared. He looked at my father. "Can you take us? Old Bitsi's car isn't big enough for all of us."

"Of course I'll take you," said my father. He looked at me. "Will you be all right? You can get a ride home with Rhiannon." He paused, then added, "Unless Rail wants you to come, too —"

"No," said Rail quickly. He muttered to me, eyes averted, "They don't let a bunch of people into the psych wards, anyway. You'd just have to sit around in the waiting room forever."

They went off toward the parking area and I turned to look for Rhiannon. The crowd was breaking up and I looked for her where we'd been sitting.

But she had disappeared. At first I stood, scanning the field, but an inexplicable apprehension filled me and I began to hurry through the crowd. Finally I turned and half ran back to the parking area. But by then my father's Chevy was gone and Rhiannon's truck was nowhere in sight.

I stopped. All around, cars were pulling away and people were slowly streaming past me. The school field was all but deserted in the early dusk. I looked into the faces of the people as they went by, searching for anyone familiar, even Betsy Warren. Even Kevin. But they were all strangers. For a moment, I couldn't think. I wasn't sure I was even breathing.

A cool breeze riffled down off the hill beyond the school. Unthinking, I turned my face to meet it. It stirred my hair and blew it softly across my face. I looked at the hill and remembered how the hawk had come swooping over it on the last day of school. Beyond the hill was the Center. All I had to do was walk there.

It would have been easier by the road. But I didn't want everyone in Hunter's Gap seeing me as they passed in their cars. I went through the row of hickory trees, trying in the darkness to avoid the poison ivy that Rail had told me grew beneath them. I went straight up the hill, pushing through thickets and brambles until I came out in the field Rail had mowed. Across it I saw the dark shapes of the buildings. There were no lights on in the house but Rhiannon's truck was there, parked in the yard.

I stood there for a long time before making my way across the open field, straining my ears. But I heard only crickets. None of Rhiannon's birds were stirring, not even the owls. When I got to the yard I took a few steps toward the shed, but there was no light on in there, either. And all the while, I could feel the tug within me, as if an invisible tether connected me to something I most longed for. I turned, walked up the steps and through the dark kitchen into the study. I was very quiet, but she said, from the darkness, "Ninian?"

"Yes," I answered.

There was the faintest stir of movement and I saw her watching me, her face pale and still as marble. "Ninian," she said again. I curled up beside her on the couch and she gathered me against her and rocked me. Her cool hands soothed my bramble-scratched skin. I closed my eyes and laid my head against her, and felt her heart beating as if it was the first sound I had ever known. I could not get close enough. Her arms could crush me and I still would not be close enough.

After a long time, her head bent over mine so I tasted the salty comfort of tears, Rhiannon sighed. "Taylor. I know it's you, Taylor. Don't worry."

I pushed more deeply against her. "I'm not Taylor," I said, muffled.

She laughed a little, down in her throat. "But you are Taylor. You don't have a choice."

"I want to be Ninian."

Her arms tightened around me a moment. Then she held me away from her. After her warmth, I shivered. "Ninian is dead," Rhiannon said.

Pandora's box, Bitsi had said. Don't open it. "I look like Ninian," I said. Rhiannon didn't say anything for a long time and I never took my eyes from hers. I pushed against her again and whispered, "I can be your daughter. I can be Ninian," and after a while I wanted to shake her because she would not answer. "How did she die?" I demanded.

"I let her die," said Rhiannon. "I was working late at night, and the static from the intercom connected to her bedroom bothered me. So I turned it off. My husband was asleep. I had to get my work done. It wasn't off for long. Ten minutes, maybe. She chewed a button off her teddy bear and choked on it." She smoothed the mussed-up hair away from my face. "Yes, you do look like her . . . like she might have looked now —" she said softly. "The first time I saw you, with your father, when you were trying to hide in Bitsi's store . . ." She smiled, something of her old, knowing smile. "She'd be your age. I wanted you to be her. It caught me, just like that . . . I couldn't help it —"

"*I* want it," I said, but she held me away from her again.

"No. You don't," she said, and suddenly stood. The moonlight through the window seemed to join her, so she was a pale shadow, hardly there.

I followed her outside to the yard, and the night washed cool over my face. "What do I *want* so much?" I cried to her. "I want something . . . I want you . . ."

She shook her head and smiled, but did not let me touch her again. "You want *you*," she said. "It's your heart you're looking for. Not mine." She turned away. "Not Ninian's," she murmured. "Not if I wished it for a million years. You can't be her."

We had reached the pines at the farthest enclosure. We pushed quietly through the branches. The moonlight sifted down over the red-tailed hawk. She sat watchfully on the highest perch and when she turned her head, the light gleamed a moment in her wild eye and then went dark. "Tim must be looking for his heart, too," I said into the darkness.

"Tim is looking for forgiveness," Rhiannon answered.

"Like you."

The hawk flapped her wings suddenly, shook herself, and hopped farther away from us. "No, not like me," Rhiannon said at last. "I don't want forgiveness. Ever."

17

I WOKE BEFORE SUNRISE, still exhausted, and lay shivering on the bare mattress I hadn't even thrown a sheet over after Rhiannon drove me home. A thick mist hung over the orchard and the fields. I hadn't undressed the night before. I pulled a sweatshirt on over my T-shirt and sat on the edge of the bed, listening to the utter silence around me. I might have been the only person left in the world. Out in the mist there were just ghosts. Only the solid objects in my room kept me from floating off into whiteness. On my desk were three of Rhiannon's books, my own notebook, and the brown-banded feather from the hawk's tail. I brushed the feather slowly back and forth across my face, trying to feel the soft promise of flight.

I went down to the kitchen. The light on the answering machine was blinking and yesterday's mail lay unopened on the table. I punched the button and listened to my father's voice. "Hi, Missy. You there? Well, I'm still at the hospital. I'm going to take Rail and the girls home after we find out what's up with Tim. The Bitsis are going to look after them for a few days . . . You okay? You asleep? Okay, it's ten-thirty. Don't know when I'll get home. I'll see you tomorrow, sweetie." A click, and silence. The machine continued to blink. Another message, from my mother. Weren't we home yet? She'd gotten to the city, she wanted to tell me she loved me, she'd be back late tomorrow. . . . Silence again. The mist seemed to swallow up even the echo of my parents' voices.

A letter on the top of the mail pile caught my eye. It was addressed to me and I recognized the logo of *The Alton Register.* I tore it open. "The editorial staff of the Register was impressed with your feature story on the Hunter's Gap Raptor Rehabilitation Center," I read. "Although it is too long to print in its present form, we would like you to revise it under staff guidance. You are eligible for the Register's Junior Internship Fellowship offered each year to a local high school student. If you are interested, we would like to encourage you to apply for this fellowship, based on the outstanding promise you have demonstrated in your article . . ."

It seemed logical, in this strange and remote world

where only I existed, to find another letter in the pile, this one from the Porter Phelps School accepting me "with pleasure" into the Advanced Writing program "which offers an opportunity for the finest writers in the school to develop professional skills . . ." I held both letters, one in each hand, studying the names they were addressed to. "Dear M. Taylor Armstrong-Brown" was the greeting from the editor at *The Register.* "Dear Miss Brown" was the salutation from Porter Phelps. The names seemed to belong to the ghosts in the mist, not to me.

I played my mother's message over three times, until I could whisper it by heart. I picked up the phone, but it was only six o'clock. Too early to call her. Restlessly, I paced the kitchen, trying to see through the mist to the barn, listening for any sign that my father was awake. Just this once, I thought fiercely, he could have slept in the house. Even his sleeping self in the bedroom upstairs would have been a comfort. I emptied the dryer of laundry, folded it, stuffed another load into the washer, and turned it on. I opened the fridge, dumping weeks of forgotten leftover Chinese take-out, curled-up pizza slices, flat soda, and half-eaten hoagies, hard as stones. The salad remaining from our dinner with Rhiannon was brown and slimy. I threw it all out. I wiped the shelves. When my mother came home this evening, the house would be perfect. Clean, neat, welcoming.

And my essay, with the letter from Porter Phelps, would be waiting for her. It would make her happier than anything. I took the letter and went upstairs. I hung my father's clean clothes in the closet in my parents' bedroom. I made my bed. Then I stuffed Rhiannon's books in my pack along with my notebook, the letters, and the computer disk containing my essay. Rhiannon was always up by dawn. I told myself I would stay long enough to print out the essay and return the books. Then I would come back home, clean the house, and wait for my mother.

I hesitated as I got on my bike, looking once more at the barn. My father must have come home very late. He probably wouldn't even be awake by the time I returned. I rode down the road in the muffling fog, unable to shake the impression that I was the only person left in the world. I couldn't see more than six feet ahead of me and the bike seemed to float in the silence.

By the time I reached the drive up to the Center, the heat from the rising sun was beginning to steam through the fog. The world had grown luminous and pink, and the smell of new-cut hay from the field enveloped me like perfume. I pushed the bike across the yard, propped it against my father's Chevy, and climbed the steps to the porch.

And stopped. And didn't move, didn't turn around, didn't look back at the Chevy which had been such a familiar sight at the Center all summer that I hadn't even registered its presence for several seconds. I held my breath, hearing only the beat of my heart. But I felt no surprise. I pushed open the screen door silently and looked through the familiar kitchen to the familiar couch in the study where Rhiannon had held me and rocked me and called me Ninian. I put my pack on the table. My father's T-shirt was draped over the back of a chair. I picked it up, rubbed it against my face, took a deep breath of his familiar scent, of marble dust, machine oil, sweat. For several minutes I heard only the uneven hum of the fridge and the click of the clock hands moving. I waited. Then, from the bedroom beyond the study, came the murmur of my father's voice and Rhiannon's answering laugh, luminous as the morning.

I took Rhiannon's books from my pack, stacked them neatly on the table, and laid the computer disk on top. I crumpled the letter from *The Alton Register* and left it beside the books. Outside, the fog had burned away and the late August sun was rising over the fields behind the Center. I took off my sweatshirt and hung it over the back of the chair, took my father's shirt, shouldered my pack, and left.

I had already started riding down the drive when the hawk screamed. I stopped. Her high, keen hunting cry struck the silence inside me and broke its back. I gasped. Rage spurted through me like blood. The red-tailed hawk screamed again.

I went to the shed, got a crate used for transporting birds, and lashed it to the back of the bike with bungee cords. Then I pushed the bike down the narrow path along the back of the enclosures. The hawk was crouched on a low perch, her eyes riveted on a flock of blackbirds in the field beyond. I didn't hesitate. I'd seen it done a dozen times. I went in, threw the T-shirt over her, and grabbed her. The T-shirt didn't wrap around her like the blanket, though, and as I clasped the hawk, half bent over to prevent her wings from beating, she raked my arm from elbow to wrist with her talons. Her beak slashed through my shirt. I shoved her into the crate.

I was glad of the pain. It focused me as I wheeled the bike down the drive and onto the road in the direction of the river. When I paused to check the straps on the crate, I heard an uneven squeakity-squeak behind me and turned to wait for Rail. I was still curiously empty of surprise, but Rail skidded his bike to a startled halt and said, "Hey, Taylor. What're you doing here this early . . ." He stopped in mid-question, looked at the crate, at the blood streaking my arm. Then he glanced with quick apprehension toward the house, where the Chevy was plainly visible parked next to Rhiannon's truck. A slow flush spread over his cheeks and his eyes flickered once to mine, then away.

"You knew, didn't you?" I said.

"Sometimes I come here early to work . . . before it

gets too hot . . . man, Taylor. I hoped you wouldn't find out. I didn't know what to do. I . . . I guess I thought it would stop . . . when your mom got home —" He swallowed and was silent.

I got on my bike. "You don't have to look so guilty," I said clearly. "You're not the one sleeping with Rhiannon and cheating on my mother." I kicked the pedal hard and left him. But soon I heard the squeak-squeak of his bike behind me. I stopped and waited until he caught up. "Go away," I said, as clearly and calmly as before. "Leave me alone, Rail. Get away from me."

"Don't *talk* to me like that!" he yelled. It startled us both and we stared at each other. "I mean it, Taylor," Rail said. He grasped the crate to keep me from going and narrowed his eyes. "What do you think you're doing, anyway? What's in the crate?"

"I'm letting the hawk go," I told him. "I'm going to set her free. I found her, and I'm going to let her go. Then I'm going to call my mother to come get me, and I'm going to tell her why, and I'm going back to the city with her and I'm never coming up here again. Ever."

He listened with his mouth open. After a pause, defiant, he said, "Well, I'm going with you."

"To the city?" I asked sarcastically.

"No," he said softly. "I'm going with you now. With the hawk. So you don't either of you get hurt."

If I hadn't started pedaling the bike down the road

as hard as I could, I would not have been able to stop the terrible thing that was rising through me and pressing against the bottom of my throat. And I had to stop it. Because I couldn't do anything until the red-tailed hawk flew free.

After a while I slowed and Rail panted up beside me, but we didn't speak. We rode toward the river through tall fields of heat-wilted corn, the sun climbing above the tassels into a white sky. But as soon as we turned onto the dirt track toward the bluffs, the stirring of a faint, cool breath came from the river far below. We stopped at the open space where the bluffs dropped off between the trees and I untied the crate and set it carefully on the ground. Then I wrapped my father's shirt tight around my gashed arm, knelt, and opened the door.

Slowly I moved my hand toward the block where the hawk sat. Without hesitation, she stepped up and grasped onto my arm. I could feel the pulse of her panting breath right through her talons. I stood, and the red-tailed hawk stayed perched calmly on my arm and blinked her eyes. She swiveled her head back and forth, her beak parted. In her dark, gold-ringed eyes the whole landscape was reflected. Trees, cornfields, river . . . and when she turned to look straight into my eyes, I saw myself there, too.

I walked to the edge of the bluffs. I lifted my arm up. But the hawk stayed with me, surveying the open air. I held my arm until it began to tremble, but I didn't drop it. Then, suddenly, she turned her head sharply, spread her wings, and lifted free. Her feathers brushed my face as she rose into the morning, beating upward, tasting the invisible currents with her wings. Higher and higher, I followed her flight into the sun. She banked and glided out over the river in a long sweep, the gap in her tail from the missing feather clearly visible. Again she rose, beating her newfound wings, circled back, swept along the tops of the trees with a long, wild cry that streamed behind her. Then, over the crest of a hill on the far side of the river, the red-tailed hawk disappeared.

I dropped my arm. I shrugged off my pack and took out the leather-bound notebook. Two more steps and I was at the precipice, the river shining a hundred feet below me. Once more I lifted my arm. The notebook fluttered open in midair, soaring out until it seemed to hover a moment in the morning light on those same invisible currents before plummeting in a spiraling dive toward the river. I leaned out to watch it go.

But something kept me tethered to the earth. Rail, his arm around my waist. Not pulling me back, but holding me steady while I tasted the open air. Then I stumbled back against him, crying so hard I couldn't take a breath. He held me wordlessly, pressing himself against me, his head bent over mine. I cried until my arms and legs were weak and I had to lean on him, and still he kept holding me, bracing his feet while my whole body shook. Finally I gasped, "Why are you here? Why aren't you with your dad?"

He murmured into my hair, "Man, Taylor. Don't you worry about that."

I clutched at him and cried harder. "I don't know why you're helping me," I sobbed. "You shouldn't be here with me . . . I've never been nice to you . . . you should be with your sisters . . . everything, and anyway . . . it's all my fault —"

Rail led me away from the bluffs to the shade under the trees and pulled me down next to him on the ground. For a moment I felt something soft on my forehead and through my incoherent gabbling, as I tried to get my breath back, I realized he had kissed me. Now he was stroking my hair as he talked. "First of all," he said quietly, "Dawn and Cattie are fine. They're staying over at the Bitsi's, an' Bitsi has them with her at the store this morning. I just didn't feel like staying in the house by myself, so I went over to Rhiannon's . . ."

"I hate her," I whispered passionately.

"Yeah, I know . . ."

"It's my fault —"

"How's it your fault?" Rail murmured into my hair.

"Because . . . because I *wanted* my father to love

her. I did, Rail. Because *I* loved her. Because I wanted her to be my . . . I wanted her . . ." I choked to a stop.

"Well, wanting something doesn't make it happen," Rail said reasonably. "I sure found that out with my mother. So it isn't your fault. People just go ahead and do whatever they're gonna do, an' half the time it's wrong but they do it anyway." He sighed. "I don't know. Maybe they don't feel it's wrong —"

"Don't tell me my father doesn't know this is wrong!" I cried.

"I didn't say *know* — I said *feel*," Rail replied, shifting a little on the grass without letting go of me. "You can know something inside out, but it won't stop you. You gotta *feel* it." He paused again, then said slowly, "Trouble is, a lot of times doing the wrong thing feels right. I know because of what my mom told me when she was leaving. 'It *feels* right,' is what she said —"

"She was just selfish!" I blurted.

Rail looked into my eyes, solemn and tired. "Guess so," he said. "Yeah, guess she was. Or else, she was just human. Like your dad, and Rhiannon —"

"I don't want to *talk* about her!"

I jumped up and walked to the bluffs, kicking loose stones over the edge and listening to them pinging down through the rocks until I couldn't hear them anymore. Rail came to stand beside me, but this time he didn't touch me. After a few minutes I said, "I had to let her go —"

"I know," he said softly.

"Will she be all right?"

He scanned the sky. "She's a strong bird — she's had a lot of practice flying and hunting. She hunts real good now. The rest is up to her."

The loss stole through my blood, a sorrow that permeated every part of me. I had lost everything. The red-tailed hawk was gone forever. My father, my mother . . . and Rhiannon. Rhiannon. All at once, my world was thick with the ghosts which had been so separate from me that morning in the fog.

"I want to go away," I declared fiercely. "I *will* go away —" But I knew, with a pain insistent as a secret, that I loved Hunter's Gap. That the reason there were ghosts at all was because I had loved.

I looked quickly into Rail's face. He smiled sadly. "Well, you can leave or not," he said. "It won't matter none, whatever. You can't stop loving people because they do wrong things. If we only got loved when we deserved it, we wouldn't none of us get any love at all."

"I've been wrong to you —"

He put his arms around me again. "Yeah. And I still love you, Taylor," he whispered.

18

I COULDN'T GO BACK to my parents' house. Rail came
as far as his road with me, but he had to go home to
wait for a relative who was going to drive him into
Alton to see Tim at the hospital. I rode my bike aim-
lessly for an hour before I ended up at Bitsi's Gas
and Lunch. I didn't go inside, but sat on the sagging
steps until Bitsi yelled, "You gonna sit on them steps
blocking the way for everyone all day?" from her
rocker. The Chihuahua yapped when I went in.

I put a pad of ruled yellow paper, a box of en-
velopes, and a couple of BIC pens on the counter.
"Would you put these on my father's credit?" I
asked her.

"I don't give credit," she said.

"You know my dad," I begged her.

Bitsi studied me shrewdly from her throne. "Think I can trust him?"

I didn't answer. At last Bitsi pushed herself up and stumped over. She wrote each item down carefully under my father's name on a slip of paper. "Where are Dawn and Cattie?" I asked, making myself sound cheerful to distract her. Bitsi's expression softened.

"Poor babies," she said. "They're takin' a nap. Always takes 'em a day or two 'fore they get back to normal."

"You mean it's happened before?"

She shot me a look. " 'Course it's happened before. Told you Tim ain't right in the head. Ain't you friends with Rail? Thought you'd know about that by now."

Obviously I wasn't good enough friends with Rail, or I would have known. Just as I should have known about Rhiannon and my father. Rail had figured it out. Probably everyone in Hunter's Gap had figured it out by now, too.

Bitsi put everything in a bag and shoved it across the counter. "You ridin' your bike?" she asked, peering out the screen door. "You better get yerself home. This heat's gonna break something awful. Lookit them big thunderheads out there."

I started for the door, then turned. "Can you add a stamp to this?" I asked. Bitsi glared at me, but handed me a stamp. I hesitated. "Is there going to be a storm?" I asked.

Bitsi gave a satisfied nod that set all her chins going. "A doozy, I bet. When me an' Old Bitsi was farmin', I could tell the weather better'n any fancy weathermen on TV. I can smell it. Compared to this here storm comin' up, them firecrackers yesterday would sound like little pops." She leaned her elbows on the counter. "Lucky thing Tim's in the hospital after all, 'cause a storm like this'n would send him off the deep end."

"Seems like he already went off the deep end," I said.

She shook her head sadly, and then her eyes sank into the crevices of her frown. "I told Junior he better do his job and find them boys what pulled that stupid prank. Wasted a lot of folks' money. Not to mention Tim. Hope your friend's birds didn't get too riled up."

"She's not my friend!" I snapped. "Anyway, what do you care? No one in Hunter's Gap wants her here. You all hate her."

Bitsi gazed at me impassively. "Told you she was Pandora's box," she said. I stomped out. In the meager shade against the side of the building, I sat cross-legged in the dust and took out the pad of paper. "Dear Editor," I wrote in my neatest handwriting. "Thank you for your letter, but I will not be able to pursue the Junior Internship as you suggested. Also, please do not publish the story I wrote on the Hunter's Gap Raptor Rehabilitation Center. There are a number of inaccuracies in it which I have just discovered. I am very sorry for the inconvenience. Yours sincerely, Melissa Brown." I put the letter in an envelope, addressed it to *The Alton Register*, licked the stamp, and slipped it into the mailbox in front of the store. Then, feeling Bitsi's eyes on me, I got on my bike and rode off.

It was Bitsi's prediction of a storm that showed me where to go. I hadn't thought of it before. Why would I? I hadn't imagined I'd ever go back. It was just a hill with a dead tree. But now there was nowhere else I wanted to be.

I hid the bike in the weeds at the side of the road a mile past our drive, and set out across the field that ran behind the orchard. I followed my instinct up through the woods, and kept climbing. By the time I broke through the thickets at the edge of the clearing, the air hung motionless and burning. Not a leaf stirred, and the grasses, bone-white now in late summer, hardly rustled when I walked across the top of the hill. Only the sycamore tree seemed to defy the stillness. Heat danced like a liquid shield along the pale mottled bark of the trunk that pierced the sky. I crawled into a hollow near the base of the tree. Using my pack as a pillow, I lay back and stared up through the maze of branches at the broken sky.

Over the woods surrounding the clearing, masses of clouds were piling, layer upon layer of mushrooming whiteness. But the sun continued to burn. In the glare a tiny dark speck circled. I sat up and shaded my eyes. But it was too far away to make anything out. Somewhere out there, the red-tailed hawk was flying on her first day of freedom. I thought of her out there alone, with the sky growing furious around her. Frantic, I tore open my pack and took out the pad of paper I'd got at Bitsi's. Grief clenched me in its talons, and if I did not do something it would rend me from throat to stomach. I pressed the pen against the paper and forced myself to write.

As long as I moved the pen, the talons could not rip at me. Gradually the movement of my hand calmed me enough so I stopped for a moment. The clouds that had been swelling all afternoon now obliterated the sun with their towering bulk. It had to be close to four o'clock. I was hungry. By now, my mother would be on her way back to Hunter's Gap from Philadelphia, driving along, not knowing what waited for her . . . and where was my father? When had he found the books, my sweatshirt, the letter? He would not miss seeing them. Neither would Rhiannon.

I felt the thunder through the ground before I heard it. When the first slender flicker of lightning cut across the clouds, I didn't flinch. I stuffed the pack deeper into the hollow and ran out into the spattering of rain. At first, the thunder was a distant rumble and the rain swept across the hill like a cool benevolent hand soothing the heavy heat. Then the thunder and lightning grew, chasing each other down the mountains, the storm shooting the rain before it like arrows. I took it full against my face. I wondered how it felt to be struck by lightning. Did it sting, or burn, or were you dead before you knew? I closed my eyes, but the lightning was so bright it seared through my closed lids.

I stood in the open while the storm slashed around me. I could no longer distinguish between the flashes of lightning and the talon-sharp pain striking through my heart. But eventually the storm retreated back into the depths of the mountains and I was left standing, soaking wet, shivering, and exhausted. I got my pack and without looking back at the white tree, I walked straight down through the woods to home.

They were facing each other across the kitchen table. I could see them through the screen door, yesterday's mail still unopened except for the two letters addressed to me. The one I'd crumpled and left at Rhiannon's was in my mother's hand. She leaped up when I came in. "Where have you been! Where have you been!" she cried. Her fingers dug into my back when she held me.

"I went for a walk —"

The phone rang and my father grabbed it. "Junior ... no. No, I was just about to call — she just walked in. Yes, she looks okay ... listen, Junior, thanks a lot — tell the others thanks, will you? Yes. Talk to you —"

He sounded so normal. My ears were roaring. I spun away from my mother. The remains of the storm dripped from my hair in cold spikes down my neck. "I am *not* okay," I hissed at him. "I hate you. You lied. You're a liar and a cheat and I hate you."

My mother looked at my father. "Get out," she said.

"We can't do it this way —" he began helplessly, but my mother said, "Go," and he left.

When the door banged shut behind him I suddenly had no strength left in my legs, and sat. I put my hands over my ears, but my mother took them gently in her own. "Sweetie, you've got to get out of those wet things," she urged.

"I want to scream," I whispered.

"I know. You can, if you want."

"Why don't *you*?" I challenged.

A red welt spread over her cheeks, as if I'd slapped her. "I've learned not to," she said, her voice clipped. "It's not the first time something like this has happened."

We stared at each other, frozen in her last words. I could see the regret darken her eyes immediately. I demanded, "You mean, not just Rhiannon?"

She shook her head reluctantly and looked away. I stamped my foot. "Why?" I cried, relentless. "Why are you still with him? I can't *believe* you'd stay with him!" I began to cough. I coughed so hard I doubled over and my mother propelled me up the stairs to the bathroom and turned on the shower.

"Get in there," she told me. "Don't come out until I say so. I'll get some dry clothes."

Under the hot, stinging shower I made up my mind not to talk. My mother would try to make me talk. Get me to work through the anger. That's what psychiatrists did. But I was more comfortable with my rage. When my mother came in with a towel, I grabbed it and spat, "*Why?* WhyWhyWhy?"

"Because I love him," she said calmly.

I slammed the door of my room, but I'd forgotten the lock didn't work, and she followed me in. "You said you'd never come into my room unless I invited you," I said, menacingly.

"I'm breaking my word, then," she said, sitting on the edge of the bed. I huddled as far away from her as I could and clamped my mouth shut.

My mother had both letters with her. She smoothed the crumpled one from *The Register* over her knee. "You didn't tell me about this," she said.

I grabbed it from her and ripped it up. "It doesn't matter," I snarled. "It's nothing. I'm going to Porter Phelps."

"Of course you are," she said soothingly. "Thank God. You'll be happy there. You'll have your own life. I don't want you to be buried out here like —"

"Like you?" I meant it sarcastically, since she'd hardly been in Hunter's Gap long enough for a funeral service, let alone a burial. I glared at her. "Why don't you leave Dad?" I demanded. "I just can't believe you'd stay with him after this!"

"Do you want me to leave him?" she cried, but immediately pulled me against her and murmured, "Don't answer that, sweetie. That's not your decision. It isn't your problem and it isn't your fault."

I let her hold me and after a while I stopped shivering. The rain had ended but the clouds still shadowed the gray early evening. My mother asked softly, "Tell me about Rhiannon."

"I hate her," I whispered.

She smiled a little. "Besides that," she said. "Before you hated her. When you spent every day with her all summer. When she was your friend."

She was huddled next to me under the thin cotton blanket. I kept my face turned disdainfully away from her. "Rail is my friend," I muttered. "*She* wasn't a friend. She was only like . . . like an *idea*."

I stopped, clamping my mouth shut, but my mother nodded her head. "Sometimes that happens," she said, smoothing my damp hair. "What was she an idea of?"

I meant to say "a mother." But instead, I blurted, "She made me believe I could fly —"

"Then she gave you a great gift."

I said sullenly, "I still hate her. I'll hate her forever."

My mother sighed and sat up on the bed, straightening the blanket. "Her gift was real anyway. Don't let her mistake clip your wings."

I couldn't wait to leave. We got ready to go to Philadelphia the next day, but when I saw my father loading things into the Chevy down by the studio, I hissed, "What's *he* doing? Is he coming, too?"

"He has to," my mother said, without looking up from a suitcase. "How else are we all going to talk? He'll stay at Dan's . . . don't worry, sweetie. We'll work things out."

"I don't see what there is to work out," I said ruthlessly. "He cheats on you. He lies. I'm sick of him. All he ever thinks about is himself. He wouldn't even stay in the house with me, when you were gone. He just left me alone. He stayed in the studio." I slammed the suitcase shut and spat, "Or at *Rhiannon's.*"

I would have been fine if Rail hadn't come over. I was ready to leave. Everything about the place made me sick . . . the house, my room with all the things that reminded me of Rhiannon, the barn. If my father hadn't been in his studio I would have gone down there, taken his heaviest mallet, and smashed the sculpture to a thousand bits. Starting with the figure of Rhiannon. I clenched my hands into fists. "Why doesn't he just *go!*" I said, following my mother to the car with a suitcase. "He doesn't have to wait for us, does he? I wish he'd leave."

But Rail arrived then, pushing his rusty bike up the drive. Just hearing the squeak-squeak of the wheels made my eyes sting. "Hey, Taylor," he called when he saw me. He looked at the car. "You're leaving, aren't you?"

"Did you think I would stay?" I muttered without looking at him. "I'm going to school, anyway. In two weeks. So what's the point of staying? I hate it here. I told you that."

If Rail hadn't dropped his bike with a clatter I might have gone on babbling forever. "Oh, yeah. I forgot," he said dryly, eyeing me. I knew that look.

"I don't want to hear what you think you know," I said. "You don't know everything."

"I know I don't believe one word you're saying," he replied, kicking gravel at his bike. I had the impression he might have meant it for me. I turned away, but he took my arm. I saw my father walking toward us from the barn.

"Let go! Let go —" I was practically whimpering. "Okay, I'll talk to you. Just let's get out of here." I twisted away and ran behind the house before my father got close enough to speak. By then I was crying again. Rail put his arms around me. "You don't have to do this every time I cry," I gulped.

"It's the only time you let me," he smiled.

I looked at him with a frown. "How'd you know I was leaving today, anyway?"

He hesitated. "Rhiannon said you were," he mumbled.

"*He* told her!"

Rail shrugged impatiently. "Don't matter," he said. "What matters is you're leaving. Man, Taylor. I won't see you again. Maybe not ever. Don't you even care?"

That was it: I didn't want to care. I didn't want anything to keep me from getting as far from Hunter's Gap as I could. All my old habits as a reporter came back to me. I had to be objective or I wouldn't get through this. I stepped away from Rail. It wasn't that hard. After all, I thought, we only started hanging out together by accident. What did we have in common, anyway, except the red-tailed hawk? And now she was gone. "I really don't care about anything," I said to Rail. "I'm sorry, but it's the truth. I'm going to be a reporter. I just can't get involved in anything the way other people do. Otherwise I won't be able to see things clearly."

I watched the shock spread over Rail's face without turning away. Without crying. Without throwing myself against him and never letting go of him. I just stood there until he found his voice. "Okay," he said softly. He walked away without saying goodbye.

I stayed in the apartment in the city while my mother and father "worked things out." That meant they went to a counselor, and spent hours talking somewhere away from me. My mother gave me her credit card. "Just don't max it out," she said, trying to smile. "You need school clothes, sweetie. Get whatever you want. And that backpack —" She looked with distaste at the pack I'd carried all summer. "It's filthy. You may as well throw it out. Get a nice new one . . ."

But I lay on the floor of the apartment for hours and hours, the old pack wadded under my head the way I'd done the afternoon of the storm. If I sniffed it, I could smell the red-tailed hawk. The chocolate bars Rail and I ate at the Center. The leather of the notebook I'd thrown into the river. The shirt Rhiannon had given me to wear the day I'd arrived soaking wet. Summer sun, sweet mown hay, eagle feathers, marble dust, the vinyl seat of the Chevy . . . I rocked the pack in my arms, burying my face in it. But I didn't go out. Not once. I didn't want to see the city at all.

On the third day, I overheard my mother on the phone to my father. "You aren't here," she was telling him. "If you were, you'd know what I'm talking about. She doesn't *do* anything. She just sits in here and watches television all the time. CNN, for God's sakes . . . she's going to have to talk to someone." There was a long pause. "Well, I don't know if it's helping us, but it might help her," she said finally. There was another pause. Then, "No, of course she doesn't want to talk to you. Why would she?" There was a click as she hung up, and a click as she called another number. Her voice was too low for me to hear. A click, and I heard her go into the bathroom. Two minutes later, the phone rang. "Can you get that, sweetie?" she called.

I picked up the receiver and said, "What?"

"Man, Taylor," said Rail. "I sure hope you don't ever get a job answering phones."

"Did my mom tell you to call me?" I asked. There was a long pause. "Did she?" I insisted.

"I wanted to myself, but I was afraid you'd hang up on me," he answered in a small voice. "Man, Taylor. Who cares if she did?"

"I care," I snapped. "She wants me to talk. She's going to try to get me to go to a shrink. Right. Like *I'm* the one who's messed up." I waited a moment, and then added, "Did she tell you to try to make me go?"

"She asked me if I ever went to one."

I was so startled I blurted, "Did you?"

"Yeah. For a while. That time I flunked . . . after

278

my mom left. And sometimes when my dad freaked out — before I got used to it."

I didn't know what to say, and after a minute, Rail said, "Taylor? You there?" I sighed. "I have to go," I said. "I'm tired."

The next night, my mother suggested going out to eat. "I'm not hungry," I told her, although I hadn't eaten all day. She insisted and I dragged myself down to the car. To my astonishment, she pulled up to a pizza place. "You hate pizza," I said, and she smiled. When we went in, I saw my father waiting for us in the booth farthest from the door. My mother held tight to my arm. "I don't want to talk to him!" I cried, struggling. "You tricked me —"

"Sit," she said.

I sat, and my father watched me from across the table. He was scrubbed clean, his hair drawn neatly back in a ponytail, a new shirt tucked into his jeans. He looked the way he had the night we'd danced with Rhiannon. We were alone. My mother had pulled her disappearing act and gone into the bathroom. "I'm not talking," I warned him.

"Fine," he said. "I'll talk." He twirled the paper slip with our order number on it between his fingers. He studied the menu board. He stretched his long legs out into the aisle. A waitress smiled at him. I glared at her. "I'm very, very sorry I've hurt you so badly, Missy," he said at last. I shrugged. He leaned toward me across the table. "Your mother and I are not breaking up over this," he added.

"Then she's stupid."

My father tilted his head and studied me quizzically. "Who are you mad at, Missy? Me or your mother?"

"If Rhiannon had been my mother, she would never in a million years put up with your lying and cheating," I shot back.

"Rhiannon is not your mother," he said quietly. "Your mother is your mother, and I am your father, and you are part of this."

"It's your mess. You clean it up."

He suddenly looked defeated. He rubbed his hand over his face. "I'm trying to," he said.

My mother came out of the bathroom and the waitress brought our pizza. I didn't take a slice, but my mother and father both ate several. As long as their mouths were full, they didn't have to talk. The smell of pizza reminded me of Hunter's Gap and the cricket-filled nights in front of the television watching Star Trek videos. My father ate in gulps, head down, and once or twice my mother glanced at him with an expression I could not figure out. Suddenly he stopped abruptly, mouth still full, muttered, "I'm going outside a moment," and left.

My mother put her pizza down.

"Was he crying?" I asked.

"Yes," she said.

Good, I was going to say. But the word wouldn't come out. I kept smelling the summer, remembering my father's arm around me, our secret unspoken and warm between us. He loved my mother and he loved Rhiannon. And so did I. Tears were running down my face and plopping onto my plate. My mother said softly, "I think we should all go back to the apartment."

My father seemed too big for the hallway, too awkward in the elevator. When my mother unlocked the door, a package propped against it fell at my feet. "Were you expecting a Fed-Ex?" she asked my father. He shook his head, looked at it, and handed it to me. "It's addressed to Missy." Then he took his too-big self to the couch and sat uncertainly on the edge.

I turned the package over. The weight felt strangely familiar. I tore it open. For several seconds I held it, too afraid to move. The leather was stained with mud and scarred with gashes, but the hawk still beat its wings in the corner of the notebook cover. Slowly I opened it. The pages were rumpled, brown in places where the mud had seeped in, but the waterproof ink hadn't run. I could read every word. Something fluttered out of the middle and I bent to pick it up. It was the hawk's tail feather, soft as the touch of its flight.

I looked up at my father. He dropped his eyes. I held the notebook tightly against my chest and felt my heart beating through the cover. "Who found it?" I whispered.

My father picked up the torn wrapping and looked at the address. He hesitated, then said, "It's Rhiannon's handwriting."

My mother took the notebook from me, and for some reason, I didn't mind when she looked inside. "Someone's taken a lot of care to clean this up," she said. "The pages are all pressed and blotted . . ." She handed it back to me, but she was looking at my father with a sad and terrible knowing, her eyes bound with love. He did not drop his eyes from hers. I felt myself begin to disappear. I opened my notebook and read. My father reached out his hand to my mother, and she took it.

I read my words and I did not disappear. I was all there, all of me, the words I had written tethering me to the bright, wondrous summer, the way the hawk had been tethered to the post when she was learning to fly. As I read, the words carried me to that high, secret hill where the wind blew and the wild hawk circled overhead. I read the words I'd written, and there was not a single inaccuracy. Every word was true. It was me. When I looked up, my parents had gone. But they had gone together. And when they came back, I would still be here.

19

I'D WAITED ALL DAY for this first moment of privacy. "Hot off the press!" called Mr. Schulman, the English teacher, when the newly printed papers had arrived just before the bell for first period that morning. There had been a rush as everyone grabbed a copy before going off to class. I'd waited until the last moment, then taken one of the last remaining copies and stuffed it into my pack. And all day, even when I saw people reading it, and even when Miss Barchik waved a copy in her hand and gave me a Victory salute through the window of the main office as I walked by, I didn't take it out of my pack.

But classes were done for the day. In a grove of trees at the far side of the building, I opened my pack at last and slowly took it out. I sniffed the new ink. I opened the front page. Yes. I definitely liked the look of my name in print. Melissa Taylor Armstrong-Brown, Editor. It needed a whole line of its own, right underneath the name of the paper: *The Flight.* I scanned the first few pages critically, checking for printer's errors, savoring my anticipation. But eventually I reached page 8, and there they were. Three poems, set on the page by themselves. I read the first line, although I knew them all by heart: "She plunges through storms and sunshine, swooping in from the edge of joy, her wings singing the fury of freedom . . ." I smiled. Yes. That was exactly how it was.

"Miss-*ee!*" screeched a familiar voice. "Missy! The bus is gonna leave without you!"

I ran from the trees and down the sidewalk to the bus. Betsy Warren was hanging on to the open door as if she thought she could anchor the bus with her puny weight. "Thanks," I said dryly as I climbed on behind her. To my surprise, Betsy followed me to my usual seat near the back, instead of sitting with Cindy the way she always did. Cindy wasn't looking good today. There was a new bruise on her chin. The school bus lumbered through Alton on its way toward the river and Hunter's Gap. Betsy plunked herself into the seat next to me.

She poked my copy of *The Flight.* "Well, I done it," she announced, after looking around suspiciously to make sure no one was listening.

"Done what?" I asked, because I knew she wanted me to.

"You know them poems you wrote — I only read them because you wrote 'em, because I hate poetry, but anyway . . ." She seemed to be struggling to say something, so I folded the paper and waited. "Well, you remember when you brought them hawks and eagles to the nursing home? You remember how I told you . . . you know. About Cindy?"

"Yeah," I said, looking out the window.

Betsy glanced worriedly up the aisle at Cindy. "You remember how you said I oughta do something . . . tell someone? Well, I did something. Today. Because when I read them poems you wrote about the hawks, it made me remember what you said."

I stared at her, and she stared right back. There was something I had never noticed before in her washed-out brown eyes. I wouldn't have guessed Betsy Warren had it in her. But there it was — a fierce, determined light, sharp as a hawk's eyes. "Who'd you tell?" I asked finally.

"You know that guidance counselor — Mrs. Ferdock? The really nice one? I told her. An' she's gonna investigate — that's what she said. I asked her if it was okay that I told on Cindy . . . you know. An' she said it'll make all the difference in the world."

"Man," I said, amazed.

Betsy giggled and stood up, bracing herself on the

jolting bus. "You sound just like Rail," she said. "Hey. He ask you to the dance yet?"

"What dance?" I grumbled.

She rolled her eyes. "Oh, you know what dance," Betsy said. "The *big* one. Next week."

"Rail wouldn't think of doing something so stupid," I said. "And neither would I."

But I smiled at Betsy anyway and watched as she made her way back to Cindy. Immediately their heads locked together and I knew they were whispering their countless plans and secrets, just the way they always did. But I kept hearing her words: "It'll make all the difference . . ." I took out the paper and turned again to page 8. I read the poems I had written. I hadn't ever imagined Betsy would read them.

The bus jerked to a stop at the bottom of my drive and I jumped out, waved at Betsy as she made a face at me through the window, and started for home. It had been a stormy, unsettled October, but today the weather was unusually sunny, although a nippy wind swept down along the mountains. I sniffed the air. Wood smoke. My father had stoked the stove in his studio against the afternoon chill. Halfway up the drive, I heard the steady, comfortable sound of the mallet hitting the chisel. I hesitated a moment in the yard. I was still holding my copy of the premier issue of *The Flight*. The tap-tapping from the studio continued and I turned into the house. I could show my father the paper soon enough.

The kitchen and living room had become so cluttered with books and papers it wasn't always easy to find my mother working under it all. My father said she'd begun to smell like a book, and she'd replied, "No worse than smelling like a rock." I dropped my pack on the kitchen table, dislodging a pile of mail. Under it was today's *Alton Register*. The headline caught my eye and I pulled the paper out. "Vinci Looking Strong for Reelection," I read.

> Senator Tom Vinci is confident about what looks like a landslide victory early next month in his bid for reelection to the senate. Despite small pockets of opposition, much of the state's voting population seems strongly behind Senator Vinci's campaign. His continued, outspoken commitment to Pennsylvania's environmental issues have earned him high . . .

My mother came into the kitchen, the portable phone against her ear. She wiggled her fingers at me in greeting. "Uh-huh," she said into the phone. I made a peanut butter sandwich. "Of course," said my mother, poking through the mail on the table with her free hand. I sat, making a little space for my plate. My father came in, raised his eyebrows at me, and I shrugged. "All right. Yes, tomorrow," said my mother. "'Bye." She put the phone down.

My father looked around the kitchen. "This is getting ridiculous, Annie," he said, pushing papers off a chair so he could sit. "You're going to have to make up your mind about renting that office in Alton." He hugged me with one arm briefly around my shoulders and I let him, but as usual, I had to fight down the same cold stillness I'd felt with him since that awful day last August. I shoved my copy of *The Flight* under their noses.

"Here it is," I announced.

My father grinned, looking over my mother's shoulder. "Only Missy could pull this off," he chuckled. "Alton High School's very first . . . what? Literary newspaper? And there you are . . ." He read silently for a while. "Editor *and* main contributor, it looks like —"

"Well, it's just the first issue," I said sheepishly. "It was hard getting people to write stuff for it. But the next issue —"

"These poems are so beautiful," interrupted my mother softly. She looked up and met my eyes. I didn't realize how afraid I'd been until that moment, of what her reaction would be. Her daughter . . . a poet. And the poems about hawks would remind her of the summer. . . .

"Thanks," I said.

"I want to read it all later," she added. "But I need to finish this up —"

"I know, Mom."

My father leaned back in his chair, contemplating her. "Annie. The office —"

My mother tried to make some order out of the chaos in the kitchen — the same chaos that had spilled throughout the house. Computer set up in the living room. Books everywhere. Papers filed on the kitchen counter. Phone calls from all over the place. "I don't see how we can afford both offices — one here, one down in the city —" she began.

"We can't. You have to choose," my father said.

I said quickly, "Aren't there plenty of crazy people around here, Mom?"

"Melissa, for God's sake. My clients are not crazy. How many times do I have to —"

"I thought the idea you had of starting a clinic for Vietnam vets was a good plan," my father interrupted. "Annie, you have to make up your mind about all this soon. This *mess* is crazy. We'll all be crazy people soon."

The phone rang. I fished it out of the papers. "Hey, Taylor. You wanna do something this afternoon?" asked Rail.

I scuttled into the living room and shut the door. "I thought you said you had to work today," I said.

"Well, I did. I mean, I got there, but . . . Dr. Williams says the bio lab can survive without me for a day." He paused. "Look. I'll come get you, okay? You doing anything?"

I grimaced into the phone. "Not much. Just listening to my mom and dad decide whether to stay married or not."

"Man —"

"Oh, don't worry. They have this discussion about three times a week. My mom doesn't seem to be leaving . . ." I stretched out on the couch. "Anyway. *I'm* staying. That's what matters, right?"

I could practically hear his grin. "Yeah."

He obviously had something in mind when he picked me up in his father's old Buick. All he would say was "Surprise," but something in his voice unsettled me. He turned left out of the drive. As usual now when I found myself going past the Center, I looked out the window in the opposite direction. "Your paper was amazing," said Rail, breaking the short silence. "I mean, I saw you putting it together and all, but the finished thing was just so . . . *great*. Especially your poems. Man, Taylor. You are a real writer."

I glanced at him gratefully. "And you're a real friend," I told him softly. But he didn't look as pleased as he might have. He was peering out the window at the sky, as if he was searching for more than what he usually stared at, and he tapped the steering wheel nervously with one hand. "We're going to the river, aren't we?" I asked finally.

"Man, Taylor. Sometimes you are a nosy reporter. Can't you be a regular human being for once, and just wait?"

I sat back and folded my arms. But I wasn't surprised when he turned down the dirt road toward the bluffs. We hadn't been there since the day I released the red-tailed hawk — the day I never referred to. I sat tensely as we bounced over the rain-filled potholes, until my attention was caught by the sky.

It seemed to be boiling with uncountable dark specks. The whole sky, from the broad-flanked mountains to the trees on the far side of the river. Boiling. Moving. Rising, falling, swirling. Dozens of specks against the sun-bright clouds. "What *is* it?" I whispered. I was filled with an almost unbearable excitement. I hardly waited for Rail to stop the car before I jumped out. Above us, the dark specks spiraled and whirled, sweeping down, swooping up, around and around until I wanted to open my arms and whirl around with them out over the shining water. "Hawks?" I breathed.

"Hawks," said Rail. "Going south."

I ran toward the bluffs, filling my lungs with the cold October wind, letting the air hold me the way it held the hawks. I did open my arms then, and whirled until I was dizzy and laughing, and even though Rail hung back a little, I could see he was smiling, too. "Come on!" I yelled to him. I wanted to run with him, the way we had that day so long ago when Rail Bogart had come out to run with me in the open field. He only shook his head, though. He took a step or two toward me, and stopped.

I saw the other person, then. Far up along the bluffs, where the ground rose steeply before the trees, a woman was standing alone, right on the edge of the rocks against the sky. The sun was behind her, so I could only see her dark form and her long hair whipping in the wind. But even before she turned and raised her arm, and even before I saw what I had not noticed before — a familiar truck pulled up under the trees — I knew. I knew, and I spun around to confront Rail. "You knew she was here!" I cried. "You brought me here, and you knew she'd be here!"

"I didn't really . . ." he stammered, a flush rising in his face. "I mean, she called Dr. Williams to tell us she'd seen the hawks kettling, that's all. That's how I knew. She said it was the biggest number she'd ever seen. But she didn't say she was going back to see them again. . . ."

I strode toward the car. Without looking at him, I demanded, "Take me home. I want to go. Now."

"No," said Rail.

I turned, stunned. He was standing where I'd left him, and Rhiannon was making her way down along the bluffs toward us. "Please . . . please," I whispered.

He shook his head stubbornly. "You gotta. You aren't the only one who's hurting, you know."

So I was trapped. Above us, the silent wheeling hawks rose and fell in the breathing air. Coming toward me was Rhiannon. Rhiannon of the birds. Rhiannon the beautiful, the magical, the sorrowful. Rhiannon, her golden laugh always calling just beyond my reach, her shadow-filled eyes shaping my dreams. Rhiannon, whom I loved and hated. I watched her come toward me, and I grew more and more afraid, until I knew it wasn't anger at all that had kept me from even thinking her name to myself all these last months. It was fear. Fear that I had lost her, fear that some essential part of myself had been cut off but I was terrified to look to see if it was gone.

But I had convinced myself that it was anger for too long. "What do you want?" I said when she came up.

She didn't say anything for a long moment, but just looked at me. At last, strangely wistful, she asked, "What do *you* want?"

I found it impossible to respond. I looked desperately toward Rail, but he had strolled some distance off, studying the hawks. I looked at the river, but the wind whipped my eyes to tears. I looked at my feet and when I couldn't bear it another moment, I looked into Rhiannon's eyes. I think she would have stood there all day, if that had been as long as it took for me to speak. "Did you find my notebook?" I croaked out at last.

She nodded. "Rail told me where you'd thrown it, so I went to look for it. I didn't think you'd have been able to get it out far enough to hit the river —"

I looked at the bluffs, dropping off in rocky outcrops and scrub-tangled ledges more than a hundred feet to the river. "You climbed down there?" I whispered.

She smiled a little. "It didn't seem to matter, right then, that it was dangerous. But I've scrambled around worse places than that, so I managed to get back in one piece." She paused. "I couldn't help reading some of it, you know — as I was drying the pages."

I looked away. She turned and started walking up along the bluffs again without looking back at me. I didn't follow at first. I wanted Rail, but I couldn't see him anywhere. And the farther away Rhiannon got, the more frantic I felt. Now it wasn't just the wind burning tears in my eyes. I stumbled as I ran, and couldn't find a voice to call her to stop. But she must have heard anyway, and turned back. I threw my arms around her.

I buried my face in her sweater and after a while my heart stopped racing. "I'm sorry. I'm sorry," I said. She held me tighter.

"You didn't do anything wrong," she murmured.

"Yes I did. I didn't even try to understand."

She looked at me with a crooked smile. "Do you understand now? Because I'm not sure I do."

"You wanted to get back everything you lost. Your little girl . . ." I took a deep breath. "And your little girl's father, right?" I looked up at her. "Was he . . . was he like my father?"

She closed her eyes a moment. Then she shook her head. "No. They're very different. He left six months after Ninian died. I made him go. I couldn't bear having a home after . . . everything. I never saw him again. Your father . . ." She stopped and looked away. In a low voice, she said, "I think your father wanted to rescue me . . ."

At the far end of the bluffs, Rail appeared, scanning the sky through a pair of binoculars. I watched him for several minutes, leaning against Rhiannon. At last I said, "I left you, too. I didn't even try to rescue you."

She laid her head against mine. "But you've come back," she smiled. "That's more of a rescue than I ever deserved."

I continued to watch Rail. "Rail says that if people had to deserve love, then none of us would ever be loved," I said.

"It's a lucky thing for me that he's right," Rhiannon whispered.

Suddenly I saw Rail move the binoculars down, then up again. Then down. He shouted to us, waving his arm and pointing, running toward us across the rocks. He was yanking the strap of the binoculars from around his neck and when he reached us, out of breath, he shoved them at me. "Look! Look!" he gasped, pointing.

I couldn't see anything but the dark specks, bigger through the lenses, weaving dizzily back and forth. "What?" I frowned. He grabbed the binoculars and gave them to Rhiannon. "There . . . there. The one with a gap . . . see? That low one? See her?"

My breath caught in my throat. I squinted against the glare and forced myself to focus. Rhiannon stood motionless, the binoculars pressed to her eyes. Some of the hawks circled lower than the others and if I concentrated, hand shading my eyes, I could see a flash of white belly or the dark tip of a wing.

Then, unbelievably, I saw it. The unmistakable gap in a widespread tail as a hawk swept low across the thermals, seeking a stronger current to rise higher into the wind. She flew so low Rhiannon dropped the binoculars and watched. The hawk swung in a loop back over us and drifted upward, banking slightly, the wide gap in the tail clearly visible.

"It's an immature red-tail, all right . . ." Rhiannon said thoughtfully. "I suppose she could have hung around here all this time — no reason not to —" She raised the binoculars again, silent.

"The gap's the same — on her left side," Rail breathed.

Out of countless hawks, would there only be one immature bird with a gap in its tail? If I'd been a reporter, I would have needed to know the facts. But the truth was, I saw my red-tailed hawk flying free, rising forever on the thermals. Her wings sang of sun and shadows, of distance and loss, and of coming home, and I had learned her song by heart. We watched until our necks ached and the wind filled our eyes with tears, and gradually the dark specks drifted farther and farther away and the sky became clear.

At the car, Rhiannon told us she was leaving. "But not until the end of the term," she said, watching my face.

"Because of *him*. Because of everything," I said bitterly.

She seemed to struggle with something. Finally she nodded. "Partly. Yes. But this is what I do, Taylor. I set up these programs and then I . . . I just go somewhere else, and —"

"You'll never find her!" I cried passionately. "Not ever! You know that!"

She smiled. "I never even knew I was looking, until the day I saw you. And saw Ninian as I dreamed she would be. But now . . . who knows? Maybe I don't have to look anymore —"

"Then stay!"

"She's gotta go, Taylor. It's her job," Rail said.

Rhiannon chuckled. "Speaking of jobs — you straighten out poor old Williams yet? You keeping him calm?"

Rail rolled his eyes. "Nothing could keep him calm. But I like the job. I'm real glad you asked him to hire me . . . he figures he can help me get a scholarship to the university when I'm ready . . ."

"So no more fighter jets?"

"Naw —" grinned Rail.

Before she drove off, she leaned out the window and said to me, "Come over soon. I'm not leaving for months. And bring those poems —"

"I will," I said softly.

I watched her until the car was out of sight. Rail dug in his pocket. "Chocolate?" he asked.

I made a face. "It's mashed. And covered in yuk."

He peeled the wrapper and took a huge bite. He chewed for a while, then looked at me and smiled. "You okay now?" he asked.

"Yeah," I answered. "Give me a piece."

When my mouth was completely stuck together with chocolate, Rail asked casually, "My dad said I could use the car next week. So you wanna go to that stupid dance?"

I almost choked. "Sure," I said. Side by side, we leaned back against the car and watched the October clouds drift high above the river's path. And all at once, as if it wasn't a mystery at all, I saw what Rail saw when he gazed off into the open sky.